W9-BYA-341

HOME
OF THE BRAVE

FORTVILLE-VERNON TWP.
PUBLIC LIBRARY
625 E. BROADWAY
FORTVILLE, IN 46040

11.69

ID
12/15

HOME
OF THE BRAVE

FORTVILLE-VERNON TWP.
PUBLIC LIBRARY
625 E. BROADWAY
FORTVILLE, IN 46040

Kristoffer Neff

WALNUT SPRINGS PRESS

To Melanie

Text copyright © 2015 by Kristoffer Neff
Cover design copyright © 2015 by Walnut Springs Press
Interior design copyright © 2015 by Walnut Springs Press

All rights reserved. This book, or parts thereof, may not be transmitted, stored in a database, or reproduced in any form without prior written permission from the publisher, except in the case of brief quotations embodied in critical reviews and certain other noncommercial uses permitted by copyright law.

Printed in the United States of America.

ISBN-13: 978-1-59992-972-9

This is a work of fiction. The characters, names, incidents, and dialogue are products of the author's imagination and are not to be construed as real, and any resemblance to real people and events is not intentional.

1

In the early morning hours of September 23, a U.S. Army C-141 cargo jet screamed across the pale sky, destined for Bagram Air Force Base in Afghanistan. Connecting out of New Guinea, where they had been delayed because of inclement weather, a team of seven Army Rangers raced against sunrise. Though the cargo jet and its crew were headed for Bagram, the Rangers were getting off early.

Corporal Taylor Sutton opened his eyes and briefly watched the stone faces of his team. There was no laughing, no jokes, no talking. HALO jumps were not something to be taken lightly.

At that moment, a specialist descended the stairs from the cockpit and began checking the heart rate and eye dilation of each man. When finished, he reported to the captain. "No sign of hypoxia or decompression. Package ready for delivery." Then he pulled the microphone away from his mouth. "You boys have a nice flight. Kick some terrorist trash while you're down there." The specialist saluted out of respect and turned to climb back to the cockpit.

"All right, men," Sergeant Heller said through his boom mike. "Make ready."

Almost robotically, the seven men lowered face masks into place that would protect their eyes and deliver vital oxygen during their descent. This part always made the child in Taylor Sutton feel a little like Darth Vader.

Mask in place, Sergeant Heller flipped a switch and the cargo door at the rear of the jet began to lower. At thirty thousand feet, the cargo bay was an instant vacuum. The sergeant motioned for the team to exit and he led the way, disembarking the safety of the aircraft without hesitation.

Each of the men followed in turn. Last in line, Corporal Sutton paused briefly. It always amazed him how at this altitude the world was a calm and beautiful thing, with no visible evidence of war and rivalry. However, he knew the opposite was true. The world was an ugly and violent place, and though he longed to remain at the edge of the stratosphere forever, he stepped out of the jet and resigned himself to gravity.

In an instant his body reached terminal velocity, and his eyes turned to his altimeter as it began to unwind at an alarming rate. To avoid panic, he distracted himself by recounting what he knew of the mission before him.

From what he had been told, recent reports revealed that a terrorist cell near Sukkur, Pakistan, was obtaining a cache of weapons including an EMP device, chemically enhanced anthrax, and enough plutonium to make a sizable nuclear bomb. As usual, the intended target was America and her allies. Sutton and the others were America's response: seven highly skilled Rangers trained in long-range surveillance. It was a black op. The blackest of black ops—no dog tags, no radios. It was do or die.

To make an urgent situation even more so, the delay in New Guinea put the jet behind schedule. By putting the pedal to the metal, as the saying goes, they had picked up some time, but they were still in a race to beat the sun. Nothing was worse than hanging from a parachute in broad daylight in a hostile land, just asking to be picked off like low-hanging fruit.

According to the latest intel, the weapons in question would be loaded on an armored truck that very morning and moved north along the Indus Highway. Relocation of the weapons gave the Rangers their window of opportunity.

From his altitude, Corporal Sutton could see the sun pushing back the night over the curve of the earth. Once on the ground he would have to hurry; the cover of night was rapidly turning the dull gray of dawn. With the altimeter unwinding at a blurring rate, Taylor focused more on steady breathing. He was 10,000 feet and counting . . . 7500 . . . then 5000. Black parachutes burst into bloom below him. At 3500 feet, a light flashed and Taylor pulled his ripcord, instantly slowing his fall. Even with the chute open, the ground was on fast approach and he had to be ready. A bad landing could mean a twisted knee, a jarred spine, or even a broken leg. More importantly, it would put him out of commission.

The ground met him solidly and he crumpled, letting his whole body take the shock. The last to land, Corporal Sutton was quickly on his feet. With a craggy gorge rising behind them and small hovels dotting the landscape before them, the Rangers scanned the area for any sign of hostiles. Confident the landing had gone unnoticed, they quickly pulled away dark outer clothing to reveal desert fatigues. With haste they bundled the clothing, face masks, and parachutes and began to bury them in the soft sand.

Three miles—or "clicks," in military terms—to the northeast lay the Indus Highway, where they were to intercept the weapons convoy. Having memorized the lay of the land via topographical maps, the men knew the valley before them was the fastest route to the highway, with the lowest visibility risk.

They were ready, but Staff Sergeant Heller signaled them to hold. "Take cover!" he ordered as the earth exploded around them. Land mines. From nowhere machine gun fire ripped through the soil, and enemy soldiers appeared from beneath tarps and the gorge behind the Rangers. A helicopter descended from the range above them, hovering, with machine guns leveled on their position. *We're fish in a barrel,* Taylor thought.

Through the chaos, Sergeant Heller spoke his last command into his boom mike. "Stand down, men. Stand down. We will have our day, but today isn't it." Reluctantly, Taylor and the other Rangers surrendered their weapons. Amid a whirling cloud of dust and debris, the chopper landed and the rotors began to idle down. From the Indus Highway, a gray armored truck turned off the road and began lumbering across the desert floor.

Within minutes, the Rangers were undressed and kneeling on the coarse sand with hands clasped behind their heads. Four of them were bleeding from near misses. Seven men from the enemy ranks were ordered forward and promptly removed their slate-gray uniforms. To Corporal Sutton's surprise, the seven enemy soldiers began to redress in the Rangers' fatigues. The Rangers started to rise to their feet, but a spray of bullets from an automatic rifle held them back.

The seven imposters, now dressed as American Rangers, disappeared into the ranks. A door on the chopper swung open. All the enemy soldiers came to attention as a dark, robust man exited. Taylor instantly recognized him as Abdul-Aziz Rais, the self-promoted terrorist general whose weapons the Ranger team had been sent to destroy.

After removing his sunglasses, the general narrowed his eyes at the Americans with loathsome examination. "Welcome to my home. I hope you enjoyed my little surprise party." He spoke English well but with a thick Middle Eastern accent. "Do you know the penalty for illegal immigration in Pakistan is death?" He chuckled without smiling. "But you are not immigrants, are you? You are thieves!"

He kicked the nearest man in the stomach, a mountain of a Ranger named Cobb, who doubled over and coughed into the dirt. The general regained his arrogant composure and continued. "But never mind, I moved my weapons yesterday." He paused to light a massive cigar.

The Rangers stole glances at each other.

"That is right. I knew you were coming," Rais declared. He took a small device from a soldier and showed it to the Americans.

On it was seven little red dots—dots from GPS transponders hidden somewhere in the Rangers' clothing, which were now being worn by their enemy. The only way the general could have tracked the GPS signal was to get the parameters directly from the programmers. Taylor Sutton groaned, betrayal burning hot in his throat.

"Even if you had missed your landing coordinates, we would have found you. But you did not miss. You landed like flies in my trap!" General Rais bellowed, then kicked Cobb one more time.

Clearly enraged, Sergeant Heller turned and punched the nearest enemy soldier in the groin. When the man doubled over, Heller threw him forward and made a grab for the man's weapon. Before the rest of the Rangers could join in the uprising, a pistol report brought Heller to a standstill. Suddenly, the fight and life were leaking out of him through a hole in his chest. As a gasp slipped past his lips, Sergeant Heller fell forward into the unsympathetic dirt.

The general took a long drag on his cigar and holstered his pistol. "Now we understand one another."

The once-distant armored truck rumbled to a stop in a cloud of dust and diesel exhaust. "So you see," Rais said, motioning to the truck, "I am no animal. I would never leave you naked and weaponless to die in the desert like little rabbits. I have arranged transportation to take you safely to your new home." He turned back to the waiting chopper and motioned for the pilot to start the rotors. The Rangers were pushed to their feet and ordered to get in the truck, but they refused.

"We are not leaving the sergeant for the dogs!" shouted Delray Fulton, a big black Ranger with a distinctive Georgia drawl. He moved to Sergeant Heller's lifeless body and picked him up as though he were a child. Armed men beat on the large man's back with their rifles, but Fulton refused to lay the sergeant down.

One of the guards grew impatient and pushed Corporal Sutton. The corporal used his forward momentum to pull the man off balance, snatch a gun from his belt, and put a bullet in his chest before he hit the dirt.

The scuffle was over before it began, and by the time the rest of soldiers reacted, Corporal Sutton had dropped the gun and raised his arms. This did not, however, stop his captors from clubbing him with a gun and kicking him in the ribs. Fulton, with the sergeant cradled in his arms, continued to receive a beating for his defiance.

The general turned at the report of the pistol. The corporal was pulled into a kneeling position, and then a soldier stood behind him with his weapon pointed at the back of his head. Undaunted, Sutton declared, "One of yours, for one of ours, *General*. We are not leaving without the sergeant. You can kill us all right here!"

General Rais merely smirked and gave an amused snort. He spoke in Arabic, and the Rangers were allowed to carry Sergeant Heller to the truck. Then the general stepped into the chopper, where the accelerating rotors whipped the dirt into a blinding frenzy.

With tears streaming down his cheeks, Fulton carried the sergeant's body to the truck. After the body was loaded, the rest of the Rangers climbed into the vehicle. What horrors awaited them, Taylor dared not even imagine.

2

Two weeks later in Fort Irwin, California, it was business as usual. Located at the edge of the Mojave Desert, the army post was perfect for military weapons development. Michael Sutton sat in an office in a large industrial building, his eyes closed as he tried to steady his heart. He closed the folder with shaking hands, the bright-red letters staring up at him: "Classified." Inside was information relating to his brother, Taylor Sutton, whose Ranger team had been declared missing in action.

Michael ran his fingers through his dark hair. "Why does Taylor always have to be in the middle of the fight?" After a long moment he forced himself to read through the brief again.

> Army Rangers LRS team designation Ghost disappeared on July 25 following HALO jump. Mission: seek and destroy (see attached) deemed failure. Satellite imagery shows military activity in area of ground zero. Satellite failure @ approx. 0600. Image was restored @ 0620. LRS team had vanished. GPS transponder signals tracked moving west (opposite of eastbound target) have also gone black. Search, via satellite and UAV, was abandoned @ 0900 hrs. Wounded: unknown. Survivors: unknown. All members of LRS Ghost team are hereby declared MIA.

A handwritten footnote was scribbled across the bottom.

Intel has reached the Pentagon that terrorist Abdul-Aziz Rais is actively pursuing the hardware and know-how to turn dirty plutonium into a nuclear bomb. It is clear the Ranger team has failed. God help those men. God help us all.

Colonel Walter Bracken

Michael thumbed through the personnel files enclosed with the brief and stopped at his brother's. A photo of Taylor, dressed in his formal uniform, stared up at him. They were five years apart, he and Taylor, and different as two brothers could be. Michael was tall and slender, quiet, but easily given to laughter. Taylor was shorter, built like a brick, and easily given to fighting. In school, Michael had excelled at everything academic, especially mathematics and chemistry, while Taylor was near unbeatable at any sport he tried—the more physically demanding the better. It was Taylor's constant fighting at school that brought their parents to realize the boy needed guidance more than restraint. Thus began his training in the martial arts and his enrollment in ROTC.

Michael closed the file, stood up, and stared out a window that opened onto an empty driveway. The sun-baked pavement shimmered.

Taylor's team had simply vanished. It didn't make sense and didn't seem possible. Feeling numb, Michael hung his head, a spontaneous prayer spilling from his lips. He pled for answers and for his brother's well-being.

With his head against the warm window, he felt for a scar on his chest. It was several years ago now, but he was lucky have only escaped with a scar. A violent attack is something that happens to others—a late-night jogger living in New York, maybe, but certainly not to a grown man in broad daylight in Salt Lake City.

A knock at the door snapped Michael out of his thoughts. He cleared his throat and said, "Come in." As the door opened, the small office filled with production noises from the outer building. The building was leased from the military by his father's company, VAS Engineering, of which Michael was vice president. VAS had been Vander Adam Sutton's brainchild before Michael was born. The company had started out in the garage but grew into a profitable munitions contractor for the army, and business was good.

A young private entered and shut the door in order to speak without shouting. Dressed in desert fatigues, he stood ridged.

"Easy, Private," Michael said. "I'm just a civilian, remember."

"Colonel Bracken wants to speak with you, sir . . . ASAP."

"Thank you. I'll be there in a minute." Michael was surprised neither by the message nor the means by which it was sent. The colonel would rather use enlisted men to carry messages than pick up the phone. It was not an uncommon joke that enlisted men were the colonel's personal carrier pigeons.

The colonel's pigeon nodded and slipped out the door.

Michael went to his desk and closed his laptop, then locked it in a safe along with other sensitive research papers. He slipped the brief under one arm and left the office.

Out in the building, machines and men moved about steadily. An occasional gunshot was heard—test fire. Across the building, Michael could see his friend Specialist Jarrett Wilkens. He put two fingers to his mouth and whistled. When Jarrett looked up, Michael motioned that he was returning the classified folder. Jarrett, who knew about the folder but not its contents, gave an understanding nod and waved.

Soon, Michael slid into the unbearably hot interior of his pickup and began the short drive across the post. He rolled down the windows and blasted the air conditioning.

His thoughts and hand returned to the scar on his chest. He hadn't been home from his LDS mission long when he and Taylor were returning from Park City with a couple of girls. The double date—hiking and a picnic lunch—had been fun. Unfortunately, they had arrived back in the city at rush hour. Rather than sit in bumper-to-bumper traffic, they had taken to the side streets. The car they were driving was old, and neither Michael nor Taylor knew the fuel gauge was broken. After a few moments discussion, and figuring a gas station with a phone booth wasn't too far, the four of them started walking.

A couple of blocks later, they spotted a gas station across a vacant lot. When the brothers and their dates were midway across the lot, three guys came toward them from the other direction. Something about the three approaching men made them all uneasy, and though it was a first date the girls instinctively clung to Michael's and Taylor's arms. Looking into the eyes of the strangers as they passed, Michael saw a wild, soulless hunger.

They all exhaled when they had passed and put a couple of steps between them. It was then Michael heard someone say, "Hey, buddy!" Michael turned in time to catch a knife to the chest instead of the back.

What followed he could only remember in bits and pieces, but if the attackers had figured on taking on two girls and a teenage boy, they quickly learned otherwise. By then Taylor was a black belt in Taekwondo, and two of the attackers were later apprehended at the emergency room of the nearest hospital.

After the fight, Taylor stayed and kept pressure on the knife wound as the girls went to call an ambulance. In the weeks that followed, Michael heard countless remarks from doctors that Taylor's quick thinking had saved his life.

Since then, the two brothers had grown steadily apart. Even though Michael had tried to set a good example for his brother, Taylor seemed determined to live a fast lifestyle, no matter how it broke their parents' hearts. Following a particularly bad incident, Taylor had completely cut himself off from the family, leaving them in a perpetual holding pattern. They had all hoped and prayed he would one day get his bearings, swallow his pride, and make things right. But now—now Michael feared that day would never come.

Michael stopped his pickup in front of the H. Norman Schwarzkopf Building, a three-story structure that housed the colonel's office, as well as the offices of a dozen other high-ranking military officials. Upon entering the building, Michael took the stairs instead of waiting for the elevator. On the third floor, he walked directly to the colonel's office. A secretary sat at a desk outside.

"Go on in, Mr. Sutton. The colonel's expecting you."

"Thank you, Wendy," Michael said with a smile, but knocked anyway. The classified brief had been loaned to him discreetly by the colonel, who was an old friend of his father's. Their history went back as far as high school. After graduating, the two of them planned to join the military. Both young men were excellent athletes and full of themselves. However, a week before basic training ended, Michael's father had caught a bullet from a misfired weapon that nearly took his leg off. Walter went on to serve honorably during Vietnam and subsequent, smaller engagements, while Vander had established VAS Engineering.

When Michael cracked open the door and spoke, the colonel was just ending a call on a cell phone. Michael noted the older man's face was flushed. It was obvious he was not pleased.

Colonel Bracken tossed the cell phone in a drawer, then smiled and said, "Come on in, Michael." He crossed the room and grasped Michael's hand and shoulder. The colonel was tall and lean with white, wavy hair and dark eyes that reflected nothing. "How are you, kid? Sorry about your brother—he's one of the best."

Michael returned the brief to the colonel. "I don't know how I'll break it to my folks. I was thinking of calling . . . "

"Perhaps you'd better tell them in person," the colonel said.

Michael sighed. "Yeah. I just can't bear to see my mom cry."

"Claire's tough. Being an army brat herself, she knows the risks. She'll be fine. Your father, however—he may want to kill somebody." The colonel paused as if to think and then continued in earnest. "I want you to know that when I saw your brother's name in that file, I called the commander at JSOC immediately. I'll do whatever I can to help get Taylor home safely."

"I appreciate that, sir."

Colonel Bracken nodded, then opened another file, also stamped "Classified." "You're still involved with Project Wakeup Call?" He set a pair of reading glasses on his long, aquiline nose.

"Yes, sir."

"Fascinating stuff," the colonel said absently. "Incendiary and armor-piercing rounds for handguns and assault rifles, I see."

"We're also developing intelligent firearms that will actually misfire when pointed at fellow soldiers. We hope to eliminate friendly fire and accidental shootings. A computer chip in the soldier's gear will send a signal to the gun and not allow it to fire. They will change ground warfare forever."

"Indeed." The colonel continued to read the brief. "Most of this was your brainchild."

Michael smiled but tried not to look proud. "Dad and I . . . the Smartgun is his baby. He's been thinking about developing it since the gunshot that ended his military career. I put most of the technical designs in place."

"There may be one scenario you haven't thought of."

"What is that, sir?"

"What if our man is being used as a human shield? What would happen then? No one could fire on his captor."

"I thought of that. If you look at the notes from initial tests, you'll see that the guns will fire within two inches of our man."

The colonel whistled. "Two inches isn't much."

"It's cutting it close, but the gap between life and death is often much less than that."

"Well said." Colonel Bracken peered at Michael over his reading glasses. "I'm just grateful you're on our side. I'm looking forward to the weapons test next week."

"Yes, sir. We'll be ready. It'll be fun." Michael stood to leave.

The colonel smiled. "You think of this as fun?"

"Absolutely, sir. Who wouldn't want a job where you design new ways to blow stuff up?"

"Even if that 'stuff' is another human? What does your God say about that?"

"We believe in defending our homes and liberties, as well as those of others. Countless members of our Church serve in the armed forces, sir, and many of them have gone on to serve in Church leadership positions."

Colonel Bracken reclined in his chair and didn't say anything for a long minute, but finally he smiled. "There were many times I wished your father had been with me in Cambodia. He's a smart, levelheaded son of a . . . well, you know. It was too bad what happened to him." He lowered his eyes as if reminiscing.

"Mom says the old wound bothers him before a storm, but he never lets on." Michael paused. "I should be getting back. Thank you for the . . . information." He glanced at the file he had returned.

Colonel Bracken nodded. "You're welcome." He closed the file on Wakeup Call and stood. He and Michael shook hands. "When you see that ugly old man of yours, tell him handsome young Walt says hello."

Michael chuckled. "I will, sir."

He was about to turn and leave, but the colonel didn't let go of his hand. The old man seemed to be searching for words and finally said, "Tell your father . . . tell him I'm sorry things turned out this way."

"I will, sir." With that, Michael turned and left Walter Bracken's office. As he stepped into the elevator he thought about the colonel's words, "I'm sorry things turned out this way." He wasn't sure what the man was apologizing for.

Michael left the building and slid into the seat of his pickup. He looked at his watch—3:00 PM. Resolving to tell his parents in person, he planned to book a flight to Salt Lake for the following morning. But first he had to give his wife, April, the bad news.

He changed his mind about going back to work; it was a good day to go home early. He pulled a cell phone from his pocket and dialed. Jarrett answered. "Hey, Jarrett. Just letting you know I'm going home early. I've got some things to take care of."

"That's fine. We're about done for the day anyway. We'll see you Monday."

"Sounds good." Michael ended the call and started the truck. He drove to the outer gates, then through them, and pointed his truck toward home.

Fort Irwin was thirty-five minutes from Barstow. With a road as straight as a high-powered rifle shot, Michael had more than once made the trip in under twenty minutes, but today he drove the speed limit. For the first time in a while, he watched for signs of life in the desert. A roadrunner sprang from the brush and crossed the highway, and a motionless jackrabbit watched from a knoll.

At the western edge of Barstow, Michael turned at a sign that read "Sierra Gardens." Typical of other subdivisions, this was a maze of narrow streets lined with contemporary homes, all of which were various shades of yellow and peach and one of three floor plans. He turned on Lucero Drive and pulled the truck into the carport of number 1021.

He shut off the engine and ran his thumb and forefinger across his eyes. He hated to be the bearer of bad news. Suddenly it occurred to him that his daughter might grow up not knowing her uncle. The thought made Michael shudder in spite of the heat.

Their home, like almost every other one on the block, was two stories with a single-car garage that was too small for anything larger than a Mini Cooper. The outside of the house had hints of Spanish architecture, with arches on the entry and domed tiles on the roof. The front yard of gravel, shrubs, and cacti was maintained by a company under contract with the homeowners association.

Michael entered the small living room and set down his laptop bag. Absently, he had brought it in even though it was empty.

At the stairwell he picked up the trail of his daughter's toys like breadcrumbs that gave away her movements during the day. It led through the family room, across the couch, and into the kitchen. He stopped to pick up an apple and began rubbing it on his shirt. He was not expected home for another couple hours and wondered what his wife did at 3:30 in the afternoon.

"April?" he called out but with no response. Then he heard laughter from the backyard. The sliding glass door was partly open and he could see his bride and daughter on the swing set in the backyard. He stood there for a while, watching the candid moment between the two people he cherished most.

He had met April at BYU after his mission. She was April Udall then, a freshman. He was returning as a sophomore. She was tall but unassuming with rich-brown hair that shimmered red in the sun. Born and raised in Valencia, she was tan and beautiful from the California sun. He was nearly colorless from two years in Alaska but still managed to get that first date. He could do little to hide his infatuation with her. At a glance, she could send him into a fits of mindless stammering. She enjoyed that.

Michael watched mother and daughter together—they were beautiful and his heart was anchored with them. He took a deep breath. He hated to break up the serene moment, but he needed to tell April. With her at his side, everything that was wrong with the world felt manageable.

He slid the door open and stepped outside into bright sun. Instantly, Suzanne squealed with delight. "Daddy's home!" She jumped from her swing and raced across the small yard. Michael crouched down and caught her up in a big hug.

"How's my girl?"

She shrugged. "I dunno."

Michael laughed. "You don't know?"

"Nope! I'm just swingin'." She kissed his cheek and hugged him, then wiggled out of his arms. Skipping back to the swing set, she began to sing the lyrics to her favorite TV show. She was a precocious four years old.

Smiling, April came up beside Michael. Her long hair was a little shorter than when they had first met, but ever radiant in the sun. Her angelic presence still stirred his soul, and he had to catch his breath. He smiled back at her.

"Hi," she whispered.

"Hi." He bent forward and kissed her. Hers was a face he could wake up to for an eternity.

"You're home early," she said with her arms around his waist. "You get fired or something?"

"Nope. Not that lucky." He paused. "We need to book a flight to Salt Lake."

April pulled back. "Why? Is everything okay?"

"It's Taylor. His team's missing."

"Are they sure? He's only been gone . . . "

"Too long." Michael met her gaze. "I read a report—a classified report. They're missing and assumed dead."

April's green eyes widened. "But there's still a chance, right?"

"I don't know. I hope there is." Michael let his breath out slowly. "I'm worried about telling Mom and Dad." Down deep in his insides, a small ember ignited, a hint of something he thought had long since been smothered.

A long silence followed as husband and wife idly watched their daughter play. Michael felt momentarily envious of her trouble-free life. Suzanne jumped off the swing and ran over.

"Can I have your apple, Daddy?"

He had forgotten he was even holding it. "Sure."

She grabbed it, took a bite no bigger than a squirrel would have, and handed it back. "Thanks. That's all." Her parents chuckled.

"Well, should we go say a prayer for your brother?" April said. "Then I'll go find us some airline tickets." She reached up and kissed Michael's cheek.

He nodded. "Good idea."

3

Half a world away, Corporal Taylor Sutton awoke in a cramped, subterranean cell—a tomb of concrete and steel—his exact location unknown. After his captors had loaded him and the other Rangers onto a truck, sleep had been administered in the form of a sharp blow to the back of the head. Now, surrounded by impenetrable walls and the repugnant odor of human excrement, Taylor waited in darkness and bewilderment. Hunger and thirst led to delirium, and time became intangible. Moments of lucidity were filled with anger and uncertainty. Where Sergeant Heller's body had ended up was a mystery, and questions about it only brought beatings from the guards.

We were betrayed, but why and by whom? Taylor thought. Missions such as theirs were only known to a handful of men with the highest security clearance—men of honor and unfathomable patriotism. The Rangers' mission had been one that held the fate of nations and countless lives in the balance. *And we failed.*

He heard guards at his door. Too weak to rise, Taylor was promptly dragged out into the corridor by his feet. He was handcuffed and hobbled, then pulled upright and escorted through the outer door and beyond to a labyrinth of dark corridors. In Corporal Sutton's delirium there seemed to be countless cages, all of them filled with the vilest specimens of the human animal, spitting and growling as he passed by.

Soon he was led up two long flights of stairs and to a large wooden door. The door opened and he was greeted by a brightly lit room as though it were something out of a dream. His eyes instinctively went to the windows to discover his surroundings, but it was night and the blackness gave nothing away. He was led to a chair and forced to sit. Tears pooled in his eyes and ran over as he squinted and blinked in the light. Once the corporal's arms and legs were bound to the chair, his escorts stepped back.

The room was finely decorated. An intricate carpet covered the center of the wood floor. Expensive-looking paintings hung from each of the clean white walls. Lights above the paintings, situated carefully to show off the artwork, wer26,e decorated with gold inlay. The domed ceiling was painted like that of a church, with cherubs and gold-laced clouds, all of it brightly lit with a row of lights hidden above a wooden tray of incredible craftsmanship. *Not what you'd expect in a prison,* Taylor thought just before his eyes discovered a door, nearly hidden behind an ornate tapestry. While he could not know for sure, he suspected it led outside.

Behind him the door from the prison opened and shut, and General Rais entered, humming. He crossed the floor and sat behind a large oak desk. After lighting a cigar, he looked at his guest.

"Give me your name, rank, and serial number!" Their eyes locked for a moment, and then the general burst into laughter. He took a long drag on his stogie and reclined in his leather chair. Taylor watched his captor with unabashed disdain.

"I am just kidding! It was a good joke. Why did you not laugh?" The general chuckled and took another puff. "I already know who you are. I know everything about you. You are Corporal Taylor Sutton. You graduated with honors from West Point, where you excelled in hand-to-hand combat. You are the third-ranking member of the Army Rangers team designated Ghost, and also the only one who dared avenge Sergeant Heller on the day of your capture. Perhaps they are not making Rangers like they used to."

Irritated by the general's arrogance, Taylor said hoarsely, "And?"

The general's eyes flashed and he pitched forward. "And you are alive because I allow it." He searched Taylor's eyes for a long second and finally said, "You are not afraid."

Taylor did not reply.

"Regardless, you will be," the general continued. "And you will die when it is time. For now you and your friends are, as they say, bargaining chips. Let me show you what I mean."

The general proceeded to dial a phone. "I would use my cell phone," he said with a chuckle, "but this one has a better speaker and you will want to listen."

After two rings, the call was picked up. "This is Colonel Bracken. Hello?"

The general smiled when Corporal Sutton gasped in horror and surprise.

"Hello, Colonel. This is General Rais."

"How on earth did you get this number?" Bracken barked.

"I have someone here who wants to say hello." The general motioned for the corporal to speak.

Not wanting to believe the obvious, Taylor said quickly, "Colonel, this is Corporal Taylor Sutton. We've been captured. Someone betrayed us, sir! And they have killed Staff Sergeant Heller. I don't know where we are, Colonel, but we're alive . . . Colonel?"

Taylor was greeted by silence. Then the general spoke. "Colonel, are you there?"

"General Rais! Why are those men still alive?"

Taylor pulled back in horror as though he had touched the devil. *The colonel is the traitor!*

The general puffed his cigar with arrogant satisfaction. "They are alive, Colonel, because I require one more thing from you. And to ensure I get it, these men will remain alive as tokens of your betrayal, just in case you decide not to cooperate."

"You fat, pompous . . . " The colonel let loose a string of expletives that would make a sailor proud.

General Rais laughed louder than the colonel could swear. "You are so very right. I am all those things, but I hold the cards. I make the rules, or these men will be free by sundown!"

There was a long, exasperated pause. "What is it?"

Furious, Ranger Sutton pulled against his restraints. "Colonel—you traitor! You'll burn for this, I swear!"

The general picked up a pistol and aimed it at Sutton. He put a finger to his lips and continued. "I have all I need, Bracken. But as you Americans say, there is some assembly required. I need someone to assemble the bomb, complete with long-range detonation. The other items are also in disrepair."

"You can't be serious," the colonel exclaimed. "I have all but gift wrapped those weapons for you. Do I need to wipe your nose too?"

"Don't patronize me, Colonel!" General Rais growled. "You are no better. Selling out your own men—even I would not do that. Regardless of what you may believe or what you see on your stupid television, there is not a bomb maker on every corner. Not of the type I require."

"I'll see what I can do." The colonel huffed. "Someone's at my door." A male's voice uttered the word "Colonel" just before the line went dead.

Taylor couldn't be sure, but the voice seemed familiar. He sat back, his head spinning. *My team and I are pawns!*

The general motioned. The previous escorts appeared beside Corporal Sutton and unlocked one of his wrists, then set a plate of food and a bottle of water in his lap. Completely deflated, he looked from the plate to the general. Taylor had no appetite—not for food, anyway.

"You should eat. If you die, my plans of blackmail will be spoiled." The general chuckled as he lit his cigar again and took another puff.

Taylor sat still for a minute. He had a choice. He could starve to death and by doing so eliminate the leverage the general had on the colonel. Or he could eat and keep his strength and wait for the opportunity to escape, to complete the mission and bring the colonel to justice. Taylor decided he would eat, but not here. He wouldn't give the general the satisfaction. And though his body yearned for the food, his appetite for information was greater. "You intend to attack America," he spat out.

The general chuckled. "Or American allies."

"You plan to escalate the war."

The general smiled and shrugged. "I will simply prolong it. Broaden it. Alienate your country. Show the world how feeble you really are. With blood in the water, the sharks will come. Also, the body count has been on a steady decline. We need the body count up." The general raised his hands in emphasis. "Especially before the American elections. Your reporters will do the rest."

"And what are the colonel's motives?"

General Rais smirked. "Who cares, but for the moment our desires are aligned. More war. I like that those words go well together."

While the general spoke, Taylor looked around the room again. For the first time he noticed a cool breeze. He searched until he found the vent to his left. It had to lead somewhere.

"Again you are looking around my quarters. Do you like them? I borrowed all this from a room at the Hotel Granada in Madrid. I stayed there once, in a penthouse suite."

"The Hotel Granada? Wasn't it destroyed?"

The general chuckled and drew on his cigar. "Yes! I blew it up. I had stayed in the room once and could not bear the thought of this work of art going down with rest of the hotel."

"You saved this room, and killed how many?"

The general shrugged indifferently. "A few hundred or so, but what does it matter? The Spaniards learned a lesson." He placed a sausage-like finger firmly on his desk.

Taylor shook his head. "If you attack with these new weapons, we'll find you and kill you."

The general snorted. "It does not matter. You may kill me, but you cannot destroy an idea. When you chop the tail off a lizard, it only grows back. I am not the head. Perhaps no one is. America and its allies believe terrorism is something that can be crushed by might. I find that amusing. Terrorism is an idea whose time has come. The powerful will always rule the weak—and we are powerful! We are recruiting from all over the globe, even from within your own borders. Thanks to the Internet, those who are tired of American oppression can unite."

"Oppression? What you're selling is anarchy. Anarchy is not freedom!" Taylor shook his head. "I heard about people like you when I was a child. You're a—a Gadianton."

"Gadi-anton? I have not heard of them. Who were they? Americans?"

"Sort of. He and his followers wanted to overthrow civilization, just like you do. Gadianton began small, moving in secret and skulking about like a cockroach until he had gained enough recruits that he felt strong and confident. But in the end his dependency on the people he despised led to his downfall." Not having thought about that story in years, Taylor surprised himself. "So here you are, planning for our destruction, all the while using cell phones and Internet and automobiles and jets, all of which were either invented or perfected in America. You're a leech despising the host. You couldn't exist without America. You're a spoiled, unappreciative child."

The general came out of his chair and planted a right fist the size of an Easter ham into Taylor's face, knocking him flat onto his back. The untouched food and water were strewn across the floor.

"You are the spoiled one, my friend! You eat when you are not hungry. You drink when you are not thirsty. You do not know what it means to be without or to watch your family butchered.

You do not understand the meaning of suffering. But you will!" The general slammed a heavy fist onto his desk.

His shouting brought more soldiers into the room. They stood above Taylor with their rifles pointed down at him. The general spat at him and sneered. "Get him out of my sight."

Taylor's chair was jerked upright and it teetered on its broken legs. He was quickly unshackled and pulled roughly to his feet. He spit the blood from his mouth onto the rug. Though the general's punch had dazed him, Taylor felt awake, shaken from the haze of starvation and thirst. He was feeding on adrenaline and ready for a fight.

If the general expected to see some sign of fear or pain, he was disappointed.

Much more coherent on the return trip to his cell, Taylor paid close attention to the route, memorizing directions. There were three lefts and a right and five barred doors as they passed through the cell blocks. He could find his way back to the general's office if the opportunity afforded itself.

Corporal Sutton also carefully studied his escorts. While maneuvering through the locked doors he could have easily overpowered them, but as gratifying as it would have been, he restrained himself. There would be other opportunities.

The clumsy guards threw Taylor into the concrete cavity and slammed the solid iron door behind him. He dusted himself off and stood tall in the middle of the cell. "Ghosts, sound off!" he shouted. His voice echoed and died. "Ghosts, sound off!"

From somewhere in the darkness came a weak voice. "Two." Slowly the rest followed.

"Seven."

"Five."

"Four."

"Three."

"Six!" Sutton said.

"Shut up, dogs!" yelled an unseen guard.

Corporal Sutton smiled in the darkness. He was not alone. Without Staff Sergeant Heller, they were only six, but six good men could do a great deal.

4

Michael could not sleep. His and April's and Suzanne's bags were packed, their tickets purchased for an 8:00 flight the next morning. How would he tell his parents their hope of reuniting with their estranged son was blasted, that they would probably have to wait until the next life? On top of that, Michael was dealing with his own guilt. Had he judged his brother too harshly? Held him to a standard Taylor simply wasn't ready to commit to?

It was midnight when Michael finally rolled out of bed and sat on the edge in the dark. His mind just wouldn't shut down.

From behind him, April spoke. "Can't sleep, love?"

"No. I can't stop thinking about Taylor or how to break the news to Mom and Dad. The last thing I told Taylor was that the family would be better off without him. Remember?"

April rolled toward Michael and reached for his hand. He felt her tender touch and curled his fingers around hers. "I remember he had it coming," she replied in a sleepy whisper. "Knowing Taylor, if there's any way to survive, he will. We have to hope."

"I know, but that doesn't make it any easier." Michael sighed. "I'm going to get up for a bit. Maybe I'll read for a while."

"I can get up with you."

"No, don't. One of us needs to get some rest or Suzanne will run all over us tomorrow." He kissed April's hand and then stood. Descending the stairs to the front room, his bare foot found one of Suzanne's toys, pointy end up, and he swore under his breath. He limped a few steps and was more careful where he stepped.

In the dark he located the lamp beside the couch and turned it on with a click. The house was silent other than the ticking of a clock from the far wall—something he never heard during the day. Michael went to the refrigerator and poured a cold glass of milk, then found a half-eaten bag of cookies and sat down at the snack bar. Ever since he was a kid he loved dunking cookies. It often cheered him up, but tonight the comfort food did little to help him relax.

Sitting alone in the shadows he could not escape the terrifying thought that his brother may have left this life believing his family hated him. It had been so long since they had been on friendly terms. Ever since that fateful night, Michael had wondered if his actions had been right. In his mind, he had hoped to be the lighthouse to which Taylor would one day look when surrounded by the fog of his misspent life. At the present moment such a thought seemed more than a little self-righteous.

It had been two years since the brothers' final falling out. The occasion had been Taylor's twenty-fifth birthday. Michael distinctly recalled checking his watch as he and April sat across from his parents at the dining room table. A banner hung from the ceiling that read, "Happy 25th Birthday, Taylor!" A lifeless birthday cake sat in the center of the table. The conversation had lulled, and their mother again looked at the clock with mounting worry on her face. Taylor was late. Very late. Michael knew their mother wanted to wait, but the food had grown cold so they had eaten dinner without Taylor. Now he had missed dinner entirely, and eating the cake without him seemed silly. It was *his* birthday after all.

"Mom, Taylor's a big boy," Michael said. "I'm sure he just lost track of time visiting his old friends." He doubted his own words.

"Maybe," she replied, clearly unconvinced. "You'd think he'd at least call."

Michael looked at his dad, who shook his head and said with a sigh, "Well, it's obvious Taylor doesn't care too much for our plans." Claire tried feebly to defend Taylor, but Van would hear nothing of it. Little could prepare them for what came next.

There was a thud at the door and a rustling. Before anyone could react, the door crashed open and Taylor spilled onto the floor, a young woman landing on top of him. The two of them laughed loudly until the woman noticed the awestruck onlookers. As she stood, clearly embarrassed, Taylor lolled his head back and said, "Hey, everyone! Why are you all upside down?" He was drunk.

Van stood up. "What in the world is going on?"

"I'm so sorry," the woman said. "He asked me to drive him to a party. I didn't know."

"The party," Van said, looking at the pathetic heap on the floor, "is over."

"I'll just go. I'm sorry." She backed sheepishly out the door.

Trying to get off the floor, Taylor yelled after her, "Call me!"

Claire pushed her chair away from the table and left the room sobbing. Van approached Taylor, who had come to a seated position. "What's the matter with you, Son? You were raised better than this." A long silence followed as he stood over Taylor. Finally, Van said, "When you sober up and grow up, you owe your mother an apology."

Their father then turned and left the room, no doubt to console their mother. Michael sat silently with his elbows resting on his knees and his head hanging. The tension in the air was as thick as a San Francisco fog. April took the cake and went to the kitchen to put it in the refrigerator, but Michael knew she was just trying to escape the uncomfortable scene.

When a pungent belch broke the silence, Michael snapped and turned on his brother. "What is your problem, Taylor?"

"Leave it alone, Mike," Taylor replied with a slur. He had worked his way up to standing against the wall, but leaned as though the earth was spinning too fast.

Michael continued undaunted. "Mom and Dad flew you out here in order to celebrate your birthday, and this is the thanks they get? This has got to be the worst thing you've ever done, and there have been some real gems over the years."

"I said leave it alone!"

"I'm not going to leave this alone, Taylor. When are you going to grow up? We weren't raised like this! Mom and Dad don't deserve this but you don't care, and that's what makes it worse."

"So you think I should live like you? An . . . an arrogant, self-righteous suck up? You're always doing whatever you're told like a good little boy. First it was seminary, then a mission, marry a pretty little angel, and pretend everything is perfect!" Spittle came out of Taylor's mouth with the last word. "Well, let me tell you what I think of that—"

Michael shook his head and closed his eyes against the pain of the memory. The argument had continued until April tried to intervene. Taylor called her a name, and Michael flattened his brother with a brutal right fist. Bleeding and too drunk to fight back, Taylor staggered from the house and into the night. It was the last time the family had been together under one roof.

Michael rubbed his face and pushed away from the snack bar. *Stupid cookies didn't help at all.* Exhausted but still restless, he found a more comfortable spot on the couch. He turned on a second lamp, and gold letters reflected in the lamplight. He picked up the Bible, which all but fell open to Christ's parable of the prodigal son. Michael read it several times and wondered if such a thing could happen—the return of the prodigal. He had to believe it could. After all, he owed that prodigal his life.

At that same hour, a single desk lamp still burned on the third floor of the Schwarzkopf building. Colonel Bracken checked his watch. Midnight. His tie was loose, his hair disheveled. He spun an empty tumbler on his desk, various thoughts and memories wandering through his mind until it settled on an old friend.

In many ways, he envied Vander Sutton. Van had never seen conflict and its horrors from the driver's seat. He had never been asked to make decisions that cost men their lives. Van had been unbelievably lucky. When they were young and naive, the world was a simple place—bravery and right were rewarded, cowardice and evil punished. They had been so very, very wrong. In reality, everything was a matter of perspective and timing.

The colonel opened a drawer and retrieved a bottle of whiskey. He filled the tumbler two fingers high, then stood and faced the window to look out across the post. Landing lights blinked in the distance.

He took a sip of the bitter fluid. It burned all the way down. Right and wrong were merely a matter of viewpoint now. One faction's hero was another faction's traitor. Who was correct? It depended on your objective and personal beliefs. There had been too many concessions, too many compromises.

He lit a cigar. The flame reflected from the glass. That too had been a small surrender along the way, perhaps his first. He didn't even like smoking. His eyes focused on his reflection; he hardly recognized the old man in the mirror.

The colonel thought about his current situation. It was deep water, as deep as it gets. And it all began with a simple conversation in the dark with an unknown individual who promised him a promotion if the mission unexpectedly went sideways. Small details about the classified mission were to be divulged, and he would be *General* Bracken by year's end. He felt deserving, since he had been previously overlooked, and something had to change. He needed a man on the inside, whoever it was.

Undoubtedly, there were others higher up on the food chain, but it was Bracken's neck in the guillotine if it all came crashing down. Of that he was certain.

He thought again of his old friend Van and wondered what it must be like to view the world through rose-colored glasses. To form opinions about topics from what one could read in the newspaper or learn from the TV—to be wholly naive. The colonel felt both jealous and bitter, for it all could have been different. It was unfortunate that Van's youngest had to be one of the sacrificial lambs. Bracken liked the kid. He liked Michael even more, yet it appeared another sacrifice would have to be laid across the altar of ambition.

Bracken crushed out his cigar and gulped the whiskey. It was time Vander Sutton made a few sacrifices of his own and learned what the world was really like.

As the whiskey warmed the colonel's insides, a cold shudder ran down his spine. Having made his decision, he picked up his cell phone. It had been specially encrypted for him by a non-military source. He dialed and General Rais's voice answered. "General, I know the man you need, but it's going to require some work on your end—some bait that can't be traced back to me."

"What do you have in mind?" asked Rais.

The colonel explained what was needed.

There comes into the life of such a man a final act, whether or not he is aware of it. That act can simply put him in the wrong place at the wrong time, or, as in the colonel's case, start a chain of events that at last culminates in his own failure. For Colonel Walter Bracken, it was that phone call.

5

A thud at the front door woke Michael with a start—the paperboy's aim was improving. Michael had fallen asleep sitting upright with his chin in his chest and now had a serious kink in his neck. As he rubbed it, he wondered when his thoughts had faded into a restless slumber. He suddenly remembered they had a plane to catch at 8:00 and jerked his head toward the clock on the wall behind him only to have a burning pain shoot through his neck again. His eyes shut against it. "Of all the days—why today," he mumbled to himself.

Taking it easier, he stood and turned to the clock. 5:30—they still had time. Perhaps April could work her magic for him. As he climbed the stairs the stiffness in his neck seemed to increase with every step, and by the time he reached their bedroom his head was tilted to one side. He found his wife in the shower.

"Hey, babe?" he said meekly.

"Hey," she replied from behind the curtain. "Did you get any sleep?"

"Sorta. I'm going to need your help when you get out." His tone got her attention and she peeked out. Her hair was slicked back and water dripped from her cute pointed nose. "What is it?" she asked.

Michael smiled sheepishly. "I fell asleep on the couch . . . sitting up. And now I can't move my neck."

"Ah, you need to visit Helga's House of Pain," April said in a Bulgarian accent.

Michael smiled. "It's not funny . . . ow . . . it's getting worse."

"I can fix it but you're not going to like it." She disappeared behind the curtain again. "Go relax on the bed. I'll be right out."

He did as he was told, but lying down took surprising effort. Every way he tried hurt, so he finally just flopped straight back. That too was a mistake. With his head resting against his left shoulder the pain was bearable and he quickly dozed off.

A few minutes later he was awakened with his wife's gentle fingers rubbing his neck. She was sitting above him on the bed. About the time he smiled and was about to open his eyes, his head was suddenly jerked wildly to the right and then the left. Both times Michael's neck cracked like a dry branch.

He tried to pull away from her, but she held him down. "Good grief! Are you trying to kill me?"

April looked down into his eyes and continued to rub his neck. With a wry grin she said, "You do have a pretty good life insurance policy, remember?" She bent forward and kissed him.

"So that's how it is. Try to kill me, then smooth it over with a kiss."

"Works every time." She smiled again and swung her legs off the bed. Michael watched her move back to the bathroom. At that moment, he was surprised her feet actually touched the floor. She was wearing black slacks and a white blouse that hung loosely about her neck. She noticed him staring and smiled. "You'd better start getting ready or we'll miss our flight."

"I'd rather just lie here and look at you." He stood carefully and came to her. "What do I owe Helga?"

Just then a small voice cried out from across the hallway. April reached up and pecked Michael on the cheek. "You can get Helga's daughter up and ready for the day."

"That's not what I had in mind." He said over his shoulder as he left the room.

Across the hall he found Suzanne sitting up in bed and rubbing one eye. His neck was still sore but he managed to pick her up and give her a big hug. He began to sing "Wake Up, Little Susie" as he swung her back and forth. Her legs dangled until after a really big swing he reached out and caught her legs and squeezed her into a ball and dropped her onto the bed.

Suzanne giggled, "Do it again, Daddy."

"No, that nearly killed me as it was. And . . . we have to get ready to go and see Grandma and Grandpa today. How would you like that?"

"Oh! I would like that bunches." She began jumping on the bed and singing "To Grandma's house we go . . . To Grandma's house we go . . . Hi ho the merry oh . . . "

Michael smiled and rummaged through her dresser until he found some clothes. He sat her down and looked into her big brown eyes. "All right, all right, baby chick. You have way too much energy this early in the morning. Let's get you dressed."

"When can we get a puppy?" Suzanne asked.

"When we get a bigger backyard."

"When's that?"

Michael sighed. They'd been through this a dozen times before. "When we get a bigger house."

"When's tha . . . "

Michael put a finger to his daughter's lips. "Let's just get you dressed, okay?"

She nodded.

After her daddy had dressed her, Suzanne looked at her clothes. "These don't match."

"Oh yeah? Says who?"

"Says Mommy." She put her little hands on her hips. "These are the kind of clothes I put on if I dress myself. Mom says I can't go out in puplick like this."

Michael chuckled. "Puplick, huh? Well, it'll have to do. Let's go eat breakfast."

"All right, but Mommy's not going to like it." Suzanne took her father's hand.

"I'll worry about that."

Over a bowl of cold cereal, she asked, "So does Mommy know we're going to Grandma's today?"

"Sure, Mommy bought the tickets," Michael said.

"Is she going to throw up again?"

He laughed and almost choked on his juice. It had been nearly a year since they had flown out to Salt Lake and April had gotten sick. He was surprised Suzanne remembered.

He leaned forward and whispered, "Let's just hope Mommy doesn't throw up this time." He hung out his tongue as though he were ill. Suzanne laughed.

At that moment April came downstairs and asked, "What are you two giggling about?"

Sitting up, Michael said, "Nothing. Just eating." He winked at his daughter. She tried to wink back, but it looked more like she had something in her eye.

April kissed Michael, then took a second look at Suzanne. "Michael, did you let her dress herself?"

Suzanne spoke first. "I tried to tell him that I couldn't go out in puplick like this."

"Traitor," Michael said.

April held out her hand to Suzanne. "Let's go get you changed while Daddy loads the luggage into the car." She gave her husband an exasperated look. Mother and daughter began some girlie conversation as they climbed the stairs.

I'm simply outnumbered, Michael thought with a chuckle. *Next time we'd better have a boy.* He swallowed the last of his juice and put the cup in the sink. Five bags waited by the door. Only one was his—maybe half of one. *That's a lot of stuff for one weekend.* He rubbed his neck, which still felt a little stiff.

6

After an eventless hour on the passenger plane, a voice came over the intercom: "This is your captain speaking. We'll be landing in Salt Lake shortly. We hope you had an enjoyable flight. We may experience some turbulence as we descend into the valley. This is perfectly normal. Thanks again for flying Global Air."

With an intense look on her face, April read the instructions on seat floatation. "Perfectly normal," she muttered. "Obviously the pilot has never puked up his toenails at twenty thousand feet."

Michael took his wife's hand and squeezed it. He knew she had promised herself not to get sick on this trip, but obviously she was struggling.

"I hate flying into Salt Lake," she said in a near whisper. She closed her eyes and took some deep breaths. "The turbulence is worse than anywhere else. We have barf bags, right?"

Michael pointed them out to her, but her eyes were shut tight.

From the window seat, Suzanne said, "The clouds look like cotton candy, Mommy."

"Yes they dooo . . ." At that moment the plane dropped and shook violently, and April's voice pitched.

"Whee!" Suzanne said excitedly. "It's like the rolly coaster at the mall! It makes my tummy tickle." Michael smiled at his daughter and put a finger to his lips, signaling her to quiet down.

The plane shuddered and shook again. Michael watched April, who looked a little green. She had a death grip on his hand and was mumbling through her teeth something that sounded like "Don't throw up, don't throw up." He grabbed one of the paper bags, just in case. Then, blessedly, the plane settled down and quickly descended onto the tarmac. With all wheels on the ground, it shuddered once more as the engines were reversed.

April let out a relieved sigh, and her color slowly began to return.

Michael smiled and rubbed her hand. "You made it."

"Yeah. It was iffy there for minute, but I'm good."

"You sure?" He lifted his hand with hers still clenched around it like a starfish on a clam.

"Oh!" April quickly let go. "Sorry." She turned to her daughter. "You all right, baby chick?"

Suzanne was plastered to the small window. "Yep. But I don't see Grandma. Does she know we're coming?"

"Nope. It's a surprise."

Suzanne turned, her eyes wide. "A surprise? A surprise!" She kicked her feet wildly from the edge of her seat. "Grandma's gonna love her surprise!"

Once the small family exited the plane and retrieved their luggage from baggage claim, they rented a car. South of the airport they took Bangerter Highway and sped toward West Jordan and the home of Suzanne's grandma and grandpa Sutton. As most people do when returning to a familiar place, Michael and April noted the changes in the city since their last visit. Suzanne, not caring anything about this, began to sing the lyrics to the latest Disney movie.

At 7000 South, Michael pulled onto the off-ramp, went through the green light, and crossed the highway traveling east. On the corner of Woodgreen and Millberg stood an old Craftsman home with a neatly manicured front lawn, and a massive oak towering out back.

Michael pulled the car into the driveway and shut off the engine. He let out a sigh as his heart thumped in his chest. "As soon as they see us, they'll know something's up. We never show up unannounced."

"It'll be all right," April said. "It's still better than telling them over the phone. At least you can be there for your dad when he starts to blame himself."

The young Sutton family got out of the car. Wasting no time, Suzanne bolted across the lawn and through the front door, squealing all the way. Her parents had barely reached the porch when Van Sutton appeared at the door, wearing reading glasses and house slippers. He was a solidly built man whose once-powerful arms and chest were growing soft in his autumn years.

He grinned. "Hey, kids. I thought that was your little hurricane that tore through here." He pulled his reading glasses down and let them hang from their chain. "What a surprise. How are you two?" He kissed his daughter-in-law on the cheek.

"We're all right," Michael said. "Looks like you're taking it easy today, Pop."

"Sure. Every now and then a man needs to shift it into neutral. So what brings you two out here so early on a Saturday?"

"Just a visit," Michael said carefully.

Looking unconvinced, Van put an arm around April's shoulders and headed for the door. "Well, let's go inside and find your mother, and you can tell us all about it."

It, Michael thought. "It" was a big it. His father obviously realized something was up, just as Michael had known he would. Michael's hands felt a little sweaty, his heart raced, and all he wanted to do was turn around and go home.

Van went back through the front door, his daughter-in-law in tow. Michael noticed his dad was wearing his old University of Utah T-shirt. There must be a game today. April and Van proceeded through the foyer, leaving Michael to close the door.

Though the city was fast changing around them, little had changed inside the walls of the old Sutton home. Family photos still hung where they had for twenty or more years. A flood of memories washed over Michael as the familiar surroundings filled his senses.

The three of them entered the kitchen and found that Claire Sutton was already spoiling her granddaughter, who sat on the counter munching a cookie.

"Well, what a wonderful surprise. I was just telling Dad we should drive out and see you guys!" Claire pulled off her apron and emerged from behind the counter. She gave April a hug, and Michael a kiss on the cheek.

"I can't believe it. I was just standing here and all of a sudden I got tackled by little Suzanne. What a surprise!" Claire's face was flushed with delight. Michael noticed her hair was a medium brown now, not the color it had been when he was a boy, or the last time he'd seen her.

Suzanne spoke up. "Do you love your surprise, Grandma?"

"Yes, I do," Claire said, then gave her son a quick glance up and down with an examining eye that never missed a thing. "You've put on weight. That's good."

Michael rolled his eyes at April.

Van motioned toward the front room. "Let's sit down and you can tell us what brings you out of the land of fruits and nuts so early on a Saturday morning."

"Maybe they just want to visit, dear," Claire said.

April helped her daughter down from the counter and told her to go in the other room and watch a movie. Like most kids these days, Suzanne first learned to walk, then how to operate the DVD player.

In the front room Van eased into his worn leather lounger, then folded the newspaper and set it on the coffee table. Claire sat on the arm of the lounger, where Van held her hand. "I still have a batch of cookies in the oven," she explained.

Michael and April sat across from them. Michael didn't sit back but perched on the edge of the couch. April rubbed his back lightly. Everyone fell silent for a minute. Michael just didn't know how to begin.

Finally, Van spoke. "What's happened to your brother?"

7

The morning raced toward noon. On a beautiful day in West Jordan, the leaves on the old oak were every shade of gold imaginable. A cool mountain breeze wove its way across the valley floor. Beside the massive tree, Michael and Vander Sutton sat on a weathered bench with wooden slats and ornately decorated armrests.

It had been almost an hour since Michael had informed his parents about Taylor's team and the events surrounding the Rangers' disappearance. His mother and father had asked a question or two, and Van had made a call to Colonel Bracken. There was little else to do and no one to petition, since the news had not come through official channels. After Van hung up the phone, there was a long, heavy silence. Finally, he stood and mumbled something about fresh air. Michael followed, while April stayed behind to be with Claire.

Now, sitting cross-legged on the park bench, Van remained quiet for a long time. A western meadowlark sang majestically somewhere in the limbs above them. "Did I ever tell you the story behind this bench?" Van asked suddenly.

"No," Michael said, wondering why his father was thinking about the bench.

"I should have. It's a good story." Van ran a hand through his salt-and-pepper hair. "I guess it has been almost thirty years now. You would've been about four years old. Your mother and I had gone out for a late-evening walk through Constitution Park, leaving you with a sitter. I remember it was a particularly beautiful evening—crisp and cold air, a fresh blanket of snow, and clear skies with a full moon. After your mother and I walked for a while, we decided to sit down. We spotted this park bench sitting next to a spruce. We cleared the snow off and sat for a while, just marveling at the stillness. On snowy nights it seems there's a great hush over the whole city, and the slightest sound travels forever. That's how it was that night.

"After several minutes, your mother turned to me with a twinkle in her eye and told me we were going to have another baby. It was a miracle. You see, after we had you, the doctors had told us your mother couldn't have any more children. They said something had gone wrong during your delivery. But here came Taylor anyway.

"Years later, when the city got new benches for the park and got rid of the old ones, we made sure we saved this one. I replaced the rotten wood and put the bench back here. I find myself sitting here whenever I need a better perspective." Van rubbed his hand across the wood slats.

After a few minutes of silence, Michael spoke. "You and Mom took the news better than I had anticipated." He glanced at his father, who only stared into the distance. "I suppose I didn't know what to expect, but silence wasn't it."

"It doesn't sound like anybody is sure of anything. Tay may still be alive. It doesn't feel like he's gone or dead. He's just missing."

Michael exhaled and sat forward. "I hope you're right, Dad. The thought that Taylor left this life believing I hate him . . ." Michael's voice cracked.

Van rubbed his son's shoulder. "I don't believe he thought that, Mike."

He turned and glanced at his father. "We never cleared things up after the fight, Dad. I was too angry after what he'd done— what he called April. But I don't hate him."

"It was no better with us. Your mom and I tried to patch things up. He just shut us all out. Honestly, I think he was more embarrassed about what happened that night than anything. It's been a long couple of years, waiting and hoping for something to heal this family."

There was a long pause before Van continued, "I believe it was Spencer W. Kimball who said that tragedy is not in death but in sin. If Tay is gone, the unfortunate thing is he wasn't ready." Van's eyes pooled with tears. "I blame myself," he said in a quivering voice. "I should have done more."

Michael sat quietly, not daring to look at his dad. He'd never seen his father cry, and just knowing he was made Michael cry as well.

After they both regained some composure, Michael said, "I need to know, Dad. How'd you know there was something wrong with Taylor before I said anything?"

"The same way you'll know when Suzanne has a problem. It will be the look on her face, the color of her cheeks, the gait in her step, or a hundred other little signs you'll pick up on from a lifetime of knowing her. It was the same when you were about twelve and brought Taylor home with a broken nose."

Michael smiled. "I don't remember that."

"And . . . well, we've been half expecting something like this all Taylor's life. It was an accomplishment just to get him grown. During his high school years, we waited almost daily for that boy to be sent home for one thing or another."

Michael stretched out his long legs and looked up through the gold canvas of oak leaves. A gust of air picked up and the tree appeared to shudder, the leaves rattling softly. "I have to admit, Dad, that I'm a little frightened about raising kids. What if April and I screw up and Suzanne goes off the deep end? Every time I see a tattooed, pierced teenager, I think, 'There goes somebody's baby.'"

"All you can do is your very best, Son. I wish I'd done more to patch up the family, but I don't take the blame for Taylor's actions. It was his choice to live a rowdy lifestyle. There was no difference in the way we raised you boys. The only difference was your response. You embraced the gospel, and Taylor rebelled.

"Think of it like this. Before you have children and you hear a crying baby, you think, 'Wow, what is wrong with those parents? Why don't they do something about that baby?' But now that you have a kid and you hear that crying baby you think, 'Wow, those poor parents. Listen to that kid!' Am I right?"

Michael chuckled. "Yeah."

"It's the same way with teenagers or any wayward child," Van went on. "Once you've been down that road, you have a new perspective. Agency is both a curse and a blessing."

"I never thought of it that way."

While father and son took advantage of the shade tree, Claire and April remained in the front room. Black cookies sat cooling on the pan, and a heavy sigh filled the air. Tears fell silently from Claire's eyes as her heart ached for her son. Distantly, she pulled at the stitching on a blanket.

"Michael said nothing is for certain," April remarked.

Claire took a long look at a framed photo of Taylor that sat on the mantle over the fireplace. Beside it were pictures of her father and Van, all of them dressed in their military uniforms.

"I watched my mother wrestle with this when I was a kid," Claire said. "My father had been captured in Korea. They didn't know if he was alive or dead for six months. I swore I would never marry into the military. Van had already been wounded and discharged when I met him. Then along comes Tay . . . ."

She didn't finish the thought but stood, walked to the mantle, and picked up the photo of Taylor. "That darn kid. He's responsible for all my gray hair, you know." She smiled to herself. "And I have lost more sleep over him than most mothers do over a house full of children. It hasn't let up since the day we brought him home."

April chuckled lightly and Claire looked up. "It's true, April. Michael slept through the night from the time he was two weeks old, but not Taylor. Oh, no—he didn't sleep all night until he was almost twelve months. It didn't matter how much I fed him or rocked him. That boy was up every two or three hours all night long. I tried to let Van sleep because he was still so involved at work, but after a time we had to start taking shifts."

"What finally changed?" April asked. She sat leaning forward with her legs crossed. Listening was one of her best qualities.

Claire chuckled and sat back down, placing the picture frame on the coffee table. "General conference."

"Really? How's that?"

"It was the funniest thing. We started to notice that whenever Dad would read to Taylor, he would fall asleep, but after about fifteen minutes of silence, he'd wake up and start screaming again. So we experimented with different books on CD and nothing seemed to work. Then one Sunday morning we were watching conference and Taylor just went limp—he was sound asleep. So that night we played a general conference CD on repeat, and that was the first good night's sleep we got since before the boy was born." Claire paused, then said with regret, "He never did stop falling asleep during general conference."

As Claire and April giggled, some weight lifted from the room. Claire looked at the grandfather clock in the corner and said, "It's about lunch time. Let's get something together." She stood, as did April. "Van gets grumpy when he's hungry."

"Well, the apple didn't fall far from the tree then, since Michael gets that way too. I am going to go check on Suzanne." She stood and stretched.

Claire went to the kitchen to get started. A few minutes later, April entered the room carrying Suzanne. The child perched on the kitchen counter, and her grandmother gave her a slice of apple.

Claire was never one to accept help from company in the kitchen, so April and Suzanne began to sing a song about apples and bananas.

Miraculously, Claire began to brighten. The singing and noises of rummaging through the kitchen, the knife on the cutting board, the opening and closing of drawers and cupboards, and the jingle of flatware all seemed to have a soothing effect, and soon the home felt warmer.

She turned and looked out the window to where her husband and son sat on the bench. As she watched them, a quiet foreboding filled her. Pushing the feeling aside, she finished washing her hands and turned to her granddaughter. "Why don't you go get Grandpa and your daddy and we'll eat."

"I can do that," Suzanne said confidently, then jumped off the counter and ran to the back door.

As Suzanne bounced out of the house, Michael and his father stopped talking. They watched her hop-scotch down the patio steps and skip across the lawn.

"Grandpa . . . " Suzanne said. "Grandma says she's making lunch and you have to eat."

Van slapped Michael's leg. "Come on, Son. We can reminisce later." They stood and walked toward the house.

Suzanne found a large fallen leaf on the lawn and held it out for her grandpa. "Here. It's for you. See how pretty it is?"

Van thanked her for it and Michael picked her up. Van held out his leaf. "So tell me, little one, what color is this leaf?"

"It's yellow, Grandpa. Everybody knows that. But there are other colors too."

In the kitchen, Michael came up behind his wife and put his arms around her. "So what's for lunch?"

His mother began to tell him, but an argument between Suzanne and her grandfather distracted her.

"I don't think this leaf has magenta or lavender in it, Suzanne," Van said as he studied the leaf.

"It does," she argued. "See right here?" She pointed to an invisible spot on the leaf. "And right there."

Van smiled and rubbed his chin as if in thought. "Are you sure? I think it's just yellow."

"You're not going to win, Dad," April reported. "Right now everything has magenta and lavender in it. They're her favorites. Right, sweetie?"

Suzanne nodded, smiling brightly. "Those are my mom's favorite colors too." Her grandpa surrendered and set the leaf on the counter. He began to walk around the counter but Suzanne spoke up. "Grandpa, don't forget your leaf."

"Oh, yes," he said. "How could I forget?" He took the leaf and smiled, then found an empty magnet and stuck the leaf to the side of the refrigerator. "We'll keep it right there."

Meals at the Suttons leaned more toward the restaurant experience than the fast-food grab and go. Lunch consisted of a variety of sandwiches, a green salad, and chips and dip. After an hour, the four adults still sat around the table, nibbling. Suzanne had grown weary of the boring grown-up talk and had wandered into the backyard.

When there was a lull in the conversation, Van said, "So, Mike and I were talking earlier and the subject of Taylor's first broken nose came up—"

April's brow furrowed. "First?"

Claire spoke up. "Yeah, that darn boy has probably broken his nose five or six times."

"Six," interjected Van. "That we know of."

April shook her head and smiled. "You know, I never noticed."

"Well, thanks to good insurance we got it fixed right every time," Claire explained. "You can hardly tell, but the last one did cause an atrocious snoring problem."

"Three times in football alone," Van continued while his wife was talking.

"So what's significant about the first break?" April asked.

Claire and Van began to relate the tale, speaking at the same time. Claire quickly got the upper hand, but Van regularly added his two bits.

"These brothers used to live across the road," she said.

"Brannon and Wacey Moore," Van put in.

"I was going to say that, dear. Those boys were troublemakers. I think they were abused at home."

Horror jolted through Michael's body as a long-buried memory erupted in his mind. His breath caught in his throat and the blood drained from his face. For a moment he was no longer sitting at the table with his wife and parents. He was twelve and dealing with feelings of unbridled hatred and anger.

It was the mention of those names that sent him reeling—names he had long since buried. And like a distant echo, he heard his mother begin to relate the associated events. Michael felt frozen and powerless to stop her. Suddenly, he realized his wife and parents were looking at him as if waiting for a reply. Bursting through the scenes of his memory, he heard his name.

"Michael!" April said sternly.

He blinked. "Sorry. My mind . . . um, wandered off."

"Wow, way off. I swear we said your name a dozen times." April looked worried.

"Sorry. What were you saying?"

"You know, it took so long to get your attention, I can't even remember," his mother admitted.

"I remember," his father said. "We just wanted to know who was with you when you found Taylor on the playground."

"Oh!" Michael feigned a smile. "That's easy enough. It was my old friend Brad Simpson."

"The kid with the hair lip?" his dad said.

Michael nodded. April gave him a perplexed look.

Claire put her hand on April's as if trying to keep her attention. "Anyway, as I was saying, by the time they crossed the field, the boys had taken off. So Michael and Brad picked him up and helped him home. When Michael brought Tay in all covered in blood and sand, I thought I was going die." She put her hand to her heart as she said it. "He was about seven and still so small."

Van looked at Michael. "That would have made you twelve, which is what I thought." Michael wasn't paying much attention. He was trying to think of a way to short-circuit the story before it went too far.

Claire continued. "After I got Tay cleaned up and settled down, I called their mother and raised a fuss, but it didn't help. They kept picking on him every chance they got. Little devils."

"Even though I've never experienced it, I've read that bullying can be a difficult thing to prove. What did you do?" April said, seeming genuinely interested.

"Back then there was little to do unless the boys were caught in the act by a police officer, or, if it happened on school property, a teacher. This went on for a while. Taylor would get beat up, and the Moore boys always had an alibi. Their mother was so gullible. Somewhere along the line, Michael got fed up and took matters into his own hands."

"We don't have to continue, Mom," he interrupted. "April's got the idea. Let's talk about something else."

"Wait," April said, turning to her husband. "Why don't you want her to tell the rest of the story?"

Michael sighed. "I did something stupid, that's all."

April grabbed his hand and teased, "Oh! So it's secret?"

"Well, no . . . " He flushed and turned to his father. "See what you started, Dad? Couldn't leave it alone, could you?"

His dad held up his hands. "Don't look at me. You should have told her."

"You better continue, Claire. I gotta know what has Michael all worked up." April squeezed his hand and smiled.

"Oh, Michael's making a bigger deal out if it than it was," Claire said.

"No, Mom, I'm not. Let's just change the subject." Michael's stern voice surprised even himself. After a long, awkward pause he added, "I apologize—that came out of nowhere. Let's just change the subject." He glanced at his wife and knew she would want an explanation. He wasn't sure he could give her one.

When the silence became too uncomfortable, Michael stood and said, "I'm going to clean up lunch." His mother protested, but he persevered. Hoping to double the effort, he turned to April. "Would you help me, babe?"

"No. I'm going to go check on Suzanne." With that she walked out the back door. Michael stared after her.

After the door shut, he grabbed the potato-chip bags and the jar of dip, trying to act unmoved. "I noticed you are wearing your old U of U shirt, Dad. Is there a game today?"

"Yeah." Van looked from the back door to his son. "Kickoff is at 3:00, but I'm not sure I'm in the mood."

"I'll watch it with you," Michael said, hoping to lighten the mood and change the subject at the same time.

His father shrugged. "I can't believe you never told April what happened."

"I had all but forgotten about it until just now. And how was a subject like that ever going to come up, Dad? 'It's a beautiful day today, dear, and by the way when I was twelve, I went to therapy because I destroyed two kids' lives!'" Michael put both hands on the table and hung his head.

"I can't believe you still blame yourself," his mother said. "I thought you were past all that. It's been over twenty years."

Michael looked up. "The therapy sessions helped me deal with it. But the blame still lies where it always has. And time doesn't heal all wounds. Some just scar over and become harder to talk about."

"I'm sorry, Michael. I didn't know."

"It's not your fault, Mom."

Van spoke up. "You are going to have to tell her now, Son. She'll be afraid it's something worse if you don't."

"I know, Dad."

The three of them looked out into the back yard, where April and Suzanne were playing. Michael suddenly wished he had only called his parents to tell them about Taylor. It would have been so much easier.

At 3:00, the microwave shut off with the sounding of a small bell. The popcorn was done. Michael filled two large glasses with ice and cola, then watched his dad dump the popcorn into a bowl. The two men took their usual spots on the couch in front of the TV as the opposing football teams lined up for kickoff. Not interested in the game, Michael's mother and April took Suzanne to the park.

"You know what this reminds me of?" he said, grabbing a handful of hot popcorn.

"No, what?" Van replied.

"We were watching Utah play Air Force—I think I was sixteen or seventeen. I had a girlfriend over and you got mad about a call by the referees and threw the entire bowl of popcorn at the TV."

"It was the Utes' Homecoming, and the call cost them the game," Van said.

Michael chuckled. "You were lucky it was a plastic bowl. As a precaution, I'm keeping the popcorn under close supervision."

Not long after the kickoff, Michael's thoughts went back to the Moore brothers. After several incidents of bullying, he had taken matters into his own hands and began watching Wacey and Brannon. In the beginning he didn't know how to stop them, only that he had to. But after a few weeks of close observation and asking around, he learned that Wacey had a habit of shoplifting and that Brannon was deathly afraid of water.

In his youthful naivety, Michael had no idea how his actions would change all three of their lives forever. With Wacey, Michael simply followed him to a store and watched him load his pockets, then alerted the store manager. How was Michael to know that Wacey had been caught shoplifting several times before and would be shipped off to juvenile detention, but that is exactly what happened.

It took a little more planning with Brannon. After Michael learned he had a crush on a girl, he faked a note inviting him to meet her at a swimming pool. When Brannon showed up, Michael sneaked up behind him and pushed him in. With a long-handled net, he kept Brannon from the edge of the pool until he promised to leave Taylor alone. Terrified of drowning, Brannon soiled himself—in front of the crowd that had gathered. Looking back now, it made Michael sick to think the boy could have just as easily drowned.

As he walked away from the pool that day, Michael was very pleased with himself. The Moore brothers would behave. Taylor was safe. However, within a few weeks, Wacey Moore was stabbed to death during a fight in juvenile detention. Soon after the loss of his brother and the disgraceful pool incident, Brannon was diagnosed with bipolar disorder and taken out of school.

Not only had Michael taken care of his enemies, he had crushed them. And it horrified him. Until today, he had managed to block most of the memories. A chill ran the length of his body as though someone had stepped on his grave.

He shook his head and looked at the TV. The Utah fans were going nuts. The Utes had just made a fantastic interception, deep in their own territory, followed by a seventy-yard carry for a touchdown.

Michael looked at his dad. Instead of cheering for his alma mater, Van was crying, the tears coursing down his weathered cheeks. Michael offered a silent prayer that somehow Taylor would make it home. He felt tears well up and cleared his throat. "Let's get out of here, Dad."

Van wiped his eyes. "I agree. Let's go." He stood and took the popcorn and cups to the kitchen counter.

"Wait. Where we going?" Michael turned off the TV.

"To work," his dad said, then left through a side door that led to a detached garage. Obviously, he intended to leave the house with or without his son.

As Michael entered the garage, the main door was lifting. "Do you want to drive my rental?" he asked. "Mom and April took your Lincoln."

"No, I have a better idea." His father pulled a dusty cover off a brilliantly silver 1964 Corvette Stingray.

"You sure? You never drive the 'Vette."

"I'm sure." Van opened the door and got into the classic vehicle. Michael ran his fingers along the contoured metal body until his fingers stopped at the chrome door latch and pressed down. The door popped open and Michael slid into the cramped interior while his father gave the throttle two pumps and turned the ignition key. Four hundred horses thundered to life as the engine's torque rocked the car. The exhaust exploded from chrome side pipes, making the garage quake.

"I had a fresh long block installed last year," Michael's father said loudly. "I haven't put three hundred miles on her since, so she could use the exercise."

Michael smiled and nodded. It was only the second time he'd ridden in his father's baby.

Van depressed the clutch and put the car in first gear. He eased the old beauty onto the highway and pointed her toward the industrial park that housed VAS Engineering's headquarters, and where he still maintained the original workshop.

The 'Vette moved smoothly through traffic, attracting double glances and ogling from every direction. The roar of the engine in Michael's ears seemed like a soothing balm. With not even one digital part, this car was a slice of simplicity in an increasingly complicated world. Michael realized his father needed to get his mind onto something other than Taylor or he would go insane. A few hours in the workshop and they would both feel better.

On a dirt floor in a small, filthy room, six American soldiers sat eating quietly. It was the first time they had seen each other in more than twenty days. Before, meals had been shoved under the iron door of each cell, and Corporal Sutton wondered why the Rangers had been brought together now. He had come to realize that in prison, routine meant safety, and change was not a good thing.

Taylor and each of his five remaining team members held a bent and corroded plate filled with a brown, semi-gelatinous mass. Soiled gray walls met the eye in every direction. High plastic windows, yellow with age, ran horizontally across one wall. A single caged bulb flickered from the ceiling, and the air reeked of long-unsanitary conditions.

The Rangers had not been allowed into the general prison population, and at present eight malicious-looking guards scrutinized them. Sweating even while idle, the Americans choked down their meal, which Taylor thought resembled and probably tasted like dog food. He ate slowly, with a heightened appreciation for the other Rangers' company.

Speaking brought swift abuse from the guards, so the men had quickly adopted a more subliminal and primitive form of communication: Morse code. While they were in their individual cells, tapping became a telegraph. It was likely their captors knew the code, so the Americans proceeded slowly, sometimes taking an hour to complete a word.

Over two weeks earlier, as each of the Rangers sat in his cell, Corporal Sutton had sent out a message in Morse code. Two words—"BRACKEN" and "TRAITOR."

A response came from the ranking officer, Sergeant Emilio Gutierrez. He had tapped out a request for confirmation, and Taylor had replied in the affirmative. All the men had trusted Colonel Bracken, and his betrayal was too heartbreaking to believe. The unanswerable question was, of course, why?

Sutton pulled a hair from his food and almost gagged. He forced down another bite, then looked around at the five men who had become his brothers in this hellish place. Gone were the high, tight haircuts and clean-shaven faces. Each man was still strong and capable, but sorrow and hopelessness grew in their eyes.

Across from Sutton sat a bullish Texan, Specialist Wesley Cobb. An expert tracker, Cobb looked and talked like a character from a western novel. On his first day of basic training, the drill sergeant had asked him if he was "corn fed like a Texas bull." Thus the nickname Corn Cobb was born, though few dared use it. An increasingly curly shock of jet-black hair covered his head, and his wide blue eyes absorbed their surroundings.

Next to Cobb sat the jester, Corporal Ian Pike. He was an Australian-born California surfer and the only son of a wealthy business mogul who had moved to the States when Ian was eighteen. If asked why he joined the military, let alone the Rangers, Ian always responded with a joke about having girlfriends on every continent. The truth had more to do with a bar fight, several felonies, and a state senator's daughter, but thanks to Ian's wealthy father and a good lawyer, the judge had given him two options: prison or military. Ian often quipped that he had chosen the greater of two evils.

Together for the first time in weeks, Taylor and the other men had to fight the urge to speak to one another. Sergeant Gutierrez had attempted to break the silence only to catch the butt of a gun to the kidney. Being adaptable, and belligerent, the Rangers began to scratch words in the dirt and make signs to communicate.

At the moment, Specialist Delray Fulton was scratching in the dirt as the others kept an eye on the guards. Hailing from Atlanta, Georgia, Fulton had grown up watching many inner-city kids lose their lives to drugs and violence. Statistically, the odds were against him living to maturity without serious trouble, but he'd done it. He was the best sniper on the team.

Fulton never hesitated to give credit for his success to his father, who had been an army chaplain in Vietnam. After leaving the service, the elder Fulton had become a lay preacher and gunsmith whose favorite pitch was "You gotta have faith in the Lord and plenty of ammo!"

Between Sutton and the sergeant sat Private First Class Todd McGillis. Because of his square build and barrel chest, the short, fiery Irishmen was often called "Tot." Born and raised in Chicago, he was the youngest member of the team. He had joined the army before graduating high school due to the fact that he was headed into his sixth year, his second as a senior. He was not the brightest young man but good in a fight.

Fulton drew the numerals 6 and 8, then crossed out the 8. Taylor understood he was suggesting a fight. Sergeant Gutierrez held up his thumb in agreement. Taylor and the others signaled that they were with him. The sergeant motioned for the Rangers to stand. All six did so in unison. The guards responded by shouldering their weapons.

"Sit down!" barked a guard behind them. The Rangers stood fast, heads hung, and again the guard ordered them to sit. All eight guards moved in slowly, stupidly.

One step too close and the Rangers burst into life. The eight prison guards were unable to fire off a single round before they had been disarmed and caught in a fight for their lives. Knees were buckled, ribs broken, and larynxes crushed.

Footfalls and the slamming of an outer door disrupted the uprising. A dozen more soldiers entered with weapons drawn. The six Rangers were armed but not ready. The escape attempt was squashed.

After their hands were bound, they were pushed out the door leading to the main yard. At the frustration and anger written in his friends' unwashed, bearded faces, Corporal Sutton thought, *Perhaps today we will die.*

10

The direct sunlight in the yard burned the eyes of the American soldiers, but with bound hands they had no means to shade them. Several hundred gaunt, vicious men gathered around the newcomers like jackals eager for fresh meat. Hot dust and the stench of sweat made the air stifling. As the Rangers were pushed toward the center of the enclosure, many of the inmates spat on them, gnashed their teeth, and spewed profanities. In the midst of this sea of guttural filth, standing in the center of the yard, was a monolith of iron strap and chain link. A cage.

Taylor Sutton glanced around the yard, hoping to find a weakness. The others seemed to be doing the same thing. The brick-and-mortar walls enclosing the yard were an easy twenty-five feet high. Every forty feet or so a turret rose, and silhouettes of armed men could be seen atop each. This was not a prison for petty thieves.

Bright and unblinking, the sun stared down from above the western wall. Sunset would come early in the yard, and the cage would soon be in shadow. On a balcony that jutted out from that same wall stood General Rais. A gunshot split the air, reducing the clamor of the prisoners to a dull murmur.

The general addressed the prisoners in Arabic, upon which some of them laughed stupidly and the general chuckled. A guard standing near him spoke to him. Staring down at the Americans,

General Rais continued in English, "I have just been told of your pathetic insurrection. It is good that you still have some fight left in you. I have been watching your American television and have found a sport that suits me—cage fighting. I enjoy the animal brutality. So I have ordered this cage built for our entertainment."

He put a heavy hand on the shoulder of a thin, pock-faced man to his left. "And I have asked my friend, the warden, to offer an early parole to any man who can kill one of you in hand-to-hand combat." Those who understood English translated for those who didn't, and the prison yard erupted in cheers.

"And what do we get if we kill them?" Gutierrez asked, though no one could hear or understand him save his own men.

At a word from the warden, the armed guards unlocked the Rangers' restraints.

"Isn't it obvious?" Cobb glanced around and rubbed his wrists. "If we win, we get to fight again."

At the sound of another gunshot, the noise again settled to a low murmur. Obviously enjoying himself, General Rais looked down from his balcony and said to the Americans, "Choose your champion."

Gutierrez turned to his men. "I'm in command. I should be the one to go."

"Like hell," Pike and Fulton replied in unison.

"We'd all like an opportunity to kick a little prison trash," Cobb said. "No reason you should have all the fun, Sarge."

The sergeant looked at his men. "So how are we going to decide this? Rock, paper, scissors?"

"I'll go," McGillis said.

Gutierrez frowned. "Why should you go, Tot?"

"Because I'm experienced in this sort of thing. Before I joined up, I used to cage fight. I've never lost."

Deciding to put an end to the discussion, Taylor moved toward the cage. He had scarcely entered it when the prison yard erupted in cheers. He knew the Rangers had seen him when he heard their supportive voices.

"Tear it up, Sutton!" That was Cobb.

"You were born for this!" the sergeant added.

Their positive affirmations gave way to cries of distress when, from across the yard, an exceedingly large man pushed his way through the crowd. Then, from across the yard, an exceedingly large man pushed his way through the crowd. The other prisoners quickly fell silent and gave way to let him through. Taylor's heart sank. It was nothing short of David versus Goliath.

At this point the Rangers made a push for the cage but were walled in behind the guards, who must have been instructed to keep them at a distance. Taylor could see the concern on his friends' faces, but he knew all they could do was watch.

The big guy approached the cage and ducked to get through the door. With the two men now inside, the door shut with a sound like a funeral chime. The fight was on.

Forgetting about the world outside, Taylor focused on his opponent, a beast that looked more animal than man with long, hairy arms and powerful, meat-hook hands. From under shaggy hair and heavy brows peered a pair of cold, dead eyes.

From a surprising distance, a large hand reached out and slapped the corporal across the face. The force whipped his head to the side, and the Neanderthal dove in. Taylor went to the ground and rolled away, kicking at a passing knee. The knee gave way and the large man fell heavily into the fence. Taylor got to his feet but so did his opponent.

A fist to the face nearly turned Taylor's lights out, but as the big man closed in for the kill, Taylor jabbed at his throat and diaphragm, leaving the giant gasping for air. Taylor took advantage of the moment to clear his head. The big man was faster than he should be. Taylor would have to just out-think him.

Seconds later his opponent had recovered and powered in with tree-dropping swings. It was all Sutton could do to avoid getting pummeled. Suddenly, the large man's breaths were rapid again, and ragged. As dangerous as it was, Taylor needed to get inside and work over the guy's ribs.

After another volley of swings and jabs, two of which made contact and nearly knocked Taylor out of his socks, he boxed the giant's ears. With the big guy holding his head Taylor went to work on the rib cage. He finished with another jab to the throat, and the Neanderthal passed out from lack of oxygen and fell to the ground. The jeers and snarls from the prison rabble faded with their champion's consciousness.

Corporal Sutton leaned heavily against the cage wall, his own lungs on fire. From above him a voice thundered, "Kill him or die yourself!"

Sutton took a deep breath and then yelled, "It's better to die than kill an unconscious and defenseless opponent!"

A soldier standing next to the general shouldered his rifle and took steady aim at Sutton, waiting for the command.

Sutton spoke again. "I'm an American and a God-fearing man, General. I'd no sooner take this man's life than I would a slumbering dog. Do what you think best."

After a long pause, Rais grabbed the rifle from the soldier, took careful aim, and pulled the trigger. Taylor braced for death. When it didn't come he believed the general had missed his target, but a glance at the Neanderthal told him his aim had been true.

The cage door opened with a clatter, and Taylor's hands were restrained again. He watched the general and his men disappear through a doorway behind the balcony. The warden lingered for a moment, and even from a distance, Taylor could feel the small man's eyes fixed on him—eyes that seemed to burn with revulsion. There was something dangerous about the warden.

With the adrenalin thinning out of his blood, Taylor noticed his ribs and face ached and his ear was ringing, probably from the first slap upside the head. Before he was pushed out of the cage, he stole another glance at the tower on the southwest corner. That was the one—the general's fancy office. It had to be. But how could Taylor get to it?

Seconds later he stood with his team again, last in line behind McGillis. "I found the general's quarters, Tot," Taylor whispered.

He would have to explain later. Instead of being led back to their cells, he and the other five Rangers were forced into what looked like vertical coffins standing at the east end of the yard. Hot boxes. The coming night would be decent enough, but with dawn would come a torture like no other. Taylor was pushed inside the first box. As he turned and before he had time to react, the butt of a rifle caught him between the eyes.

Taylor awoke a few hours later with a thundering in his head as though the butt of the gun was repeatedly pounding against his skull. It was disturbingly dark in the box, and he had to check that his eyes were actually open. He inhaled and exhaled slowly. The box smelled of death and was so narrow he could only stand or squat. Near the top, a small opening covered in chicken wire was the only ventilation. *Perhaps it was required by the Geneva Convention,* Taylor mused. It would do him and his comrades little good tomorrow.

His dangerous circumstance did not escape his attention. Having just fought in the heat, he would have little fluid in him to make it through the next day. He focused on conserving energy.

Nearly blind, he strained his ears for any sound from the others. He heard nothing and began to suspect he was alone in the yard. He had to risk an outburst. "Rangers, sound off!"

No reply.

He spoke again. "Rangers!"

Instantly, he heard footfalls, followed by what could have been a Louisville Slugger slamming into his box. "Shut up!" barked a gravelly voice.

If he was alone, what had become of the others? Perhaps they had been clubbed with the rifle as he had been. Time slowed to a snail's pace and he continued to listen for any sound from the others. But all that filled his ears were his own slow, even breaths.

Sometime during the night, in one of the painful shifts between squatting and standing, Taylor found the moon shining bold and free out in the cool reaches of space. It was the same moon that had stared brightly down during all those camping trips with his family. He closed his eyes and could almost smell the evergreens as a gentle mountain breeze rattled the leaves of the aspen trees.

His family would know he was missing by now. What lie Colonel Bracken had concocted, Taylor could only guess. He sighed. He had left things in a train wreck as far as his family was concerned, showing them little more than contempt. What he'd give for a cell phone now.

In recent days, he'd found himself growing more anxious about his mother's worrying. He had not been a good son— downright awful was closer to the truth. He had never intended to leave things as he had, but now he found himself in a place where he was completely unable to make amends. If he escaped alive, she would never let him hear the end of it.

Unknown to his family, he had been cleaning his life up, trying to right his course, even attending church once in a while. But where they were concerned, Taylor feared he'd procrastinated too long. He made up his mind that if somehow he survived, he would ask them for forgiveness. This decision gave him renewed desire to survive, yet he also knew he had to put his family out of his mind. Such thoughts could drive a captive man crazy with desperation.

Taylor returned to a squatting position and tried to sleep.

The following day burned with a blistering heat. On such days, the general population of the prison was kept in their cells. Intense heat could drive men over the edge of insanity, giving way to riots.

In the courtyard, the world became a glistening, shimmering mirror of reality. High in their watchtowers, guards consumed water by the gallon as their earth-tone uniforms turned dark and soggy.

During the previous night, the general had received an encrypted message and a series of numbers. In the early afternoon, he sent for Sutton.

The corporal's box was unlocked, and a puddle of a man spilled out onto the ground. He was unconscious and appeared to be barely alive. Two guards dragged him to the general's quarters.

11

Slowly, through blurred vision and a crippling headache, Taylor Sutton managed to regain consciousness and find his bearings. He felt a cool breeze across his face and was grateful for it. He wondered for moment if he was again in the mountains of Utah on a camping trip and all else had been a nightmare. Moving his eyes, he believed he saw his dad standing over a campfire, but then Taylor blinked and the truth came into focus. General Rais stood looking out a window. Taylor made a feeble attempt to rise and found he was strapped to a chair.

Rais turned and said coolly, "I see you are yet alive. The wonder of modern medicine." Taylor's eyes moved and focused on a bag of clear fluid hanging from a chrome tree and a long clear tube that went into his arm. He pulled at his restraints.

"What is this? Why am I here?"

"You needed fluids to bring you back from the dead. It would have been easier to let you die in that box, but plans have changed and I need you alive."

"Why? What can I do for you? Give you reason to shoot some more prisoners?" Taylor's voice was raspy and his head spun.

The general produced a walking stick and swung it down onto the top of his desk, splintering it into toothpicks. "You think you are so strong, so brave. Believe me when I say, you will beg for me to kill you!" He motioned for the men behind Sutton to stand him up.

As Taylor's restraints were unfastened, the general returned to the window. "Come. You need to look outside."

Taylor was forced to his feet and roughly moved toward the window. He peered down at the empty prison yard. Empty, except for several hotboxes.

"It is a very hot day. I have heard that after a day like today a man's brain would actually be hardboiled inside his own skull." The general paused. "You are the only one I need alive, Corporal. The rest can die today."

Taylor recalled the previous night. "I don't think there's anyone else in those boxes."

The general nodded at a guard, who spoke into a radio. Seconds later, another guard appeared in the yard below. He went to the nearest box and unlocked it, whereupon a man fell out of the box and landed face down in the dirt.

Taylor fought against his captors, but his arms felt like soggy noodles. He was still too weak from heat exhaustion. "You let those men go or you'll get nothing from me."

"You are in no position to make demands!"

The corporal pulled at the handcuffs on his wrists. "What do you want? Why me?"

The general's eyes brightened. "Why you? Because the good colonel knows that you know all about him. As long as you are alive, he will do what I demand. It is the only reason you are alive. I will kill you when it is time, but right now I want you to say two words for me as clearly as possible."

Taylor didn't like it. "Two words and you will let those men out of the boxes?"

"Two words into a recorder. With emphasis, of course."

"What words?"

"I have thought about that. The most effective thing will simply be 'help me.'" You could even throw in a 'please.'"

"'Help me'? You want me to ask for help? From who?"

The general smiled. "That is not your concern."

Taylor wasn't sure if was out of pure defiance or some sense of duty, but he flatly denied the general's request. He turned again to look at the hotboxes dancing behind the ocean of heat waves. "Those men are Rangers. They'd rather die than assist you in any way, and so would I."

"Very well." The general nodded at a man whom Taylor had not noticed before. It was the pock-faced man—the warden. He held up a syringe, his cold, unfeeling eyes focused on the cylinder, and tapped it calmly. The man's serenity was disturbing.

Taylor bent forward then snapped his head back, making contact with a man's face behind him. He mule-kicked and felt a knee buckle, but before he could make a fight of it, a needle was injected into the IV tube and within seconds the world around him bent like a funhouse mirror.

"I knew you would not cooperate, but we can achieve the same end through . . . chemical coercion." General Rais lit a cigar and took a long drag.

Taylor found himself again in the chair. His eyes felt like they would swell to bursting, and a horrible metallic taste filled his mouth—no doubt the effects of the drug. The warden began asking him questions and Taylor could not stop himself from answering. It seemed as though his voice was coming from somewhere other than his mouth, like an echo. The general's office spun like a carnival ride, and then everything went black.

Sergeant Emilio Gutierrez listened intently as he lay on the floor of his windowless cell. To his right, a rat scratched its way across the floor. Above him, a small ceiling vent chirped with each rotation. He waited for the sound that would betray Corporal Sutton's return to his cell, but it had been hours and there had only been a rodent and a chirping fan. When the sergeant focused his eyes on the sky beyond the vent, his cell did not seem so confining. Light and shadow chased each other around the sky. The light grew increasingly dim. Sunset. Emilio muttered to himself, "All day in that hotbox—Sutton's a dead man."

Emilio Gutierrez was a full-blooded Mexican with narrow dark eyes and black hair. Born to parents of questionable immigration status, he had been taught from an early age to love America and freedom. His grandfather had fallen prey to the desert heat near Yuma while crossing the border and therefore had become a martyr for liberty in the eyes of his family. It was this love of liberty that inspired Emilio to become an Army Ranger. After Staff Sergeant Heller's death, he found himself in command under the worst possible circumstances. Privately, Gutierrez doubted his abilities.

An hour later, with the light beyond the ceiling vent a slate gray, Gutierrez hung on the edge of consciousness. A crash echoed down the hall and stole through his door. It was the sound of a cell door clamping shut. His eyes flew open. He had waited and prayed to hear that sound most the day and wondered now if he had imagined it.

To his knowledge, the only one not in his cell was Sutton. The closing of a cell door at that hour was a good sign that they had brought him back . . . alive. Gutierrez went to the door and lifted a small flap. He listened closely as the footfalls of two guards progressed down the corridor and though the outer door. He would have to risk speaking. He was too anxious to learn of Sutton's condition to worry about code.

"Rangers!" he said. "Sound off!"

In the cell next to Gutierrez, Private McGillis replied, "Five!"

Fulton called out, "Three!"

"Four." That was Cobb.

And finally Pike. "Seven."

Gutierrez waited for a "six," but it didn't come. "Two!" he said after a minute. Either Sutton was unable to reply or had not actually returned from the hotbox. Perhaps someone else now occupied his cell.

From across the hallway, McGillis whispered, "Sergeant!"

"What is it?"

"Before we got separated in the yard, Sutton said he'd found the general's quarters."

Gutierrez thought about that for a second. "Then let's pray Sutton is still alive. If he spent all day in them boxes, he's dead for certain."

"Sir?" McGillis said.

"Yes, Private."

"You homesick?"

"We all are. Just hang in there."

McGillis didn't reply and the sergeant thought he heard a whimper and a sniffle. All was quiet for several minutes. Soon, Fulton began singing Bill Withers' classic "Ain't No Sunshine." It was a fitting ballad as absolute darkness enveloped them.

12

Three cell doors from the sergeant, Corporal Sutton struggled to regain his faculties, but whatever drug they had given him was potent. From somewhere in the hollows of his mind, he heard his team sound off, and though he tried, the word "six" barely spilled over his parched lips.

Nightmares filled his subconscious as the drugs mixed up his mind. Vaguely, he recalled the general's quarters, an IV, and sitting before a digital recorder and being forced to say something—to plead for something. He had been robbed of his ability to resist. There had been a name associated with that pleading, yet he could not recall it. Perhaps it had all been a dream. Taylor strained his memory, but as with a dream, the harder he tried the more it slipped away.

Just as dawn came, Taylor finally broke from his chemical prison and called out, "Six!" It seemed as if the word rang the walls.

"Six . . . I am alive," Taylor muttered to himself. The drug had left a crippling migraine behind, and when he had screamed out, it felt as though his head would explode.

"Sutton . . . Sutton," Specialist Cobb called out. "We thought you were a dead man!"

Knowing Cobb was in the cell across from him, Taylor edged his way to the small opening in his door. He could see the specialist's eyes peering out of the opening in his own door. "I feel like a dead man, Cobb. How're you guys?"

"We're all fine . . . been in here since the fight."

Sutton thought for a moment as the obvious began to come into focus. "I was afraid you were all in those hot boxes with me."

"No, sir. You're the only one they put in the box. Guess he musta been punishin' you for winnin' the fight. How in the world did you survive?"

Taylor tried to think. "I . . . I'm not sure. They drugged me. I know that. I remember the heat of the box and maybe the general's quarters, but after that everything gets fuzzy."

Without warning, a liquid sprayed into the small doors where Sutton and Cobb lay speaking to each other. The stench and burn were distinctive—pepper spray. Taylor rolled away from his door. A malevolent chuckle came from the hallway.

"Why don't you come in here and fight like a man!" Cobb screamed.

Taylor heard Cobb moaning and knew he'd taken a direct hit in the eyes. The spray into Taylor's cell had been less exact and only grazed one eye, but compounded with his present condition, it was enough. He sat up and glanced around his tiny cell with his good eye. For the first time, he noticed a cup of water and a small package in the corner. Tilting his head back, he dribbled the water into his eye. It was the equivalent of throwing water on a grease fire. "Ah! Stupid," he growled. "I knew better."

He drank what was left of the water and, keeping the peppered eye closed, picked up the package. It held several strips of beef jerky and a small foil packet. The packet contained two small pills and a strip of paper that read, *The pills will help your head. Swallow the note.*

Taylor thought about that. At first he was suspicious, but then he realized whoever left the note didn't want it found and that the only way to destroy it was to have him consume it. In Taylor's mind, it gave the man, whoever he was, some authenticity. If the desire had been to poison Taylor, the finding of the note would have been of little consequence, not to mention that there had been plenty of opportunities to kill him already.

He swallowed the pills, then the note.

There was something else about the handwriting on the note that interested him, but at that moment he began to hear a low rumble across the hall. He flattened out again and strained his neck to look out the hole in the bottom of the door. The stench of pepper spray stung his nose, but all he could see for his effort was the scuffle of feet. Listening, his ears told him much more. Cobb was in the middle of a fight.

In his cell, Cobb was just regaining his eyesight when he heard the lock unlatch. "If it's a fight you want, you'll have more than that," a voice said. Then the door swung wide and a young guard burst in with a club. *Amateur,* thought Cobb.

A fight in close quarters is difficult because it is nearly impossible to get far enough from your opponent to deliver a powerful blow. But Cobb had, as a youth, found his first employment as a cowhand, and more than once he had faced livestock in tighter spots than this. The guard thrust the club toward Cobb's midsection, which brought the man in close. A tight uppercut put the guard on his heels. Cobb followed up with a couple of quick jabs and an elbow. Then a wild swing of the club caught Cobb in the neck and set him back, coughing.

The guard regained his bearings and swung hard at Cobb's head. The high swing struck the ceiling, breaking his grip. Cobb used the moment to step back and kick the man hard in the chest. The kick knocked the air out of the guard and sent him flying to the other side of the cell.

The winded guard clutched his chest, grasping for air in low, raspy gulps. Cobb was certain the fight was over until the guard lunged for him. He sidestepped the attack and the guard fell into the nearly closed cell door. The guard's head went into the opening and the weight of his body pushed it shut. A sharp crack sounded and the guard went limp and crumpled to the floor.

"Now that was straight-up clumsy." Cobb squatted on his heels and checked the man's pulse. He was dead.

Cobb rubbed his neck where the club had made contact. He reached across the body of the guard, grabbed him by the belt, and turned him over.

He found keys on the man's belt—and not just the key to his cell, but to all of them. The convenience of it all made Cobb uneasy. "Feels like a setup," he mumbled, but he took the keys and went to the cells that held the other Rangers.

When he opened the last cell door, Sergeant Gutierrez's, Cobb said, "Boss, we have ourselves a problem."

"You look terrible, Cobb," the sergeant replied.

A single bulb glowed meekly from the ceiling, barely holding back the shadows, but Cobb knew the sergeant could see his red, swollen eyes.

"It's pepper spray, sir."

The six men converged on Cobb's cell where the guard lay. Gutierrez entered the cell and squatted next to the body. "We all heard the fight. How'd it start?"

"I was talkin' to Sutton here when I got maced, and before I got my eyesight back, this dude comes in swingin'. I tried to take the wind out of him. But he fell into the door and broke his neck. It feels like a setup, sir."

"Why do you say that?" Gutierrez moved into the hall with the others.

"The guard's just a kid and certainly not a fighter. I've had bigger scraps with my nieces and nephews."

"You think this guard was on a suicide mission? To what end?"

"You tell me. He's here alone with all the keys necessary for our escape." Cobb handed the keys to the sergeant.

Gutierrez looked at the keys. "You may be right. No one has come to check on him and we've been heavily guarded since we arrived. It's too pretty. Question is, what do we do now?"

McGillis nodded. "I say we take the opportunity."

"I'm ready for a good fight," Fulton said.

"So am I." Gutierrez motioned to the outer door. "But we have no idea what waits for us beyond that door. And—"

"—With no weapons we'd be like bobbin' targets in a shooting gallery at a county fair," Cobb finished for him.

The sergeant smiled. "Basically."

"So what's the plan?" McGillis asked impatiently.

"I say we sit this out and wait to make our own opportunity," Sutton said. With the fight and the dead guard, Cobb had all but forgotten the corporal was once again among the living.

"How are you, Sutton?" Gutierrez said.

"Been better." His ashen features made it obvious he was not up to par.

"How'd you survive the hotbox?" asked the sergeant.

"Like I was telling Cobb before all this, I don't really remember much after the heatstroke set in. And I also think they drugged me."

"Drugged you? Who drugged you?" questioned Gutierrez.

"And where can we get some?" Corporal Pike put in. Everyone turned to look at him. "Just joshin' you, of course."

"I believe I was in the general's quarters again," Taylor continued. "I remember an IV and being forced to say . . . something." His voice trailed off as if he strained at the memory.

"What do we do with the dead body, sir?" McGillis asked Gutierrez. "We're in it—don't you see? They're gonna want blood for this, and we can't throw Cobb to the wolves."

While McGillis spoke, Gutierrez had hung his head and pulled at his beard. Now he said, "I swear, Tot, you nag like my mother. Of course we're not throwing Cobb to wolves!" The sergeant paused. "I'll take the heat. I'll lock all you back up and wait for the guards to come down. If they're setting a trap and we don't show, they'll get curious and—"

Cobb began shaking his head in objection and finally cut off the sergeant. "No way! Nobody's taking the blame for something I did."

"You're too valuable to lose, Wes," Gutierrez said. "Nobody's a better tracker!"

"Like we can spare you, Sarge," Fulton argued. "We already lost Heller."

Pike cleared his throat. "I've a better idea—a shell game."

"A shell game?" McGillis said skeptically.

"Sure. We drag the guard to the center of the hallway and leave all our doors open. It'll be like one of those riddles where a dead man is found in the middle of the desert, etc., etc."

"He was a skydiver," Fulton said in answer to Pike's riddle.

"They're not going to like it," McGillis declared. "They might kill us all."

Pike smiled. "It'll go off like a bucket of prawns in the sun." When the team stared at him, he said, "Ya know—cause a commotion."

Gutierrez nodded. "I think it's our only play." He and Pike went to Cobb's cell, grabbed the guard, and moved him into the hallway. "I'd be willing to bet that whoever laid this little trap doesn't have the approval of the general, who has gone through a lot of effort to keep most of us alive. Someone else sent this young guard in here fully expecting him to get beaten. It would be one thing to report, after the fact, that we had made an attempt at escape and had all been killed. It is quite another to report that a guard was killed and that our cell doors had all been found open. This will be the safest course."

Trusting in the sergeant, Cobb returned the keys to the dead guard's belt loop, and the Rangers went back to their cells.

After a few minutes of beleaguered silence, Cobb heard someone's stomach rumble.

"Crikey, that was me!" Ian Pike piped up. "I think my stomach is digesting the large intestine."

"I have some beef jerky left," Taylor said.

"You have what?" Cobb sprang to his feet.

"Beef jerky, or at least I hope it is beef. Could be camel for all I know."

Cobb was first through the door. "Call me what you want, just don't call me late for a meal!"

All the men converged on Taylor's cell. "Sorry. I thought you all would've had the same," he said. "Found it in here when I woke up." The remaining meat was split between the men.

"We haven't eaten since before the fight," Fulton said, grinning. "And what we had then was closer to Alpo."

Taylor cleared his throat. "There's something else odd here. I also found two pills with the jerky and a note instructing me to take them to help with the effects of the drugs."

Gutierrez put some jerky in his mouth. "You didn't take them, did you?"

"I did. I had a terrible headache, and whoever it was didn't want the note to be found."

"So what did you do with the note?"

"Whoever left the pills told me to swallow the note."

The sergeant frowned. "So you swallowed it?"

"Of course! We can use all the help we can get."

"You just swallowed what could have been poison and the note?" Pike said.

"That's what I thought at first, but then it occurred to me that if it was poison nobody would care if the note was found. But if it was help, then it would be a huge deal. Was there anyone in my cell while I was outside?"

McGillis said, "You're insane."

"You're bleedin' bonkers, mate," Pike agreed.

"We wouldn't know. Anybody could have come and went. We were stuck in our own cells," Fulton said. Then suddenly he brightened. "Wait. I actually did hear something late last night. It was a wisp across the floor, like the scuff of a boot. I tried to look under the door but it was too dark."

Sutton suddenly snapped his fingers. "There was something else that bothered me about the note."

"The taste?" Pike said sarcastically.

Sutton smiled. "No. The handwriting—the note was written by a woman!"

"What?" said the other men in unison.

"Sounds crazy, I know, but I am sure of it."

The men began to filter back into their cells. Shaking his head, Cobb said, "You sure they didn't give you peyote, Sutton? Because that's crazy."

"If there was a woman in this prison, mate, she'd have come to see *me*." Pike smiled.

Cobb rolled his eyes. "You're full of crap."

Soon it was just Gutierrez and Sutton in the cell. "You have to believe me, sir. There's a woman out there who helped me."

"I believe you're tired and coming out of whatever drug they gave you. Get some rest." With that, the sergeant turned and left.

The waiting commenced again. Soon the outer door would open and the guard would be found lifeless on the floor of a dead-end hallway. What would come next remained a mystery. Taylor lay on his back on the concrete floor and thought about the note, the pills and the food. It had to be a woman!

A few minutes later, Ian Pike spoke up. "With all this time on my hands I have figured out the mystery of Stonehenge. Anybody care to know?" Nobody responded because they knew he would continue without encouragement. "It was started by a guy who was probably the world's first procrastinator, or his wife had the biggest honey-do list ever. You see, she wanted a huge stone fence around her garden and so this poor bloke gets started only to put off finishing the project until he finally died and left it half done. I know this because my uncle was the same way only he couldn't finish a vinyl fence. The house burned down with half a fence. Anyway, there you go. Mystery solved."

The other men chuckled. As an encore to Pike's story, Fulton began singing "Rock of Ages," and the men laughed again. His baritone voice resounded majestically from the tight walls of the prison, and Taylor was grateful for the song.

The Rangers' respite was cut short by the rattling of the lock at the outer door. Unable to see the door from their cells, Corporal Sutton and the others waited in apprehensive silence. The corporal heard several guards enter, and when they came into his view he noticed they held automatic weapons at the ready. They found the fallen guard where the Americans had left him and all the cell doors ajar. One of the guards checked the cells and reported his findings into a radio. After a long pause, an order came. The body of the fallen guard was retrieved, but all the cell doors were left unlocked.

Sutton looked across the hallway at Cobb. They watched the guards retrieve the guard's body, weapons ready. Briefly the hallway was empty, but soon footsteps sounded and a thin, impish man entered. He squatted in the hallway where the dead guard had lain. "You Americans think you are so smart. Leaving the dead guard in the hall poses the question as to who murdered him. Since all the cell doors are open it is apparent that you intend to leave that question unanswered. Unfortunately for you, General Rais is away. He has, up until now, kept you safe— protecting you—until his plans bear fruit. I am not motivated by such things. I am Aman Shamir, the warden, and I enjoy the torture of men."

With eyes of a cold-blooded serpent, Shamir stared blankly forward. His disturbingly calm voice was familiar to Corporal Sutton, who shuddered involuntarily. "I will make an offer just this once," the warden said. "Whoever reveals the murderer first I will only torture a little." He flashed an impish grin toward Sutton, sending needles coursing up Taylor's spine.

From his cell, Sergeant Gutierrez spoke. "What will Rais say when he returns and finds us dead?"

No longer smiling, Shamir responded, "I never said I would kill you. But you will certainly yearn for death."

The soldiers remained silent.

The warden stood, his appearance the very embodiment of evil. "No confession? Very well! Let us begin." The outer door opened wide with a thunderous clap. A dozen guards rushed the open cells. The Americans were forcibly bound and their heads bagged. In the chaos, McGillis burst out, "Brilliant plan, Sarge!" and got a fist planted in his abdomen.

13

Michael and his family flew back to California on Sunday after attending church with his parents. An uneasy silence had grown between April and him since they left Salt Lake. Now they sat together for a late-evening meal of leftover meatloaf and potatoes. Suzanne had fallen asleep on the drive from the airport, so the only sound was metal utensils on ceramic plates.

Michael cut some meatloaf and held it up on the end of his fork. "Meatloaf isn't one of those things that gets better with age."

April simply replied, "Mmm-hmm."

After another minute, he set down his fork and wiped his mouth. "Okay, this is killing me. Are you mad because I acted strange when the subject of the Moore brothers came up?"

"I don't care about the Moore brothers," she said. "Your mother told me all about them."

"Then what's with the silent treatment?"

April stared at him for a long moment. "Are you going to leave me?"

Startled, Michael choked out, "What?"

"Are you going to leave me?"

He frowned. "Of course not! What are you talking about?"

The corners of her mouth came up in a small smile. "Your mother is convinced you're going to take off to try to save Taylor because he saved your life."

"I don't even know where he is, April."

"But if you did?" Her eyes bore into his soul like a laser.

Suddenly thirsty, he took a long drink of milk. Questions about the Moore brothers would have been easier. Michael's love for his wife and daughter was unmatched, but he also believed if a man could do something he should do it—especially if he owed someone his life. Deep inside, he knew he could save his brother if the opportunity afforded itself. But here again, he had his wife and daughter to consider. He swallowed. "No, of course not."

"Good. Fine," April said, though she didn't seem convinced. The silence returned.

On Monday morning Michael returned to work at the post but found it difficult to focus. Minutes stretched on forever. The more he thought about Taylor, the more he became convinced he could rescue him, as ridiculous as it sounded when spoken aloud. The idea that Taylor might, at that moment, be enduring unimaginable torture and pain ignited an intense anger in Michael's heart.

Later in the week, the weapons test for Project Wakeup Call went perfectly, but even that success seemed meaningless. More and more, Michael became distracted and paced the floor, often losing an hour or more deep in thought. When he did come to his senses, he was drenched in sweat and holding the scar on his chest. Shaking off those moments only intensified the feeling and fueled the fire in his soul.

It was 2:00 AM on Friday when Michael's cell phone rang. He snatched it up on the first ring, almost as if he had expected the call. "Mike," said a weak voice he instantly recognized. "Mike . . . help me. I'm alive—we're all alive."

"Taylor? Taylor! Where are you?"

"Mingora . . . somewhere." Taylor's voice sounded airy and vacant.

"Mingora? Taylor?" Michael shouted, but the line had gone dead.

In that instant, he realized he had lied to his wife. He turned to her, knowing his yelling would have awakened her. Michael wiped his eyes. "It was Taylor. He is in Mingora."

"I heard. Are you sure it was him?" April clicked on the light beside the bed and sat up.

"He said he needs my help. And why do you ask that?"

She rubbed her eyes. "Because he was missing, and out of nowhere he calls in the middle of the night and asks for your help. When was the last time Taylor asked for your help, Mike?"

"He's asking now." Michael lowered his eyes.

"You promised me, Michael. You promised!"

"How can I turn my back on my brother? He needs me." Michael lifted his gaze to meet his wife's. She was right, but how could he live with himself if he could do something and didn't?

"I know he saved your life once, and for that I'm eternally grateful. But you don't have to throw it away! I need you! Suzanne needs you! And if I remember right, Taylor turned his back on you first." April's tears flowed freely now. "He insulted your parents, he insulted me, and you flattened his face for it. The ball was in his court. He should have came crawling back months ago—asking *our* forgiveness!"

"I don't know what to say. He didn't, and he may never. He has a streak of pride a mile wide, but he is still family and right now he needs my help."

"How can you help him, Michael? You're not military. You're not a killer. This is not like when you were boys. Whoever has him is not some playground bully." April's voice broke and she shook her head. "I can't believe your mother was right. She told me this would happen. I was naive enough to think I knew you better."

"I can do this, April," Michael said softly. "Just listen to me." He moved to sit next to her on the bed.

She pulled back and looked at her husband as though he were a stranger. "I will not bury you, Michael. If you do this thing, you do it alone!" At that moment Suzanne cried out and April shot him one last now-look-what-you've-done glare, then took her pillow and left the room.

"April, would you just—" His words caught in his throat as her silhouette disappeared into the darkness. It was useless to try to convince her.

Michael was wide awake now and began to pace the floor. He was certain now that he had to do something. He could only hope April would someday understand. After a few minutes, he moved to the kitchen table and sat down with a pen and paper to organize his thoughts. There were three main obstacles: the expense of the travel, acquiring weapons once he got to Pakistan, and finding Taylor's exact location. Michael considered involving his dad, but did not want to worry him or his mom, even if she expected this. He doubted Colonel Bracken would be able to help, either. Like it or not, Michael was going solo.

Curled up next to her daughter, April had little hope of falling back to sleep. Her heart ached and her tears dampened the pillow below her head. She couldn't believe Michael would leave her to go on a suicide mission for a brother he hadn't spoken to in over two years. It shouldn't surprise her—not really. Ever since they had come home, Michael had grown increasingly distant and restless. Deep inside she knew this was coming, and tonight's call was the clincher.

How frustrating that Claire could be so right about her son, and April so wrong about her husband. It cast shadows of doubt into April's heart about everything. Countless dramas were built around the theme of women who married well only to find the man they loved was someone else entirely. She found herself checking and reevaluating every memory she could conjure until her mind spun.

Who are these people, the Suttons? she wondered. On the outset they appeared to be a perfectly normal family. She had fallen in love with Michael first, then his family. They were beyond kind, and she had not detected anything out of place. Sure, they had their quirks, and recently, where Taylor was concerned, their fair share of grief. But there was obviously something April had missed. What could explain her husband's irrational desire to leave her and their young daughter to follow an estranged brother halfway around the globe on a suicide mission? What had forged such a bond? She had a sister and a brother, but even if one of them had saved her life, she doubted she could risk leaving Michael without a wife and Suzanne without a mother. It had to be something in the Suttons' genetic makeup, maybe something buried in their Irish heritage. Suddenly April decided she never wanted to have sons.

She listened to Suzanne breathe and stroked her hair. This is not the way her life was supposed to go. April's father had been the leaving kind, circling around at an odd birthday here and there. When she was young, she looked forward to those occasions. Once she grew up, she realized the circles were nothing more than holes in her life.

In Michael Sutton she believed she had found the polar opposite of her father. A man of integrity, who loved the gospel and honored women. She also loved his a gift for all things electrical—from computers to toasters, he could fix them. He was a problem solver, an inventor of sorts, seeing solutions where others only saw obstacles. She had predicted he would be as regular as clockwork, and he had been for the last five years. But now this.

As she thought about Michael and his gift for solving the elusive, a small flicker, like a spark in the present darkness of her heart, caused her to almost smile. *If anyone could pull it off, he could.* She quickly snuffed out the thought, still angry that he would even consider risking his life. Yet the spark had left enough residual solace that exhaustion finally won out and April drifted to sleep.

Dawn had barely stretched its wide arms across the sleeping desert when Michael was ready to head into the army post, anxious to get busy with his plans. He sat at the kitchen bar looking from the front door to the clock and then his watch. Amid all the turmoil in his mind, he recognized his wife was worried and distraught. He knew her well enough to see that the anger was a shield to hide her true feelings. How could he help her understand he would do the same for her? To know he could save a life and to not act made him feel sick inside. Though he was anxious to be out the door and moving forward, he also needed to try to make peace with April, so here he sat.

When she slowly descended the stairs, he sat up straighter. Their eyes met and she paused as though not expecting to see him. He noticed her red pajama top matched her bloodshot eyes. She crossed the kitchen to the refrigerator and grabbed a bottle of Michael's Mountain Dew from the door. He watched in amusement as she guzzled half the bottle. Typically, she never touched soda pop, especially the caffeinated kind.

"I don't know how you can stand this stuff," she said, then belched adorably. She didn't return the bottle but kept it and slid into a bar stool next to him.

"Did you get any sleep?" he asked.

"A little. Why do you think I'm drinking this crap?" April pushed the bottle aside and laid her head on the counter.

"I'm sorry," Michael said. "I am sorry for this. I know I hurt you."

"If you're sorry, don't go," she replied, her head still down.

"I have to."

April sat up straight and glared at him. "Do what you think you need to. Just don't expect me to be here if you get back."

"What do you mean?"

"I mean that I love you more than my life, more than anything or anyone in the world, and I thought you felt the same."

"I do. It's just . . . " He paused. April stood to leave and he grabbed her hand. With tears in his eyes, he pulled her close and for a long minute held her tight.

"Don't you see?" he finally said. "I would do the same for you, for Suzanne. I love you both more than my life and would readily give it. I am not the man who finds comfort in hoping and praying for a good outcome. I have to go make it happen or die trying."

"That's not very comforting. I don't want to be a widow because my husband thought he was Rambo."

Michael let go and stood up. "That's not it. You know me better than that."

"Do I? I've racked my brain most of the night about this. What makes you want to go after a brother who has all but written himself out of the family? The thought that you'd leave Suzanne and me to go who knows where scares me to death."

"It scares me too," Michael admitted.

"So why?"

Lowering his voice, he said, "Because love him or hate him, Taylor is still family, and I would go to the ends of the earth for my family. And for some unknown reason I *know* I can save him. What I did to those boys years ago—" Michael stopped, searching for the words. "I know how to turn a person against themselves, how to exploit their weaknesses or even strengths."

"These are not playground bullies, Michael."

"I know."

This time April pulled him close. "Then let's go tell someone like Colonel Bracken that we got a phone call from Taylor and let them handle it. Don't you think they will go after their own?"

Michael didn't have an answer, and the question still hung in the air as the doorbell rang.

"Expecting someone?" he said.

"No. But Allie from down the street was coming by later. Get the door. If it's for me, I need to brush my hair."

Walking to the door, he could make out two figures in dark clothing beyond the marbled glass and knew it wasn't Allie from down the street. He opened the door and found two stone-faced men on the welcome mat. "Can I help you?" Michael asked.

After each flashed a badge, one of the men spoke. "My name is Smith. This is Wakefield. We're with the Defense Intelligence Agency. Mr. Sutton, we understand you received a phone call at 2:00 AM today." It was not a question.

"That's correct. How did you know that?" It was a knee-jerk response, for in an instant Michael remembered a project he had helped the NSA complete two years prior.

"That's none of your concern," Wakefield replied. "We just do. Does your wife know about the call?"

"She does."

"Can we speak to both of you?"

"Certainly." Michael opened the door wide and pointed to the small living room. "Have a seat. I'll go get her."

The men remained standing until April entered. "Honey, this is Agents Smith and Wakefield. They're with the Defense Intelligence Agency." Smith was tall and pasty with broad shoulders and something like a quarterback's stance. Wakefield was black, not as tall as Smith but thicker in all the ways a lineman is thicker than the quarterback. April greeted them with hesitation.

Michael took his wife by the hand, and everyone sat down but only on the edge of the cushions. "Thanks for waiting. I had to pour my daughter some breakfast. So what's going on?" April looked from her husband to the visitors.

Wakefield began. "Ma'am, we're here in response to the phone call your husband received during the night. " His accent was Southern but not Deep South; Michael figured Arkansas.

April nodded. "Okay."

"We felt it best to apprise you and your husband of the situation. We understand the anxiety under which people operate when a family member is missing, especially under these circumstances. Unfortunately, we are not certain the voice was authentic. *If* it was your brother, Mr. Sutton, he was under duress. We are also confident it was a digital reproduction."

"So spell it out. What are you saying?" April said indignantly.

"Ma'am. What we're saying . . . " Wakefield fumbled.

He is definitely the rookie, Michael thought, reading between the lines and reading the agents.

"The fact is," said Smith, picking up the ball, "it was not a live voice. So—"

"Don't get your hopes up," Michael interrupted. "That's what you're telling us. You're saying that even though Taylor said Mingora, which is in Pakistan, which is where his team went, don't believe that either."

"I am sorry," Smith said. "But that is correct."

"So where did you trace this mock phone call to?"

"We can't say," Smith responded.

"Can't say, or don't know?" Michael didn't wait for a reply. "If you're still using the Alacrity Tracer, you probably don't know. It's famously inaccurate and constantly in need of recalibration with global positioning satellites. When was the last diagnostic ran?"

The agents looked at each other with puzzlement on their faces, no doubt wondering how he knew about the NSA's top-secret satellite.

"You two should do your homework. I helped design that piece of junk."

"I assure you, Mr. Sutton, the Alacrity is working just fine," Smith said. "We know exactly where the call originated from."

"Okay, so when does the military intend to go after those Rangers? You do take care of your own, don't you?" April's desperation was obvious.

There was a long pause as the men shifted in their seats. Michael watched them intently; one of them was going to crack. He was betting on the rookie.

As predicted, Wakefield spoke first. "That's up to JSOC, but we currently are unaware of any plans. It was a covert op, and since relations with Pakistan are less than optimal . . . "

"So you did trace the call to Pakistan?" Michael said, trying to hold back a smile.

"We cannot say," Smith barked. Eyeing his partner he repeated, "We *cannot* say."

The agents stood and buttoned their suit coats. Smith glared at Michael. "Before we leave we must inform you that a gag order is in effect. Neither of you are allowed to speak of this—to anyone. Do so and you will find yourselves on trial for treason. Go to work. Let life get back to normal. In all reality, nothing has changed since you were first apprised of your brother's capture."

Michael extended his hand to Smith. "I have two questions. Why is the Defense Intelligence Agency involved? And why are you spying on Americans?" Smith did not shake Michael's hand but followed his partner to the door. Wakefield opened the door and both men exited. "Have a beautiful day, gentlemen," Michael called out. Neither of the agents responded.

After he closed the door, Michael followed April to the kitchen, where Suzanne was slurping her milk out of her cereal bowl, her hair standing up in every direction. Both of them watched as she finished her breakfast, Michael feeling envious of the innocence and simplicity of youth.

"Michael . . . " April began with a sigh.

"Actually, sweetheart," he interrupted, "I think you are right. I'll go talk with Colonel Bracken to see if there are any plans in the works, especially since the phone call."

Her whole body seemed to breathe a sigh. "Thank you, honey." She wrapped her arms around Michael as he pulled her in for a kiss. "So what was with the whole Alasi whatever?"

"The Alacrity Tracer. It's the NSA's spy satellite used to track terrorist activity. It's very reliable. I was just winding them up to see what I could get out of them. They basically said they knew exactly where the call originated. So even if Taylor was forced to lie, they should know the truth. It's not like the movies where it takes forever to trace a call. It's instantaneous. That's why I'm going to talk to the colonel. If the military can do anything, it will be now."

"Huh. You're pretty smart for a guy." April smiled.

"Thanks. Would you like some breakfast?"

"Oh no. Mountain Dew is all I need."

Michael grinned. "How 'bout eggs and toast?"

"Sure." She bent over to kiss Suzanne on the forehead. "Would you like some eggs, honey?

"No," the four-year-old replied. "That's where baby chickens come from—yuck!"

April and Michael laughed.

On Wednesday evening, April sat at the dinner table with Suzanne. She looked at her husband's empty chair before she blessed the meal. They were having clam chowder, his favorite. But even Michael's favorite dish wasn't enough to bring him home on time. Last night he had come home with more devastating news. According to Colonel Bracken, JSOC had no intention of going after the missing Rangers. Apparently, intelligence pointed to a major military coup that would occur within the next few weeks. Michael had argued that would make the matter even more urgent, but, April thought, no self-respecting colonel is going to listen to a civilian.

Almost as soon as April said amen, Suzanne dove into her soup. "This is good, Mommy. I like ham chowder."

April grinned. There was no way she was going to tell her daughter that it was *clam* chowder, and that clams are little creatures that resemble characters from *SpongeBob*.

Suzanne slurped her soup. "Aren't you going to eat, Mommy?"

"Well, I was hoping to eat with Daddy, but he's working." It was all April could do to fight back the tears. "I can save him" was the last thing he had said to her before he left through the front door. She had spent the entire day crying whenever Suzanne wasn't looking.

April glanced from the empty chair to the cell phone beside her bowl. Michael had said he wasn't going to tell his parents because he didn't want them to worry. She thought about the "gag" order mentioned by Agent Smith and wondered if he was bluffing. She decided to throw caution out the window and dialed her in-laws' number. If Michael was going to come home, he would need all the help he could get. And Vander Sutton was a brilliant man.

14

It had been two days since Michael's wife had accepted the fact that he was going to try to rescue his brother. She wasn't a fan of the idea, but at least she wasn't packing her bags. At first Michael felt liberated, but the angry fire in his heart did not cool and now he felt the weight of his undertaking.

The first order of business was to learn everything he could about the region and the people. Formerly a city of culture and attraction, Mingora was now at the heart of the turbulent Northwest Province. Located in the beautiful Swat Valley at the foot of the Himalayas, it had once attracted both summer travelers and winter skiers, but warring political factions had changed all that. In addition, Pakistan's most vicious and degenerate resided in Mingora, within the walls of the infamous Slohman Gaul prison. According to the latest reports the area was currently at peace, but like the rumblings in the earth before a volcano erupted, all signs pointed to a violent upheaval in the north.

As Michael studied maps of city and terrain, he wondered about the call being faked or recorded, as Smith and Wakefield had insisted. But that would mean all this was for nothing—a possibility Michael wasn't ready to accept.

There was plenty to worry about and even more to plan for as he set his mind to the task of getting to Mingora, finding his brother, and getting out alive. It would be necessary to discover the exact whereabouts of his brother and any other survivors, procure weapons, and most importantly, plan an escape route.

It was very late, but Michael forced himself to continue poring over maps and satellite imagery. He had also been studying about this General Rais, whom the Rangers had been sent to eliminate, but Michael's mind was growing numb. He had slept on his office couch the previous night, surviving on snack food, and suspected he would do the same tonight. There was a knock at the office door before it opened.

"Jarrett? You scared me!"

"Sorry, Mike." Jarrett chuckled. "I thought you'd left the light on. Didn't expect to find you in here." He walked a few steps into the small office and left the door wide behind him.

Michael put a hand to his heart. "Actually, I should thank you. I was about to go get something to wake me up, but you coming in did that just fine."

"You all right? You and April all right?"

"Sure, Jarrett. Why do you ask?"

He pointed to evidence that Michael had slept on the couch. "You haven't been home in two days."

As much as Michael liked and trusted Jarrett, he knew he could not include him in his plans. It had become increasingly obvious that he would have to break a few laws to get everything done, and he didn't want to jeopardize someone else's future.

"I know, Jarrett. But this is pretty important. I am against a deadline on this project and I've got to get it done." Michael collapsed in his chair and tossed a pencil onto the desk. He was about to say more when he noticed a man standing in the doorway. Michael's heart skipped a beat. "Dad!"

The old patriarch stood with clenched fists, a furrow cut deeply between his brows. His eyes were red.

Jarrett turned to face Vander Sutton and quickly excused himself.

Moving to shut the door, Van spoke with his back toward Michael. "Got a call from April. Turns out my oldest son has lost his mind."

"So much for a gag order," Michael muttered.

Van faced his son squarely. "She said something about that too. She called from a neighbor's phone. It is odd that the DIA would be involved, but that's not why I'm here."

Michael started on the defensive. "I can't believe she asked you to talk me out of this. I thought she . . . we . . . agreed on this."

"No, that wasn't it." His father spoke with calm measured words. "Surprisingly, she was supportive, even proud of you. But she thought we should at least know what was going on. It should have been you that called. I came here on my own accord to try to talk you out of this."

"Why? It's what you would do."

Van moved away from the door and leaned a heavy arm a filing cabinet. "You're not me."

"I'm more you than you think."

"You don't have the heart for this."

"Don't have the heart? You think I'm incapable of following through, that somehow I will baulk when the crap hits the fan?"

"Are you ready, Son, to look a man in the face and pull the trigger? To watch the life drain from his eyes? And if you do, are you prepared for them to haunt your dreams? Are you ready to become *that* man? War is an ugly thing, Michael. You can't—you can't calculate it. There's is no equation for it. It's just ugly."

"I know I calculate and recalculate, but when I act, it is without reservation. If I don't go, Taylor may never come home and I will regret having not tried. That will haunt my dreams and every waking moment, Dad."

Van rubbed his bloodshot eyes. "I don't know about this, Michael. Taylor may have saved your life years ago, but war is a horrible thing. You cannot promise you will come home. There are no guarantees and no foolproof plan."

Michael shifted his weight. "I've thought about that. April and Suzanne have been at the forefront of my mind. It kills me to think I might make April a widow over this, but something deep down in my soul is driving me on. It is more than his saving my life—Taylor is family! I know you well enough to realize that if the roles were reversed, and you were a young man, nothing would stop you."

"You're not hearing me, Michael." Van hammered a fist on the filing cabinet. "I don't want to lose another son!" The walls of the small office seemed to shudder as a father's fear finally surfaced.

Michael sighed. "You won't, Dad. In fact, you may get us both back."

"You can't guarantee that." Van's chin quivered.

"You're right, I can't. And maybe you're right—maybe I don't have the heart for this. Honestly, I wish it was me out there. I wish Taylor was here and I was there, because I know . . . " Fighting tears, Michael choked out, "I know Taylor would come for me. He would find me, no matter the cost. You have reminded us a hundred times that since the days when Washburn Sutton fought in the Revolutionary War, the Suttons have never backed down from a fight. And you used to tell us how Washburn's great-grandchildren fought in the Civil War and became known as the Fighting Suttons because of their valor. That blood must still run in our veins. This war came to our door, Dad. I cannot live with the thought of not answering."

Van hung his head for a moment before he glanced up with moist eyes. "Fine, Son," he said quietly. "But you are going to need some help."

Michael's father turned to the door and opened it. Colonel Walter Bracken stood just outside. He was dressed as Michael had never seen him before, in jeans and a T-shirt. The colonel walked in and said, "I told you he wouldn't change his mind, Van."

"It doesn't surprise me either, but I had to try." Turning to his son, Van continued, "The colonel has agreed to help us . . . unofficially. Tell us what you have so far."

15

In the upper east corner, in his personal living quarters above the Slohman Gaul Prison, Aman Shamir sat behind a desk with his heavy black boots perched on one corner. Between two fingers of one hand, a cigarette smoldered. The other hand idly turned a cup of tea. He was exhausted. Torture was tiring work, even for a young man, which he was not. Above him, a small window was wide open, allowing the cool night air to settle around him.

Unlike the general's office, Aman's was nothing fancy. The mud-gray walls were bare, save a mirror and a plaque. A single wooden chair sat in the corner. To his right, a door led out into the prison; another door adjacent led into a small apartment. He prided himself on his simplicity.

Typically, a smoke of fine Turkish tobacco and a cup of tea soothed his nerves, but tonight Aman stared at his desk, brooding. Etched in the wood were a thousand pen strokes from his heavy hand, pen strokes that had ordered the deaths or spared the lives of a thousand men. From this very spot he commanded men and they obeyed. From within these walls, he was God. No man questioned Aman's authority. That was until he formed an unlikely union with Abdul-Aziz Rais, an ambitious and self-aggrandizing man.

Rais had money—lots of it—and the need for an army. With Aman's prison filled beyond capacity and his income menial, it seemed to be the perfect opportunity. But recently he had been losing control of the situation. He had let greed get the better of him, and now he had six Americans in his prison whose lives he desperately wished to end. And yet he was prevented from doing so by Abdul Rais. The large man was beginning to wear out his welcome. Something would have to be done.

Suddenly, as if conjured from Aman's thoughts, General Rais entered the small office. It was obvious he was unhappy.

"What is this?" the general barked. "In my absence, you have been torturing my prisoners? You are not to go near them! I told you that! After my plans have succeeded, you can do with them as you wish, but not before."

Aman Shamir coolly crushed the cigarette stub into a tray. "Calm yourself, Abdul. They are well enough. I hardly touched them. Before I got to them, I had an attempted prison break by a dozen men. I had to put them first. I am losing control of this prison, thanks to you."

"Thanks to me?" repeated Rais incredulously.

"Yes. Thanks to you and your games. You should have shot the American the other day. The prisoners saw that you were shut down by him. He controlled the fight and you! If we do not make an example of him, we will have to kill every man in here. And there goes your army."

The general hit the desk with a force that bounced Aman's boots off the corner. "I need them alive, especially that one! Soon I will have completed my plans and will be far away from here, and you will have your money."

"The sooner, the better, General!" Aman Shamir turned and closed the window. Though they were high above the ground, he did not like speaking of this business near an open window. "If my superiors learn that these prisoners are filling up your ranks, I am a dead man. We all have to answer for our sins to someone. As far as your Americans are concerned, I am justified in my designs. They killed a guard."

"Who killed him?"

"Not your pet, if that is what you are wondering."

After a brief pause, the general said, "Let us restore some order then. We will put the man who killed the guard in the cage tomorrow and ensure that he loses."

"What if he does not lose?"

"You shoot him like a dog anyway."

Aman Shamir smiled slightly. "Very well. We shall retrieve your Americans from the catacombs then."

The warden's concern that their conversation would be overheard had been valid, but it was not from the window. Though the door to his apartment was made of a solid wood, it hung sloppily from the frame, and from around the frame slipped every syllable. This exchange, as had many others before, did not empty into a vacant apartment but into the keen ears of a perceptive young woman.

She was also a prisoner, but not for any crime. She was a slender, dark-haired girl of nineteen with olive skin and dark-brown eyes that held strength even a life as pathetic as hers could not erase. Her name was Nasira, and Aman Shamir had kept her locked away in his apartment for the better part of her life. Though he allowed her freedom of movement about the apartment, she was forbidden to leave.

He had found her many years earlier, lost in the catacombs below the prison. She was ten, and being full of curiosity had wandered into the catacombs. All her sobs and pleas to be free had been in vain. He refused to find her family and forbade her from asking about them. Saying fate had brought her to him, Shamir kept her. And like a dragon who kidnapped a princess, he locked her away in his tower. For many years, she dared not leave, being surrounded by the most dangerous of all animals—man.

Recently, however, especially after the arrival of the American soldiers, she began to risk all and venture out. On one of her trips she had left medicine and food for one of the Americans—a man brave enough to defy the general and warden and live.

Listening to Shamir and the general, Nasira knew it was time to act or forever forget about leaving her apartment-prison.

In near darkness, Taylor touched his face. It felt foreign, as though it were made of clay. His nose was broken, he was sure of that, and he could only see out of one eye. His cheekbones were soft and puffy, his beard matted with dried blood. The guards had been using him as a punching bag, and he felt certain they were only getting warmed up. Since he and the other Rangers had been in the lower cells, the warden had not made an appearance, for which Taylor was grateful. The man had an air of evil about him. Taylor had heard screams and prayed they were not from his brothers.

He licked his cracked lips with a dry tongue. What he wouldn't give for some lip balm and a drink of water. Nearly blind, he reached out with his other senses. Someone was coming.

A steel door swung wide and a sickly yellow light spilled onto the floor. Taylor's heart pounded as he fought the urge to cry. Soon his would be the voice that cried out in the darkness and in vain against the soulless men. Until this moment he had always believed there would be more time. He had believed in the Ranger's inevitable escape and victorious emergence from captivity, but suddenly an ugly alternate reality emerged and he could hardly believe it. Today, he was going to die—if he was lucky.

Even with only one eye, he recognized the pitiless stance of the warden and he shuddered so deeply he almost crumpled to the floor. The warden barked an order and two guards entered. Taylor was unchained and pushed to the door. *This is it,* he thought. He was not ready to die, but at least he understood it. Death was absolute; death was freedom. It was torture he feared most. His mind raced. He had to fight! Once outside the room he would make his stand and die like a Ranger.

The yellow light grew brighter. The pace of his breathing increased as the adrenalin coursed through his veins and his muscles tightened. Just as he was about to make his move, he saw Fulton's dark silhouette, then Pike's. His brothers—they were here. His heart leaped in his chest but he was unsure. Perhaps they were to be tortured together.

In the pallid light of the corridor he saw them all. Fulton and Pike, Gutierrez, Cobb, and McGillis. They were all bruised and beaten, but they were alive. Cradling his obviously broken forearm, McGillis seemed the worst off.

The warden gave an order in his native tongue, but Taylor understood regardless. They were going back to their cells. There would be no further abuse, at least not today.

In their cells, they found food and water, and they went to it like men possessed. The series of events seemed peculiar to Taylor, but at the moment he was too famished to make more than a passing note of it. Clarity would come soon enough.

16

The following morning Cobb found himself in the cage, pitted against a thick, barrel-chested man with powerful arms and a face that seemed to be chiseled from stone by a blind mason. The two had been hand selected by the warden to fight in the cage. *Where do they get these guys?* Cobb thought. Something in his gut told him this was retribution for the slain guard, which meant either the guard had been sent to Cobb's cell specifically, or one of the other Rangers had given him up. The latter was unthinkable.

A short, brutal blow rattled Cobb's head. There was no time to think about how he ended up here. He swung at his opponent and missed. He had been beaten badly the previous day in the lower cells while awaiting a torture that never came. He had little use of his left arm, since the ribs on that side had been bruised or broken. He dodged an incoming haymaker and cringed in pain.

Snarling, the man lunged and caught Cobb in his fractured midsection. The air forced from his lungs tasted of blood—a punctured lung in a place like this meant slow death. As the man pressed forward, Cobb drove down hard with a right elbow and his opponent buckled under the Texan's weight. Cobb followed up with a knee to the chin that knocked the man backward.

The cries and shouts from the prison mob were almost deafening. It was a fight to the death, and Cobb doubted he would have the restraint Sutton had shown in the previous fight.

As Cobb cleared the pain from his mind, something occurred to him. His legs were in perfect shape. The previous day's beatings had left them unharmed. He watched his opponent circling. Wild with anger, the man came in for the kill, but Cobb anticipated his opponent's action and speed. He landed a front kick that must have fractured a rib or two. He followed with a kick between the legs that caused a howl of pain from every man in sight. Cobb finished with a powerful roundhouse that caught his opponent in the face. The man twisted head over heels and landed face down in the dirt, unconscious.

A hush fell over the crowd. "Finish him," ordered the warden from the balcony.

Cobb looked up and then into the crowd. "I do not take orders from cowards like you. I am an American soldier. We are not trained to kill the defenseless—" His words were suddenly cut short. He looked again at the warden, who now held a smoking rifle. Cobb touched his chest—it felt warm and wet. Searching the crowd, his eyes met those of Gutierrez and the others. They were screaming and scrambling to get to him. Silent words fell from his lips, and his knees buckled. Night seemed to be falling on the world—falling on him. The pain in his body subsided and everything went quiet.

Later, the five remaining Army Rangers sat in silence, each in his own cell. The previous night's food and drink had come as a reward, Taylor now realized. One of his team members had talked. The thought made him sick to his stomach.

His eyes turned to the septic bowl of food sitting on the floor. After what had just happened, it was an insult. He looked about his cell; it seemed smaller, and darker. The loss of Wesley Cobb crowded out the idea of escape, and the hope of freedom began to slip from the corporal's mind.

Taylor thought of Ian Pike. His lean figure had grown leaner, his eyes hollow. He and Cobb had been good friends. It was a dark day for all of them, but especially Ian.

From out of the darkness, Pike suddenly spoke. "Heck with it, mates. I'm eating."

Taylor heard shuffling from Pike's cell, and when the Australian spoke again, his mouth was obviously full. "Like Cobb said, 'Call me whatever you want. Just don't call me late for supper.' Here's to you, mate!" Taylor wasn't sure, but it sounded like Pike was on the verge of tears.

Then Pike chuckled and said, "Wes was as game as Ned Kelly. Did you see him kick that man? There is no way that bloke will ever have offspring!"

"I personally like the roundhouse that finished him off," said Fulton. "The guy looked like he'd been hit by a truck."

"I tell you, Cobb was a fighter! The man was awesome, a real ripper!" Pike went on. "We should drink to his memory! Everyone grab your nasty brown water. Pretend it's a longneck if it helps."

Taylor picked up his cup and held it high. "To Specialist Wesley 'Corn' Cobb. Hurrah!"

"Hurrah!" repeated Gutierrez, Fulton, and Pike.

Taylor noticed McGillis had remained silent.

"Thank you, Pike," Sergeant Gutierrez said from his cell. "We needed that."

"You're welcome, sir."

A few minutes later, Fulton broke out with "Jesus, Lover of My Soul." The hymn restored some light to Taylor's darkened mind and lifted his heavy heart. It may well have been the best hymn he'd ever heard.

17

The V-22 Osprey's landing was surprisingly smooth for a flying tank with massive turboprops pointing skyward, the twin blades fracturing the air in great swaths. Michael had experienced much bumpier landings in commercial airliners. Being fastened securely to the wall like a piece of equipment, however, made him appreciate reclining chairs.

One of the many things he'd learned in the last two weeks was that a person did not simply catch a flight to Pakistan with motives such as his. Michael had relied heavily on his father and Colonel Bracken, and the two astute men had quickly formulated a plan. Posing as a photojournalist for *National Geographic*, Michael had flown out a few days earlier with the 132nd Regiment. A digital camera hung around his neck, and he carried a computer bag as well. Michael Sutton was now, as Walter Bracken had described the typical news reporter in the battlefield, an "overzealous, overbearing, sycophantic suck-up."

Feeling as if he had been traveling forever, Michael looked forward to having solid ground beneath his feet. This was the fourth leg of a five-leg flight, and he knew what it meant to have jet lag.

The cargo bay door lowered in front of him and he could feel the excitement in the air as the men of 132nd inhaled the jet-fueled atmosphere of Bagram Airfield. He had made it to Afghanistan. It was dark, 9:00 PM local time, and Michael looked forward to a bed or a cot or even a soft patch of dirt. His eyes burned every time he blinked. Tomorrow he would catch one last flight to Jalalabad, a mere hop compared to what he'd been through. Flying east around the globe had shortened the days, and he felt as though he'd aged considerably.

The soldiers of the 132nd quickly unfastened their harnesses and stood. They marched away into the darkness without a word. Michael looked to his left and right and found he was alone.

"All right then," he mumbled, then unfastened the five-point harness that had held him tight for the past several hours. When he stood and stretched, every bone in his back cracked like dry cedar. He retrieved his overnight bag, and suddenly a man in camo was beside him.

"Evening, sir. The name's Private Scott." The young man extended a hand, which Michael shook readily. "I have been asked to escort you to and from your barracks."

"I appreciate your promptness. It's been a long day."

"You're welcome. Long flight?"

"Flights," Michael replied. "I feel like I've been on the move forever." He doubted the young man was yet twenty-one. Not of legal drinking age back in the States, but old enough to offer his life for his country.

"I will show you to your digs for the night, sir."

"You can knock off the 'sir's. You're the one with the military rank. The name's Michael."

The young man smiled. "Yes, sir. I have a car this way."

Michael followed him out onto the tarmac. Though the night wind was cool, heat radiated from the ground. It had obviously been much warmer during the day. He looked around. Bagram was a small, bright city pushing back the night in the middle of the bleak desert.

Private Scott walked to a small car and opened the rear hatch.

"For some reason I expected a Jeep." Michael set his bag and computer in the back.

"Well, this isn't *M.A.S.H.* But since the military bought train loads of these cheap little British cars, we tear 'em up."

"British, huh? That explains the driver's side being on the right."

"Yeah, that was weird to get used to, shifting with the left hand and all."

Michael and the private got in and sat shoulder to shoulder.

"Roomy," Michael said.

Private Scott started the car and lugged the engine as he engaged the clutch. The small engine strained against the weight of the two men. "You'll be staying at Camp Albert tonight," the private explained. "It looks like a shanty town, but the beds are good. I'll pick you up at 0700."

"Fine." Michael hung his head. He did not like being in motion again.

Scott cut left then right, weaving back and forth, dodging every obstacle—seen and unseen. The little three-cylinder motor wound tight each time the private depressed the clutch with gusto. Wondering if the kid had recently watched the *Fast and Furious* movies, Michael knew he had been safer strapped into the cargo bay of the V-22.

Finally, the car squealed to a halt. Michael peered out and saw a plywood cabin that had to be smaller than the master bathroom in his house. "We're here," Private Scott said.

Michael got out and looked around. Even in the darkness, he could see that Camp Albert consisted of cookie-cutter cabins, all of them painted an awful salmon color. Most of the cabins seemed vacant, but randomly, a cabin door stood wide, the light spilling into the street. Music and laughter came from those cabins. Michael thought of dorm life during his college days—nobody stayed alone in his own dorm, and every night was a party of some sort. He smiled to himself. Private Scott, still playing valet, opened the hatch and pulled Michael's bags from the back of the car.

"Number 75, right in front of you. Remember, 0700 tomorrow." The private handed the bags over, got in the car, and sped away.

Michael turned the knob and pushed the door open wide. He found the light switch and glanced around the room. All he cared about at the moment was that there was a bed. He closed the door behind him and dropped his bags near the bathroom door.

Forcing himself to stay alert for another minute, he knelt down at the side of the bed and offered thanks to God for his safe arrival and pled with all his heart for his dear wife and child. They would be worried for him. Lastly, Michael pled for success in the endeavor he had undertaken. He felt that without the Lord's help, he was on a fool's errand.

Michael stood and stripped off his shirt and shoes, then lay down on the bed. His ears still rang from the thundering engines of the V-22, and it felt as though his body was still in motion.

It had only been a week since the final plan had been laid out, and his life had been a whirlwind ever since. The plan was patchy at best, but Michael's anxiety and impatience had won out. It had all been nailed down late one evening when Colonel Bracken had shown up at Michael's house. It was just him and his dad at home, since April had taken Suzanne and gone to visit her sister, wanting to escape the tension. After the colonel showed up, the three of them sat down at the kitchen table. "We have the last piece of the puzzle," the colonel had said as he opened a manila envelope and removed a couple of photos. He passed them across the table.

Michael and his father looked at them. "What are we looking at?" asked Van.

"These are satellite photos of a ski lodge east of Mingora. The satellite is designed to pick up heat signatures. It is used for night ops. The seven multicolored shapes you see are warm bodies. Rangers—sleeping perhaps, but alive."

"What are the other shapes?"

"You're looking at the shape of a man from the head down— guards no doubt. I count a dozen."

"A dozen! That's going to be a challenge," Michael said. "How do we know these are our seven men?"

"I've had a contact in Pakistan do a little recon for us. He confirmed there are seven American soldiers being held here. As for taking out a dozen guards, it's just a matter of the proper application of explosives." The colonel smiled, but neither Sutton reciprocated.

Bracken cleared his throat. "I've had my office work up some theoretical scenarios for getting men out of situations just like this. They are diversionary tactics and require some practice. We could set a practice range at the post if you'd like. There are a couple of outbuildings away from the main lodge; these could be blown up easily enough."

"Wow," Van said. "I don't know about this, Son."

"Let's just work on it, Dad, and see if we can come up with something viable." Michael sighed. "If not, we'll have to forget it."

The three of them had pulled an all-nighter, but a plan had come together. Now he was thousands of miles from that kitchen table and committed to a plan that any sane person would call suicidal. Slowly his thoughts gave way to his exhaustion, the room stopped spinning, and Michael fell asleep.

It seemed to Michael that he had scarcely closed his eyes before a bugle playing reveille pounded in his brain. It had to be worst way to wake up. Even a country song would have been better—and he hated country music.

Sitting up, he rubbed the sleep from his eyes and tried to focus on his watch. At first he believed it said 12:20 AM. His body and brain wanted to accept this as fact, but on closer inspection he realized was actually 5:00 in the morning.

He sat quiet for a moment trying to clear the cobwebs and figure out what time it was back in California. "It'd be 5:00

yesterday," he muttered. "That's odd to think about." He rubbed his chin, which felt like a cactus. "Better shave."

Michael quickly showered, shaved, and dressed. He was grateful for clean clothes, for he had been in his current ones since the trip began. He stuffed the dirty clothes in his bag, knowing he would have no time to wash them.

Just before six AM, he threw the rest of his belongings into the bag and sat on the bed to call April. He had modified his phone before he left; it would get a signal anywhere on the planet now. On it were the GPS coordinates of Taylor's last known location—a ski resort lodge sitting on the edge of Mingora on the western slopes of the Himalayas.

Michael thought to check one more thing while he had some privacy—the laptop. It was a parting gift from his father, who said it would help with his new identity. Van had instructed him to press control-alt-delete the next time he was alone.

Michael pulled the computer from its case and opened it. It looked like a standard laptop, though it was a little bulky and out of date. His fingers quickly found the buttons and pressed them.

Click.

The laptop opened again. Curiously, Michael lifted the keyboard and looked inside. He found a gun.

"How very 007!" He retrieved the gun and read the side: "Glock 10 mm."

While examining the weapon, Michael picked up his phone to call his wife and noticed a video message from a familiar number. He gave the icon a tap. A video quickly loaded. His father appeared on the small screen and began to speak.

"Michael, this is Dad, of course. We ran out of time, so I put this together for you the night before you left. I couldn't bear the thought of sending you out without giving you everything I could to help you come home. You've already found the gun. As you can imagine, it is not an over-the-counter pistol. The ammo is sharing space with the computer's battery. It is not typical, either.

The gun has improved recoil for greater accuracy, but more importantly the ammo is something I've designed but never had the stomach to market. The idea came from Russian nesting dolls. Each 10 mm round looks like a hollow point, but inside is a small Titanium round about the size of a .22. As you may have guessed already, the rounds will pierce body armor. Most militants in that part of the world use a form of Kevlar called Twaron. It is more susceptible to double stress. The impossible feat with body armor has always been to hit the same spot twice. With these rounds it isn't necessary. As the main bullet mushrooms and strains the armor, the piggyback round tears through. Since they are small, you'd better make them count. They are the only ones of their kind, so don't waste them. I hate talking like this . . . I hope you don't have to use them, but it would be stupid to not be prepared. Don't forget that the most important weapon you have is your great mind. I love you, Son."

The video closed. Michael put the phone on the nightstand.

Never one to pass up a new gadget, he released the battery from the back of the laptop. From the meticulously machined cavity, two 15-round magazines slid into his hand. He looked closely at the round at the top of the clip. He could see the tip of the piggyback bullet inside. "Only my dad would come up with something like this."

Michael put away the magazines and began to reassemble the laptop. "Dial April," he told his cell phone, which came to life and dialed home.

18

Aviation Lieutenant Henry McNally looked at his watch and groaned—it was 0700 exactly. He was scheduled to deliver a Kiowa Warrior to Jalalabad by 0800 and had no intention of letting a "muckraker" make him late. There were other names for news reporters, but McNally preferred not to use profanity.

McNally leaned against the helicopter and looked at his watch again. The muckraker was a last-minute addendum to his flight plan, and he did not like last-minute changes. Whoever it was had some pull from high places.

Standing alone on the tarmac, the lieutenant could see a great deal of the hustle and bustle that typified life at Bagram Airfield. Like busy little ants, thousands of camouflage clones raced about each day, most with menial tasks that often led one to wonder about the sanity and purpose of it all. Only a few people there had anything of real importance to accomplish. The flying of the Kiowa to Jalalabad was a perfect example. McNally had flown this same chopper up from Jalalabad just last month and it had only sat here since then. He looked at his watch again.

In the daylight, Private Scott was much more cautious behind the wheel. Driving as he had last night would result in a citation, and he had enough of those. One more and he'd be walking. The photojournalist in the passenger seat seemed to enjoy the opportunity to look around—it was obviously his first time in Bagram. The private glanced at the lanyard and ID badge around the man's neck. They were new.

"What you photographin' down at Jalalabad?" Scott asked.

"Just the locals," replied the photographer.

Scott glanced at the single bag on the back seat. "Packin' light for such a long stay." He was beginning to wonder if this man was really who he said he was.

"I hope to be in and out. How'd you land this detail—playing taxi for me?"

"Most days I'm just a file clerk for the general. He walked out of his office and pointed at the first fool he saw."

"Which one?" his passenger asked.

Confused, Scott said, "Me. That's why—"

"Which general?" Michael interrupted.

"Oh! That makes more sense. Gibbons. But he's not here very often. He bounces around a lot. Last month he was—whoa!" Just after turning a corner, Scott had to slam on his brakes. "The lieutenant is going to kill me if you're late. Is that a camel?"

Both men opened their doors and stood to get a better view of the situation up ahead. They were on Disney Drive, a very American-looking street. Up ahead there seemed to be a problem with a man, a camel, and the driver of an SUV.

Private Scott squinted into the early morning sun, then looked at his watch. "You have a helicopter to catch, sir. We need to hurry." He got back into the car, as did Michael.

"Here goes another citation," Scott muttered. "Camels are supposed to stay out of the base. Somebody's head is gonna roll." The private backed up the car, turned around on a lawn, and drove over the sidewalk, where he knocked over a trash can and nearly hit a cat. But moments later they were on their way, leaving the camel/car pileup behind.

Driving more like he had the night before, Private Scott headed for the landing strip. He knew where he'd find the lieutenant, who would be growing very impatient by now. Scott glanced in his rearview mirror—no flashing lights. So far.

Just ahead he could see where the road ended and the tarmac began. The time was 0720. He whipped the car through a pedestrian gate and onto the tarmac, knocking off the passenger mirror as he did. He quickly spotted the chopper and pilot. Even from fifty yards away he thought he could see the pilot's scowl. Scott picked up his speed.

Michael forced himself to steady his breath. This would be his first ride in a helicopter. The private had done well getting him here—who could have planned on a camel crash? He thought he heard a tire squeal as the little car came to an abrupt halt next to the chopper. The pilot wasted no time yelling at them; he simply climbed aboard and began take-off procedures.

Michael opened the car door and began to get out.

"Don't forget your bag," the private said.

Michael reached into his pocket and pulled out a fifty-dollar bill. "That's for getting me here on time. I'll give you another hundred if you'll take care of the bag and wash my clothes for me. I'll be back through here soon."

Scott dropped the bag and gasped. "I knew it! You're CIA, aren't you?"

Michael didn't have time to argue or explain. Something caught his eye and his attention. A flashing light. Someone was coming to talk with the reckless driver in the little car. "You have company, Private." He could hear the young man swear as he dropped the fifty on the seat and shut the door.

CIA, Michael thought, almost laughing. *Let the kid think what he wants as long as I get my clothes back.*

"So you're the newspaper reporter," the pilot said as Michael sat down beside him in the helicopter.

"Photojournalist," Michael corrected as he began searching for the seatbelt.

"Let me guess, this is your first chopper ride."

"Yes. And my first seatbelt, it would appear."

The pilot shook his head. "You're the greenest muckraker yet. It's a five-point harness. Pull that strap up between your legs . . . those around your hips and these over your shoulders. By the way, I'm Lieutenant McNally."

Michael had it done in seconds. "Sorry we're late, Lieutenant," he said, trying to talk through his nervousness. "There was a traffic problem with a camel."

McNally only nodded.

Even through the helmet, Michael heard the vicious slicing of the blades through the air. Lifting off felt something like an anti-gravitational ride at the county fair. He thought of April. She wouldn't make it five minutes. This brought new meaning to the term "motion sickness," even for him.

McNally pointed the Warrior southeast toward Jalalabad and they were on their way. The chopper steadily climbed. If Michael's memory served him correctly, they would skirt the bluffs of the towering Cengay Ghar mountain range before landing in Jalalabad. There he would meet another Private Scott, of sorts, and drive across the Pakistani border. The thought of crossing into potentially hostile territory was daunting.

After fifteen minutes of silence it was obvious Lieutenant McNally was not a talker. "How long is the flight from Bagram to Jalalabad?" Michael asked.

"About forty minutes."

"Been flying long?"

"Forever."

"Like it?"

"Yep."

As the attempt at conversation just funneled into nothingness, Michael closed his eyes. The negative G force was nearly unbearable, giving him the feeling of complete weightlessness. He had only eaten an apple and granola bar that morning, but it may as well have been a rock as his stomach bounced off his diaphragm. He held onto the seat with white knuckles, determined to keep down his breakfast.

On the desert floor below, there seemed to be little life, either animal or plant. Occasionally a dirt track cut across their flight path like two fingers tracing random lines in the sand, running to some unseen destination.

It surprised Michael how little the desert below them differed from the California desert between his house and Salt Lake City. Only here there were more rocks. He never saw the sand dunes so popular in modern movies when depicting this part of the world. He mentioned this to McNally with no response.

Soon they approached Jalalabad. Unlike Bagram, which appeared to have sprung up from the weeds, Jalalabad was an established city. After the bumpy ride, it was a beautiful sight.

An airfield outside the city was McNally's obvious target. Michael was grateful to finally hear the turbine overhead idling to a standstill. When they landed, he unfastened his harness and removed his helmet. Clutching his laptop case and feeling as though the camera around his neck weighed a ton, he stepped from the chopper. He leaned against the Kiowa for a moment to get his legs back.

McNally rounded the nose of the helicopter, eyeing him suspiciously. Michael tried to ignore him as he let his stomach settle and knees stop shaking.

"So, what's the truth, muckraker?" the lieutenant asked.

"I don't know what you are talking about," Michael replied, a little breathless. "What's a muckraker?"

"It was a term Roosevelt used for a reporter or photojournalist, which you are not. I've met them before, lots of them, and if they're not running their mouths, they're taking pictures. You didn't take a single shot while we were up there. A real photographer would die to have a half hour up there on a clear day like today. So again, what's the truth?"

Colonel Bracken's last words of advice rang in Michael's ears: "Fly under the radar."

"Well, believe me or not, that's what I am."

McNally looked him up and down. "Whatever you say. I need to report in, and I am sure somebody is looking for you. Let's go." He motioned for Michael to follow.

"I'll be fine, thank you," Michael replied.

"Suit yourself," McNally said, then turned and walked away.

Michael did not know what else to do but walk in a tangent direction. A direction he hoped would lead him off the airfield and into the welcomed sight of another greeter—Private Scott's counterpart. Colonel Bracken had taken care of him so far. Michael prayed he would not be abandoned when he was so close. Placing all his faith in one individual, family friend or not, was a little unnerving, but so far the plan had gone smoothly. From here, he was supposed to secure transportation and continue southeast to the border and to Peshawar. The trip would take about an hour and a half, not including a delay at the border.

With Michael's long stride, he was soon off the tarmac and out of the accusing pilot's line of sight. He had no idea what to do from here. He had fully expected another randomly chosen file clerk to appear from nowhere and point him in the right direction. It also occurred to him that he had no idea where the road lay that would take him to Peshawar and finally Mingora. He touched his phone for security; Google Maps would fix that problem.

After deciding it would be a good time to get something to eat, Michael wandered for upwards of an hour and soon found himself in a busy street market. The kiosks were elaborately decorated in yellows, reds, and blues. Vehicles of both three and four wheels clattered along cobblestone streets, streaming black trails of exhaust. He began taking photos, glad he had the camera. If nothing else, he could show the pictures to April and Suzanne when he got home.

Home. It seemed very far away.

He was startled from his thoughts when a vehicle nearly ran him over. It was scarcely larger than a tricycle, and a small putter came from a tiny motor. He peered into its shaded interior and recognized Lieutenant McNally at once.

"Hey, I've been looking for you," the lieutenant announced.

"Yeah?"

"I was rude back there. Let me buy you a drink."

"I don't drink."

"Not even water?"

Surprised at McNally's cheerful mood, a 180-degree turn from earlier, Michael asked, "To what do I owe this sudden benevolence?"

"Benevolence? You sound like a stuffy reporter. I'm off duty until tomorrow and I really just want to apologize. Come on, get in the taxi. I know where the best water is in town."

Michael chuckled and got in. "This is a taxi? I've ridden in go-carts larger than this."

"And more powerful, no doubt."

18

Sitting at a roadside kiosk, Michael drained the last drops of a refreshing Mountain Dew. He took a large bite of a mutton kabob and found it to be delicious. Bright colors met his every gaze, and people moved along the street riding every sort of vehicle imaginable, like something from a Dr. Seuss book. With the city's enchanting effect, Michael had to continually remind himself that he was not there for pleasure. There was a long and dangerous drive ahead of him, and his next contact had yet to appear.

One of Michael's many talents was that of listening. Most people, he found, enjoyed talking about themselves, and McNally, now more relaxed, was no different. Michael enjoyed learning about the pilot's life, which had been quite exciting at times. He was a widower with a child back in the States. The boy wasn't really a child anymore—he was married with children of his own—and he wanted nothing to do with the military. He just couldn't understand his father's decision to stay in Afghanistan. As McNally spoke, Michael mostly nodded and laughed, all the while watching for a man who might be looking for him.

McNally's cap and sunglasses sat on the table beside his drink. Crow's feet framed his eyes, and deep furrows crossed his forehead. Time had not been his friend, Michael decided, for the man's face almost resembled a topographical map.

He had grown so used to the pilot's ramblings that he looked up when it stopped. The pilot's observant eyes bored into him. Michael swallowed his food. "What? I was listening."

"I know, but I've been doing all the talking." McNally leaned forward. "Here's what I figure. You are not a government man and you are not a photographer. You are, however, waiting for someone. You're smart enough to not draw attention to yourself, but you are waiting for that person to find you. You're edgy, so whatever is ahead of you is new. So . . . "

Michael sighed. "Well, you've got me. I am waiting for someone who should have been here by now. Not that I haven't enjoyed your company."

"You're not going to say anything more? Fine. I'll tell you one more thing I know. The man sitting across the street at your four o'clock has been watching you for the last fifteen minutes. Good people don't do that."

Michael said nothing but glanced to his right and saw a man across the street. The man got up and began to cross.

"I like you," McNally said, "so if you're in trouble, let me help you."

Traffic momentarily blocked the approaching man. "I'm not in trouble, but I am here to help someone who is," Michael confided. "I wish I could tell you more."

The man was Middle Eastern and moved with agility and confidence toward their table. He was smartly dressed with a polo shirt and a sport jacket even though it was a warm day.

McNally spoke quickly. "If that changes, call me." He slid a card across the table. Michael was not sure why, but the pilot's concern made him nervous.

Michael palmed the card as the Middle Eastern man walked up and asked, "Are you Michael Sutton?"

"Yes." Michael took the man's extended hand.

"I am Marcus. I will be driving you." He turned to greet McNally, who seemed reluctant to even shake his hand.

"I have been watching you from across the street to make sure it was you. I have been sent by a mutual friend to help you on your way." He looked at McNally.

"Great," Michael said. "I was starting to think I'd be making this trip alone."

"It is too—how do you say?—risky to go alone." Marcus had dark-mocha skin and heavy eyebrows like Groucho Marx. He spoke English well but with a thick accent.

McNally stood. "I should be getting back to the base. And you have obviously found your next travel companion. God speed, Michael."

Michael stood and offered his hand and the pilot clasped it tightly. Seconds later, McNally disappeared into the busy street.

"Come, Michael Sutton. I have a car waiting."

He hesitated, looking after the pilot, but ultimately followed Marcus around the corner, where a small Fiat sat. Getting in the car, Marcus began to speak. "The colonel has arranged what you Americans call a care package. It is near."

"Care package," Michael repeated. "Whatever you call it, I hope it is loaded."

Marcus did not reply but started the car and moved into traffic. Michael looked around the interior of the vehicle, which would seat four men at the most. "Whatever the care package is had better hold a lot more passengers."

"All has been arranged, Mr. Sutton. Do not worry. Just do not lean on the doors. They will open and you will fall out. It is a Fiat, after all."

Michael pulled his arm off the door rest, fastened his seatbelt, and began to take mental notes on his new escort. For starters, the man smelled of too much cologne as though he were covering up other odors. Old scars circled his wrists, perhaps from restraints, and a couple of times Michael caught sight of small round marks on his forearms. The closer he looked, the more he noticed the man was covered in scars.

He must not have been careful in his observations, for Marcus soon broke the silence. "I was in a car accident a few years back. It was very bad. I was thrown through the windshield and onto the concrete. I almost met Allah that day."

"Sorry," Michael replied. "I wasn't trying to stare."

Soon Marcus began to point out some of the sights of Jalalabad, both historical and modern. Michael almost felt like he was on a tour. Most the city streets were divided and insanely disorganized. Little three-wheeled cars used both for taxi service and deliveries darted haphazardly in and out of traffic. Marcus pointed out the stately Shahi Palace, the governor's residence, and no less than two dozen mosques. Michael remembered his camera and began snapping digital shots of everything in sight.

"What are you doing?" Marcus asked.

"Just taking a few shots for the wife and kid." He snapped a picture of Marcus.

Marcus pushed the camera down. "Don't act like tourist. Nobody likes tourist. You want to get to Mingora safely, you do as I say."

For some reason, Michael wasn't surprised by the man's reaction to the camera. Perhaps McNally was right, he thought, remembering his words—"Good men don't do that." With a picture of Marcus on the camera, all Michael had to do was wait and see. If the camera disappeared, Marcus was more than a driver and Michael would know not to trust him.

Marcus turned the Fiat into what seemed to be a blind alley. "We are here."

The alley was just wider than the little car and allowed no room for a direction change. "I see why you drove this car," Michael commented.

The alley was not completely blind, for a garage door opened to their left. Marcus pulled the Fiat into a dimly lit garage, and the door quickly closed behind them. He got out as the little car sputtered and then died.

Michael climbed out as well. When his eyes adjusted to the semi-darkness, he saw several vehicles, including a beautifully restored 1966 GTO. "I hope that's the care package," he said.

"No, no, she's mine. This is your care package." Marcus pointed to a multicolored truck. A fiberglass ice cream cone stuck out of the top. Paintings of various ice cream treats adorned the sides.

"We're driving an ice cream truck all the way to Mingora?" Michael asked.

"Yes. Hide in plain sight. But these treats are not for children." Marcus opened the back. Behind the hidden panels lay a cache of weapons that would make any revolutionary jealous.

"What about food, water, and basic medical supplies?"

"It's all here. Take a look for yourself."

Michael opened some cabinet doors and took a mental inventory. There was no telling what condition he would find his brother's team in.

"Come, we should going," Marcus said impatiently.

Michael looked at his watch. The early start and early lunch with McNally made it feel later than it was. It was not yet noon, but they should have been in Peshawar by now.

Marcus got in the driver's seat and Michael climbed in the passenger's. Marcus pushed a button and a garage door opened opposite the one they had entered. Everything else in the garage darkened around the large bright square. The truck started quietly and moved out of the garage, and the door shut securely behind them.

Soon they headed southeast across the desert floor on what seemed to be a main highway. When a helicopter flew overhead, Michael thought of McNally and remembered to ask Marcus, "Why were you late meeting me?"

"I was driving others. You were early. I was told to meet you at the airfield. When you were not there, I went to find you."

Recalling the busy street where they had met, Michael figured Marcus must have a photo of him; otherwise, he would have never located him. "I guess I'm lucky you tracked me down. Kinda like looking for a needle in a haystack."

"No. Americans are easy to find," Marcus came back. "You all love to eat."

Remembering the ten pounds he had recently put on, Michael couldn't argue about his love of food. "So how do you know the colonel?"

"He is a friend of a friend. He needed someone in Jalalabad. I was available. You are starting to sound like a news reporter." Marcus flipped the lanyard around Michael's neck. "It is fake, remember? You should take it off before the border."

Michael did not apologize for being inquisitive. He glanced at his camera. He had set it on the floor between them as bait. They did not speak again for a long time, and even as jet-lagged as he was, Michael had no desire to sleep. Marcus soon turned on the radio and began to sing along.

20

Michael quickly realized the ice cream truck's top speed was fifty miles per hour, and that it was not equipped with an air conditioner. After a sweaty couple of hours listening to Marcus sing to Pakistani music, he began to question his own existence. Michael was drumming his fingers on the door in frustration when the truck rolled to a stop behind a line of cars. Marcus shut off the engine.

Michael frowned. "What's going on?"

"There is always a wait at the border," Marcus replied. "Can't let in the crazies, you know." He got out of the truck. "Your turn to drive."

Feeling hot and sticky, Michael got out and stretched. While he had not anticipated this delay, he was grateful for the chance to get blood to his feet. Plus his back was killing him.

Marcus took a blue booklet from his pocket and handed it Michael. "The border guards will ask for papers. Give them these."

"But I have a passport."

"Give me."

Michael retrieved his passport from his laptop case and Marcus took one glance at it.

"No, that will not do. An American does not get half the way around the world without any stamps. Take these. It will make everything easy."

Michael opened the passport. Inside there were stamps from all over the globe. He looked at the picture inside the front cover. "Uh, this looks nothing like me."

"It does not matter. Tell them you shaved. All they look for is stamps."

"And changed my skin color? I'm not a human chameleon."

"Trust me," Marcus said. "I am driver. The queue is moving."

Michael got in the driver's seat and started the truck. The traffic moved slowly.

An hour later, the brakes squealed for the last time in front of the guard shack. The sun was high above them.

In Pakistani a young guard said, "Papers." Marcus translated for Michael and they each handed over a blue booklet. Continuing in rough English, the guard asked Michael, "What have you inside?"

"Ice cream," Marcus said from the passenger seat. "Everyone loves ice cream."

"That's right," Michael put in. "People in Peshawar love their ice cream."

The guard seemed doubtful. "We should have you open the back."

"Here, we will show." Marcus moved to the back and retrieved a large ice cream container. He opened the lid and placed what looked like a large amount of money on top of the frozen treat.

"Hey! Hey!" Michael took the ice cream and held it out. "Look here! That is a lot of pistachio ice cream for two men."

"It's avocado," Marcus corrected.

Michael gave him a disgusted look and turned back to the guards. He lifted the lid slightly. "Now that's what I call a cool treat."

Smiling, one of the guards took the container and motioned for the gate to be lifted. He returned the passports to Michael.

"Thank you very much," Michael said as he began to drive away. "You had better put that in the freezer!" As he pulled away, he saw the guards retrieve the money from under the lid and take the tub inside the shack.

A minute later the road dipped below a ridge and continued southeast. "Avocado, really?" Michael said. "That's disgusting."

"I say the same thing about pistachio." Marcus pulled a cell phone from his pocket and punched out a message.

"What are you doing?" Michael asked.

"Just drive."

A few minutes later, a black column of ascending smoke caught Michael's eye. "Is that the border?"

"Perhaps," Marcus said. "Must have been a car bomb. It happens far too often these days."

"We are lucky then." As Michael said it, he thought of the ice cream tub and Marcus's cell phone call. He glanced at his camera. It still sat where he left it.

"Yes, we are very lucky," Marcus replied.

General Rais's cell phone beeped annoyingly. He entered a code to unlock it and then read the message: "Border open—cargo secure." He smiled to himself as he put the phone in his pocket. Glorious days were ahead, days when men would amass to be counted with him.

"Sanjif!" he bellowed. A small Indian man in a black suit appeared. "Yes, sir?"

"We are going to the lodge. Get the car." And by car he meant his Humvee complete with bulletproof doors and windows.

21

Later that evening, after the apathetic night shift came on duty at the prison, Nasira was busy with plans of her own. In the candlelit apartment, she worked as quickly as possible. She pulled her dark hair into a ponytail and tucked it into a jacket collar. She hid the rest of her hair beneath a beret and adjusted it as she had seen the warden do with his a thousand times. Standing in his boots in front of a mirror, she judged she was near his height. She took a lump of coal from the small stove and rubbed it on her face to give herself thick eyebrows and a beard. Under his jacket, she wore several shirts to give her slender frame a more masculine appearance. This was not the first time she had done this.

She turned and looked at Aman Shamir, her captor for nearly a decade. Thanks to an evening tea loaded with eszopiclone, he snored even through her noises. He always needed to use drugs to sleep, but tonight she had doubled his normal dose. She knew she could have given him even more and killed him. But murder was something he did, and she wanted nothing to do with it.

Nasira took Shamir's keys and slipped out into the dark corridor. She locked him in as he had done to her countless times. She would need time—a lot of time. When he awoke, he would be hung over and as angry as the devil.

As she moved down the corridor, she transformed her gentle gait into the warden's arrogant stride. Wearing his clothes made her skin crawl, but it was a necessity. They smelled of cigarette smoke and sweat. And him.

Nasira passed through the corridor and descended a flight of stairs. Soon she would pass several guards. Knowing her hazel eyes would give her away, she lowered her head and held her hands behind her back as Shamir often did while in thought. No one ever dared disturb his thoughts.

Two guards snapped a salute and came to ridged attention as Nasira approached in the warden's clothing and manner. They lowered their eyes as if to avoid the warden's. Nasira did not return their salutes, which was typical of Shamir's condescending manner. He would no sooner acknowledge an inferior man than he would a dog or a rodent. The warden's beret was pulled low over Nasira's eyes, and she passed from shadow into darkness.

She moved more confidently, unlocking doors with Shamir's keys as needed. Soon she would be at the American's cell block.

A guard approached and did as the other guards, except he did not lower his eyes. Nasira could not pass close scrutiny and had counted on fear. She thought fast. The guard would need to focus his eyes on something else, if only long enough for her to slip past. One step closer and she would be visible, even in the low light.

In donning Shamir's garb, she had not forgotten his gun or night stick. She pulled the gun, cocked the hammer, and pointed it at the guard's face.

"Oh, Warden Shamir! I am so very sorry, sir. I did not see it was you, sir." The man went to his knees.

Nasira released the hammer and was about to continue, but she knew compassion was not in the warden's nature. Regretfully, she pulled out the night stick and struck the man at base of his neck. The guard buckled and Nasira turned quickly away, feeling sick to her stomach. *Almost there,* she told herself.

At the American's cell door, another guard lingered—under the warden's orders, no doubt. Nasira would have to speak. She had spent many hours imitating her captor's voice but never felt confident if forced to say much.

The guard came to attention and saluted.

"Leave," Nasira barked in Shamir's voice.

"Yes, sir," the guard replied.

Nasira stepped closer and realized the guard had only one good eye and had turned with that eye toward the wall and his back to the cell door.

"Wait," Nasira growled. "We are moving these dogs."

"Do we need help?"

"No."

Nasira stepped out of shadow and to the door. The guard unlocked it, entered, and shut it behind him. It occurred to Nasira then that most of the guards rarely or never heard the warden's voice.

Once in the block she moved to closest cell. It was the man she had helped before. She unlocked his cell and opened the door. A square of flickering light stretched across the floor. She stepped forward, expecting to find a sleeping man. Suddenly she heard a sound behind her. Before she could turn, strong arms wrapped themselves around her neck.

"I didn't expect to see you, Warden," whispered the man behind her. "Did you enjoy killing Cobb? Now I'm going to kill you."

She pulled on his arm and managed, "Wait! Please wait!"

Taylor released his chokehold and the figure fell to the floor, coughing. This was no man, the corporal realized. He bent and touched the person's back. As he did, the figure moved and Taylor's feet were swept out from under him. Suddenly on his back, he felt a cold stick pressed against his throat.

"I have come to help you," said a woman's voice.

Taylor couldn't believe his ears but quickly remember the note. "I believe you," he said.

"Good." The stick moved away from his throat. "We are wasting precious time."

He stood, as did the woman. "Was it you that brought me medicine the other day?" he asked.

"Yes."

"Why are you here? Why are you dressed like the warden?"

"In the morning you and the others are going to be tortured and killed."

"What about General Rais?"

"He has no more need of you. His plans are nearly finished. He has someone else."

"Who?"

"Another American."

"So the general has given us over to the warden." Taylor lowered his eyes in thought. "How do you know all this?"

"I listen." The woman moved out of the cell and began to unlock the other doors. "We do not have much time."

As the team gathered, Gutierrez spoke. "Did I hear a woman's voice or was I dreaming?"

"You did," Taylor said. "She is the one who helped me and left us food."

"How can we trust her?" McGillis asked.

"We have no other choice. She says that tomorrow we are to be tortured and killed."

Pike stepped forward. "M'name's Ian Pike. But friends call me Pikey."

"Or donkey," Fulton said, faking an Australian accent.

Pike chuckled. "Watch it. I was talkin' to the sheila."

The woman didn't crack a smile but walked toward the cell block door. "Move out as if you are bound. We are leaving." She pulled the door wide and was greeted by three guards. They entered the cell block, weapons drawn. "Are you in need of assistance, sir?" the lead guard asked the warden.

"Yes," the woman replied. Fortunately, Taylor thought, she had been in the shadow of the door as the guards entered, and they kept their sights trained on the Rangers. Still posing as the warden, the woman shut the cell block door. She pulled the pistol from its holster and pressed it to the back of the guard's head nearest her.

"Drop your guns," she said. The guard with the gun to his head froze, but the other two turned in disbelief.

It was all the time Taylor and the other Rangers needed. Seconds later, they were standing over the unconscious guards. "What do we do now?" Fulton asked.

"I cannot get into the lower chambers guarding six prisoners alone. You, you, and you, put on their clothes." She pointed at Gutierrez, Pike, and Sutton. "You two put on these restraints." She tossed handcuffs and ankle chains to Fulton and McGillis.

The men quickly undressed the guards, then dumped them in the closest cell and locked the door.

The woman posing as the warden and the three Rangers in guards' clothing left the cell block with two "prisoners" between them. According to the woman, few guards remained between here and the lower levels. Taylor and the others remembered the way, having been led there once before. Returning was a disheartening thought.

At the door, the "warden" removed a key and unlocked the final door. A putrid smell escaped, and the sick yellow light spilled out. They entered quickly. The woman locked the door behind them and spoke. "We should be fine now. Nobody comes in here unless it is necessary."

With his good arm, McGillis suddenly pinned her to a wall. "Why should we trust you?"

"Private, let her go!" Taylor ordered.

"How do you know we can trust her?"

"Because she wouldn't go to all this trouble for nothing."

Gutierrez stepped forward. "I am your superior officer, McGillis. Let her go. We at least need to hear her out."

McGillis let her go. "Fine, but I don't trust her."

She pushed the little man away and turned to the others. "I offer you life, and this is the thanks I get? If you get caught, you will die. If I get caught, I will be sent back to live with that animal, the warden. You have been prisoners for a few months. I have been here for ten years, hidden away in his apartment."

"So why now? Why not weeks ago? Why not—" McGillis seemed to choke on the words.

The woman turned to Gutierrez. "I wish to make a deal. I will get you out of the prison if you get me out of Pakistan. General Rais no longer needs you alive. I overheard him speaking to Shamir last night. There is another American. With him here, all of you can be dealt with as the warden sees fit. He will bring you down here and you will never leave."

"So what, you brought us down here early?" McGillis snapped.

Pike slapped McGillis in the back of the head. "That's enough, little chook."

"We are wasting time," she cried. "We must walk. I will tell you what you want to know, but we must keep moving."

"You have your deal," Gutierrez said earnestly. "You get us out of here, and I swear we will get you out of Pakistan."

Taylor saw a spark of hope in her bright eyes as she replied, "Very good. Follow me." She began walking very quickly.

"What do we call you? What's your name?" the sergeant said.

"My name is Nasira Habeeb."

Though the lower levels were warm, even stifling, a cold evil filled the air. Through the open doors, various torture devices could be seen—tubs of water, chairs with binders. Taylor ignored them, praying this would not be their fate.

As they went, Nasira pointed out emergency flashlights, hidden in various places. These they collected. She explained that electricity was often a problem, and no one wished to be down here in the dark.

They came to a door that was chained shut. "This leads to the catacombs," Nasira announced. "The prison was built on the remains of an ancient fortress dating back to the Mogul Empire. The catacombs are still intact, and some branch out beneath the city. When I was a little girl, I wandered into a tunnel and was found here. This was before the warden barred the door. Even then, these halls were used for torture. He believes I have forgotten, but I remember how I got here. It kept me alive through many lonely days—knowing that someday I would leave." She backed up. "Someone shoot the lock, please."

Using the sidearm he had stolen from the guard, Taylor blew off the lock. As the door was pushed open, dank, stagnant air washed over everyone.

"I'll take point," Sergeant Gutierrez announced. "Sutton, bring up the rear."

Nasira turned. "Sutton? Who is Sutton?"

"I am," Taylor said. "Why?"

"Is that a common name?"

"Not really. Have you heard it before?"

"Yes. When General Rais was speaking to the warden, he said he had the other Sutton. What does that mean?"

Taylor tried not to panic. "I hope you misunderstood."

"No. I understood perfectly. This man is to assemble the general's bombs."

Taylor gasped. "Oh, no . . . Michael!"

"What are you talking about?" Fulton asked.

"My brother's here! Somehow the colonel baited him into coming . ."

Sudden realization took hold as everything came into focus. Taylor groaned. "That's what happened. That's why we were kept alive."

"Mind cluing us in?" Fulton said.

"When I was drugged after the fight, I couldn't remember what I was doing in the general's quarters. I remember now. They had me ask my brother for help. They tricked him. Now the general has him. That is why we are expendable."

"What makes you think your brother would come here after just one pleading phone call?" McGillis said. "I have three brothers and they wouldn't."

"You don't know my brother. Nasira, did you hear where they were going to hold him?"

"Yes. They have the old ski resort on the west of the city set up for his arrival. Something about him assembling weapons."

"You do listen, don't you," Taylor remarked.

"I do, but it is in the wrong direction for us to escape before the warden comes after us."

"Sergeant, we have to— I have to—"

"We will, Corporal. Let's get out of here first. Nasira, stay just behind me. Point the way."

Five Americans soldiers and one brave girl disappeared into the dark labyrinth.

22

Though the shot was too far away and too buried to be heard, Aman Shamir awoke as the door to the catacombs was blown open. He sat up in the light of early day, rubbed his eyes, and wiped the dried saliva from his mouth. His head throbbed with every pulse of blood through his constricted veins.

"Worthless girl," he muttered, recognizing the effects of too much sleep medicine. It was not the first time she had made the mistake.

"Nasira!" he called in a loud whisper that made his head want to explode. No response. The apartment was deathly quiet. Again he called her name, and again, nothing.

He got feebly to his feet, then stumbled to the kitchen and felt the teapot. Cold. "Sleeping in," he growled. "I will beat her."

He looked for her on the floor where she slept and only found empty blankets. Confused, he found a light switch and gave it a turn. The room lit up faster than his pupils could contract. Shielding his eyes, Shamir staggered around his apartment until he was confident the girl was not there.

Realization was a slow, sobering pill and he fumbled to the door leading to his office. It was locked. He returned to the door leaving the apartment—also locked. In spite of his migraine, he screamed at the absent girl. The apartment had no windows and no one would come looking for the warden. No one dared.

"Have you seen him?" asked Kazim, a young guard who was pacing the floor of an observation room.

"Not so far today." Jamal slapped a small, flickering monitor, trying to improve the picture.

"Good. The warden makes me nervous."

"Just do your job and stay out of his sight. There are a hundred guards in this prison with more seniority, so chances are he will never speak to you anyway." Jamal had worked in the prison for seven years and had recently helped Kazim, his cousin, secure a job as guard. Jamal's current post was to sit in a room and watch security monitors on the various cell blocks. There were more blocks than monitors, so they would cycle every minute or so.

"I heard," Jamal went on, "that he was up early this morning. He clubbed Tamir for staring at him."

"Just for staring at him?" Kazim dragged his hands through his hair. "I don't want to get clubbed, Jamal. You said this was a good job."

"Tamir is an idiot. Don't worry. I said the pay was decent, not the work, and certainly not the boss. Besides, we suppose he was headed to the Americans' cell block. He has been dying to torture those men for weeks. That means he'll be busy all day. We won't see him."

Just as Kazim relaxed enough to sit down, Habir, the shift supervisor, walked past the observation room. "Does it take two of you to watch those monitors?"

Kazim jumped out of his chair so fast it toppled over. He stood at attention. Jamal didn't flinch but casually turned. "Good morning, sir."

"Good morning?" Habir huffed. "Which one of you would like to haul the waste buckets out of the solitary cells this good morning?"

"Don't look at me, sir," Jamal said. "I'm doing my job."

Kazim's nose puckered and he glanced at Jamal. Obviously, blood may be thicker than water, but not the contents of a waste bucket. The shift supervisor pointed at Kazim. "All of them."

In the solitary cells located in the prison's basement, below the modern plumbing system, prisoners had to use waste buckets instead of toilets. Emptying the buckets was the lowest of all chores in the facility.

Soon, Kazim unlocked the first of several solitary cell blocks. Feeling apprehensive, he beat on the first door and said, "Waste bucket!" As he lifted the small opening at the base of the door, a wide-bottomed bucket appeared. The contents sloshed and narrowly missed his shoe. Kazim saw the near miss as a foreshadowing.

At the third door, the bucket was full to overflowing. "Are you serious?" Kazim gasped. A sadistic chuckle came from the other side of the door.

Wending his way up the stairwells from the lower cell blocks, Kazim mumbled, "A hundred guards in the prison with more seniority . . . so crap does run downhill."

On the third level was a makeshift well leading to the main sewer. After dumping all the buckets, it was necessary to wash the waste down with a high-pressure hose. Kazim dumped the second bucket and vomited violently. He no longer appreciated his cousin helping him get a job.

After hours of carrying buckets up stairs that seemed increasingly steep, Kazim came to the cell block housing the American soldiers. Exhausted, he sat down on a three-legged stool. The first near miss had been the only one of the day; several times urine and excrement had spilled onto his feet and lower legs. The odors on his clothing were also burned into his olfactory senses. Whatever they fed the prisoners had become unnaturally foul on the back end. Kazim dry heaved. If his stomach was not already completely devoid of contents, he would have vomited yet again. He was starving but dared not eat until he finished. Five more cells to go.

Grudgingly, Kazim unlocked the last cell block door. The hinges groaned under the weight of the large, heavy door. He went to the first cell to his left and said, "Waste bucket." He lifted the small door, but no bucket came forth. Then he remembered one of the Americans had recently died; this must be his cell.

Kazim went to the next door and knocked. "Waste bucket!"

Nothing.

Now he recalled Jamal saying the warden had taken some of the Americans downstairs. Kazim checked his keys and found he could not enter individual cells. His heart gladdened a bit.

He tapped on all the remaining doors with no response. Empty cells meant no buckets.

He was finished!

Kazim was about to walk out of the cell block when he heard a groan. He stopped short of the outer door and turned, not sure he believed his ears. Nothing.

He turned again to leave but heard a low mutter. This time he went back to the cells and waited to hear which one the noises came from. After several seconds, Kazim heard a low voice, though he could not understand it. He moved to that door. "Hello? I mean . . . waste bucket."

"What? Waste bucket?" said the voice from behind the door.

"Yes, waste bucket." Kazim lifted the small door near his feet. Instead of a bucket, a hairy hand gripped his boot. Kazim squealed, jumped, and released the trap door. The door came down on the forearm, and the man swore. "You idiot! I am not a prisoner. I am a guard! Now get us out of here!"

"Yeah, right, " Kazim said, thinking it was a trick. "Wait, did you say 'us'?"

"Yes, you fool! There are three of us in here."

Kazim lifted the small door and bent to peer inside the cell at three men in their underwear. They seemed to be getting their bearings after a long night at the whiskey glass. "What happened?" he asked.

"Get us out of here," the guard repeated.

"I don't have the keys."

"Then go find someone who does!" barked the man. "There are three Americans running around in guard uniforms! Perhaps they have already escaped!"

Kazim let the little door shut—a jailbreak, and it was his first week on the job. He retrieved the radio from his hip. "Jamal, this is Kazim . . ."

23

As Michael drove, the rocky desert unfolded before them. The highway had skirted Peshawar and continued unhindered to Mingora. Mud hovels dotted the landscape.

Marcus had grown friendlier and more talkative since the border, and Michael appreciated the conversation, since it kept his mind off the difficulties ahead. Still, he felt uncertain about Marcus. Michael could read most people when he needed to, but it was difficult to get a bead on this guy.

After a lull in the conversation, Marcus spoke again. "I like you. I would like to help you in Mingora."

"I can't put anyone else at risk. Besides you're just the driver, remember, even though I've done most the driving."

Marcus smiled. "I offered to take over."

"I expected to travel this leg of my journey alone. As far as I knew, you were supposed to set me up in a truck and turn me loose. I am grateful you have come this far."

"I like this truck. I want it back."

Michael shook his head, grinning a little. "And you don't think I would return it to you? What else would I do with it? It's an ice cream truck!"

"Judging by the weapons in here, you are not in Pakistan on a holiday. It is not likely I will get my truck back in one piece if I leave you to it."

"That may be, but if it gets destroyed, I will buy you another one. I will drop you off outside Mingora and pick you up on our way out. If we don't connect, I will leave the truck in the alley behind your warehouse. I'm sorry, but that is just the way it has to be."

The truth was, Michael would have loved the help, but after the explosion at the border he just didn't trust the man. His thoughts went to Marcus's reaction when his picture had been taken, and Michael's gaze inadvertently went to the camera.

Marcus's eyes followed. "It is a nice camera. Is it new?" He picked it up and turned it over in his hands.

"Oh . . . uh, no." Michael had not meant to be so obvious about the camera.

The ice cream truck continued to roll down the dusty highway. They passed a sign: "Mingora 25 km." Michael's heart skipped a beat. He felt pathetically prepared for what lay ahead of him.

It was mid-afternoon. He would wait until dark to move on the building that held his brother. A few more miles and he'd drop Marcus off. As they got closer to the city, houses replaced the mud huts, and highway traffic grew heavier.

"Where would you like me to leave you? Is there a bus depot or something?"

"I do not know . . . anywhere," Marcus replied.

A few minutes later, Michael spotted a bus stop. "I can find my way from here, Marcus. Thank you for everything."

The bus stop was occupied. "Pull up just a little farther," Marcus directed.

Michael did so. When he stopped the truck, Marcus held up the camera and said, "You have been glancing at this thing for hours. Have you been expecting me to steal it?"

"What? No."

"Perhaps you have been expecting this." Marcus ejected the memory disk from the side of the camera, and with no more effort than snapping a twig he broke the disk in two.

Michael noticed Marcus's Middle Eastern accent had slipped, but he felt more concern at the realization of his worst fears. He was sitting next to the enemy! Michael's first thought was to get out of the truck, but suddenly a fist slammed into his face. Lights exploded in his brain like fireworks. He made an attempt to recover, but a second blow left him slumped against the door. For a moment he struggled, but then everything went dark.

24

It had been a full hour since Kazim found the guards in the solitary cells. Now a dozen other guards stood outside the warden's apartment. Habir had summoned a man, a machinist, who worked with an acetylene torch at the hinges of the solid steel door. The scorching flame reflected in the black, soul-less goggles of the machinist, and soon the hinges turned to little molten raindrops that fell and exploded across the floor. The door fell inward with an echoing thud.

Habir and the machinist looked into the smoky apartment. Inside, they found the warden sitting quietly. The interior of his apartment had been destroyed as though by a caged animal. Aman Shamir looked up and crushed out his cigarette. "I need every available man and as many weapons as you can scrape together." His voice was deathly calm.

Habir replied, "Yes, sir. We can't find the Americans. We may have had a prison br—"

The warden's dark eyes seemed to burst into flame. He produced a pistol and fired a shot that ricocheted off the doorjamb and nearly hit Habir. "I know!" Shamir barked as loudly as the report of his weapon. "Now get me those men and guns!"

The warden fastened on a pair of boots and adjusted his beret. Habir thought the boots looked old and the hat worn—not up to Shamir's usual standards, but of course he said nothing.

The other guards scattered in fright. Suddenly alone with the warden in the corridor, Habir stood at attention. He spoke as Shamir approached. "I have every available guard assembling for your command. The prison is locked down. All" —Habir swallowed— "remaining prisoners have been accounted for."

"Very good." The warden did not break stride, and the captain had to walk briskly. "Stay behind with a skeleton crew. I want every able body ready to leave immediately. We will find the Americans."

"Sir, the guards who were found in the Americans' cells . . . They said there was a woman disguised as—"

The warden stopped. Habir held his breath. Turning slightly as if he wanted to see the captain of the guard from his peripheral vision, Shamir spoke in a near whisper. "Leave her to me." The warden looked away, then added, "As for the guards outsmarted by a woman—kill them."

In defense of the guards, Habir almost pointed out that the woman had also outsmarted the warden. But then, valuing his life, he held his tongue.

As he watched the organization of the hunting party, Aman Shamir's thoughts raced. The escape of the Americans was unfortunate. Instead of torturing them as he would have liked to do, he would now hunt them and shoot them like animals. It would be good sport, but he preferred torture—it was less work.

Nasira's betrayal constituted another matter altogether, an insult of the highest order. Shamir had once considered her arrival a blessing. She had been an angel—his angel. Finding her that day in the lower cells could not have been pure chance; she simply had to be a gift from Allah. She could have run or screamed, but she seemed above that. Even as a child, she had been strong and beautiful. Shamir had spared her from his basest desires, never wanting to soil the gift.

But now—now he knew her for what she really was. Not an angel, but a demon. The devil's own daughter sent by some unknown power to wrest from Shamir's heart the last lights of human decency. He would make her suffer in ways yet to be imagined. There was only one way out of Mingora, and though she had a considerable head start he would spare nothing to find her.

Soon, he had an army with weapons loaded. His guards were few, but they were courageous. No one escaped Slohman Gaul Prison.

Habir approached with a young man at his side. "This is Kazim, sir. He was the man who discovered the guards. And even though he is very new here, he kept a level head and was quick to report."

"Very good," said the warden without a hint of affability. "Do you drive?"

"Y–yes, sir," Kazim stuttered.

"You will drive me." Aman Shamir leaped into the military Jeep at the head of the brigade. Two heavy doors swung wide, and the cavalcade tore into the streets.

It had been a long hour in the absolute blackness of the catacombs. Sergeant Gutierrez and the four remaining Rangers under his command were weary from starvation, yet the thought of freedom kept their steps from faltering. As they approached a dead end and a passage opened to the left, Nasira instructed, "Turn here."

"I can't believe you still remember the way after ten years," Gutierrez said, trying to sound more amazed than doubtful.

."I used to draw it out on a piece of paper from memory until the warden became suspicious. I knew that one day God would provide a means for my escape. Turn again." Nasira paused. "In the beginning he always kept his apartment door locked from the outside whenever he was not there, which was most of the time. There were a lot of lonely, lonely days. I worried a great deal about my family and where they must think I was. I worried that they believed I was dead. They surely would never find me. All I could do was weep and wait. The crying finally stopped, but the waiting felt like eternity. Now turn here."

The sergeant turned into what appeared to be another dead end until he took another step and a way opened to the right. The men behind them followed silently.

"So you waited," Gutierrez said.

"I waited and listened. In the solitary confinement of that monster's apartment, I learned the value of silence."

"One day I noticed that if I listened at the vent in one of the apartment walls, I could hear some conversations taking place in the prison. A few weeks ago, I learned that the general had captured several Americans. My heart leaped. I already knew how I would get out of the prison, but I had nowhere to go after that. There is no such thing as a homeless woman in Pakistan. There would have been questions and I would have wound up back here. The warden will come for me. I have to get far away."

"You speak very good English," Gutierrez said. "Did the warden teach you?"

"No. He forbade me from speaking English, but I have always known how."

For a moment the only sound was the shuffling of feet across the hard-packed dirt. Thinking of Nasira's dilemma, Gutierrez asked, "Couldn't you have gone to your family? Don't they live Pakistan?"

"No. They live in New York City."

He stopped and held a flashlight beam toward Nasira, looking at her with new eyes. "You're an American citizen? Hear that, men? She's American."

She shielded her eyes from the bright light. "Yes, I am. Now put the light on the ground. We are almost there."

"How did you come to be prisoner to a madman?"

"I have already told you. He found me. I had heard about these catacombs from a friend and was curious. I came down here one day with a flashlight and thought I heard a child crying, so I followed the sound. When I got to the end, Aman Shamir found me and wouldn't let me go."

"What about the crying?"

Nasira didn't answer.

"Did you find the child?"

"No," she said somberly. "It was a man."

Gutierrez could only guess at what would cause a man to cry like a child, and it sent chills down his spine. The darkness seemed deeper as Nasira moved out ahead.

"We are here," she announced. She took a few more steps and looked up. Directly above her in the low ceiling was a storm drain. "We need only to remove the lid. When I was young, it was only a tin plate, but this looks heavier."

"Perhaps it was put there to keep other youngsters from disappearing," Gutierrez commented.

The three tallest Rangers—Fulton, Gutierrez, and Pike—all pushed in unison, and the heavy lid moved aside. Instead of a cylinder of sun bearing through the hole, only the gray of shadow greeted them. Fulton popped his head out. "We're inside a room."

"That is actually a good thing," Gutierrez said. "Nothing attracts attention quite like people crawling out of the sewer."

Minutes later they all stood around a black hole in the ground. It seemed unreal, but they were free. The room they found themselves in was nothing more than four corrugated tin walls and a shallow roof. Needles of sunshine leaked through holes made in the tin by missing nails that had once held it to the frame.

After moving the lid back over the hole, Gutierrez took a new look at Nasira, and he noticed the other men staring too. Somewhere in the darkness she had removed most of the warden's clothing, and now she wore a T-shirt and camo pants. Her dark hair, tied back, stretched nearly to her slender waist. The remaining streaks of coal on her face did little to hide her natural beauty.

"What? It was hot in those caverns and I was wearing six layers of clothing."

The sergeant forced back a chuckle. "If we are to move about the city unnoticed, Nasira, you are going to need some clothes. Same goes for you two." He nodded toward Fulton and McGillis, who still wore prison rags.

"Any chance we could scratch up some tucker, Sarge?" Pike asked.

Fulton laughed. "We told you, bro. You're gonna have to speak American."

"Grub, chow, groceries," Pike said, mocking Fulton's Southern drawl.

"Yes to all of the above," Gutierrez replied.

"Good. I'm so hungry I have the shakes. I'm shaking like a dog poopin' peach pits." For a second everyone looked at Pike, who then added, "That was Cobb's favorite saying."

"One of many," Taylor said. "I remember once—"

"What are we going to do about money, Sergeant?" McGillis interrupted. "This isn't a country where you want to get caught shoplifting an apple, no matter how hungry you are."

"I've got that." Nasira reached into a pocket and produced a handful of bills. "The warden's personal collection."

The men smiled. "You really do have this all planned out, don't you?" Fulton said.

"I should. I had the time," she said wryly.

The three men dressed as guards left the tin room to search for food and clothing. Fulton, McGillis, and Nasira had nothing to do but wait. The room grew warmer and soon began to feel more and more like an extension of the prison they had just left.

After fifteen minutes, McGillis began to pace the floor. "What if they got caught?" he growled.

"Did you hear gunfire?" Fulton said.

"No."

"Then they are fine. None of us will go back to that prison alive."

McGillis did not seem reassured.

Nasira sat quietly on the ground. Fulton joined her. Agitation and impatience is often contagious at stressful times, but to this Nasira was immune. She was accustomed to waiting and was unmoved by McGillis's growing anxiety.

Another minute and they heard gunfire and the rumble of a distant explosion. The door to the tin room burst open. "No time for a picnic," Gutierrez said as he entered, followed by Taylor and Pike. The sergeant and Taylor carried clothing, while Pike held a woven basket full of food and water. Nasira and Fulton came to their feet.

"What's going on?" McGillis asked.

"We don't know, but everyone in the city seems to be on the move. Get changed quickly." Gutierrez tossed a long Moroccan robe or *dishdasha* to Nasira, one to McGillis, and one to Fulton.

Nasira's was flower print. "Perfect," she said.

Gutierrez also had a change of clothing for himself. "They will be looking for three guards . . . thought I'd change it up a bit. I also picked up these *kufi* caps, and a *smagh* for blondie." He nodded toward McGillis.

"You're kidding—I gotta wear a towel on my head?" said the private.

"Yes. Your blond hair is a dead giveaway. You look great in a dress, by the way."

McGillis was short enough that his dishdasha drug the ground. When he put the smagh on his head, everyone started laughing. "What?" he exclaimed.

"You look like a little girl," Nasira said. They all laughed again, and even McGillis had to admit he looked silly.

"Well, at least it was easy to get my arm through the sleeve," he said.

Nasira tied her hair up and pulled an ornate *hijab,* or scarf, over her head. The change of clothes was a good disguise for her and hid the warden's boots, which she still wore.

With beards and dark complexions, Gutierrez and Fulton could pass for Pakistani men. The basket held fruit, six bottles of water, and large, fresh portions of nan bread. After everyone changed clothes, Gutierrez divided the food, but when it came time to hand Sutton his portion, he was gone.

"Sutton, you fool," the sergeant said.

Nasira gasped. "Where'd he go? He was just here."

"After his brother, I'm sure." Pike shook his head. "While we were out, he said his brother was his problem, not ours. He wanted us to get out while we could."

"So, let's get out," McGillis said.

Fulton turned on the smaller man. "What in the world is the matter with you, Private? All you care about is yourself."

"All I care about is the rest of us getting out alive. Haven't enough of us died here?"

"Stop," the sergeant ordered. "We are going after Sutton and his brother. No arguments. Grab everything you can carry and let's go."

25

As Michael Sutton began to regain consciousness, he noticed two things. First, two men were arguing, and second, the air was heavy and musty. Third, his head was killing him.

"We are wasting precious time," thundered a voice with a thick Middle Eastern accent. "You shouldn't have punched him out."

"As I said before, it was unavoidable." Michael recognized the second man as Marcus, the driver, his Middle Eastern accent now gone.

"There are a dozen ways to render a man unconscious without affecting the way he might think later. A concussion is not one of them. The others will be here in less than a day and our bomb technician is unconscious. I should kill you."

"You know better than to try."

"If these weapons are not ready by morning, I will kill you."

Marcus laughed.

Michael raised his head and the talking stopped. Someone stood beside him and put a cup to his lips. Michael drank too quickly and started coughing. He sat up, the blood pounding in his head. He touched his face; it was swollen and tender.

"We will give you something for that," Marcus said.

"Enough, Sister Teresa! I need him up and going!" The voice caused Michael's head to pound even more. He felt a needle poke in his shoulder and tried to pull away, but Marcus held him fast.

Michael turned his head and watched as a syringe was emptied into his arm.

Marcus chuckled. "You'll be feeling better in minutes. It's a little adrenaline concoction."

Though his vision seemed fuzzy, Michael looked around. The last light of day was setting in large, west-facing windows of a large hall, the high ceiling held aloft by several massive pillars. From the schematics he had studied, he knew this was the vacant ski lodge. In its recent past, this hall would have been used for large parties.

As his head began to clear, he recalled details. To his right would be a large fireplace. Behind him was the kitchen, and beyond that, an exit to a parking lot.

The man with the booming voice approached. He was large and walked with the solidity of a mammoth. "It is good to finally meet you, Michael Sutton. I have heard great things about you."

"Oh yeah? From who?"

"Never mind. That is not your business here. My name is General Rais."

Michael smiled weakly. "Is your name supposed to mean something to me?"

The general's face turned red and he looked like he wanted to kick Michael in the head. "It will. I have a chore for you. I have brought you here to assemble some—what is the name you people use?—weapons of mass destruction." The general lit a cigar.

The sun dipped below the horizon in a beautiful display of purple and orange, a striking contrast to the situation in which Michael now found himself. Just as the room grew dim, floodlights snapped on, illuminating an area of the floor immediately around the three men.

"You are mistaken," Michael declared to the general. "I have come all this way to free my brother and his Ranger team."

Rais chuckled. "That didn't work out so well. No, you are here because I want you here. I am the master of these events. I secured the weapons. I captured the Rangers like butterflies in a net. I kept them alive in order to bring you here. You and your brother are my puppets."

"*You* made the phone call."

"Correct."

"I knew Taylor would never ask for my help willingly."

"Also correct. Coercion can be accomplished with a wide variety of means."

"Where is he?" Michael asked.

"Not here. Never was."

"They were. Where did you move them? I won't assemble a Lego toy for you unless you let him go!"

The general laughed again. He picked up a photo from off a nearby table. "Are you referring to the satellite images?" He held up the photo. It was identical to the one Michael had seen at home. "What you saw were seven mannequins wrapped in electric blankets," the general said in a sinister tone. "Pretty good, huh? Forget about your brother. He is as good as dead."

Michael hung his head.

"Understand this—you have come all this way to assemble my bombs or I will kill you right now. Marcus will then fly to California and visit your wife and daughter and perhaps drive over to Utah and kill your parents."

Though the threat to his family burned like a branding iron, Michael did not look up. His jaw tensed and his heart sickened. He wondered about the feelings that had brought him to his current entanglement—the consuming desire to free his brother. Had Michael been foolish? Second-guessing was a luxury he did not have now. He was here, a prisoner, and no one would come for him. He kept his head low, not in submission as the general would suppose, but in calculation.

"Do you understand me?" the general roared.

Michael raised his head. "Why me?" he asked, trying his best to turn his anger into what seemed like fear.

"Because the items we have need a brilliant mind. And contrary to what you might see on television, a good bomb technician is hard to find on this side of the world. Sure you have the locals, but I'm not dealing with C4 and fertilizer."

"What makes you so sure I can do this?"

The general sighed, then said as if from memory, "You graduated valedictorian from West Valley High School with aptitudes in electronics and mathematics. You passed the entrance exam for MIT but decided to waste two years preaching Christianity. After you returned home, MIT approached you, but you opted to go to Brigham Young University, where you graduated with degrees in electrical and nuclear engineering. And, again wasting your gifts, you decided to work for your father's pathetic little company, VAS Engineering. Doing what? Designing weapons. As you can see, I've done my homework."

"If I do this for you, a lot of people will die and so will I."

"Yes, a lot of people will die, but they will not be your people. I will not insult you by promising freedom. I will promise to leave your family alone, however. Your daughter will grow up and perhaps your wife will remarry a man who would have stayed home when his brother called. A man not at all like you."

"Lives will not be spared if you do not do what I ask. They, like you, will die anyway; it will just be slower and more painful, especially for you."

Michael had finished his calculations and made his decision, but he waited for a little more compulsion so as to appear unwilling. It came quickly when Marcus violently jabbed a pressure point in his back. A searing, crippling pain shot down Michael's spine. He let out a painful cry and pitched forward onto the floor. Footsteps approached and then Michael heard the general's voice.

"Marcus is talented in many painful applications. But he is nothing compared to the man who will, by tomorrow, be having a field day with your brother. Help me and I'll have your brother and his team killed quickly, mercifully. If you refuse, I will send Marcus to California, to 1021 Lucero Drive. That is correct, isn't it?"

The pain in Michael's back disappeared as quickly as it had come. He got to his knees. "Fine! Just leave my family alone."

"I knew you would see things my way." Rais turned and disappeared into the shadows outside the reach of the spotlights.

Holding out a hand to help Michael stand, Marcus asked earnestly, "How is your back?"

"Fine."

"Very good," Marcus said. "I am sorry that was necessary."

Michael looked at him quizzically. How could someone appear so genuinely nice and yet be so quickly brutal? Perhaps Marcus suffered from a type of schizophrenia or he was just a plain old psychopath. At this point, Michael honestly didn't care which. "I don't know what you want me to build," he said, "but I am going to need a lot of equipment."

"We have all you will need," came the reply from the shadows.

More floodlights came to life with the loud snap of an electrical breaker. The hall that had appeared empty from satellite footage now contained some of the finest machinery Michael had ever seen. He forced himself to seem unimpressed.

"We brought you everything you are used to working with in that dumpy army warehouse, except everything here is top of the line," General Rais stated proudly. "You have until tomorrow morning to complete the assembly."

"And what I am assembling?"

"Only three small projects. We have a broken but, I am told, repairable EMP device, enough plutonium for a suitcase nuke, and sufficient anthrax for a nice biological weapon."

"You make it sound like I'll be baking cookies!"

"I have faith in you, Michael Sutton." The general sucked deeply on his cigar.

"I don't know if I can get it done that fast. I'll have to work through the night. I haven't done that in years."

The general walked over to a refrigerator and opened it. It was full of sugary snacks and caffeinated soda. "All your favorites."

"I'm going to need the laptop I brought with me."

"We have a better laptop."

"Perhaps, but I need formulas and notes that are in mine."

The general scanned the contents of the refrigerator. "It will be useless to try to use your cell phone or any wireless connections while you are here. I have purposely selected this location. There is something about the steel in the roof or its location that creates a dead zone."

"Regardless, I will still need the laptop," Michael said.

Rais shut the door and snapped his fingers. Six armed guards appeared from the shadows; one of them held the laptop, which he gave to the general.

Michael sighed. "I really don't work well under the gun." In truth, he worried about the prospect of being so heavily guarded.

"Oh, these guards are for me. These are dangerous times, Michael Sutton. Marcus will keep an eye on you." The general set the computer on a table and, turning to leave, added, "And yes, Michael Sutton, you are under the gun. I will see you in the morning."

As the general moved into the shadows, only the red glow from his cigar could be seen.

"Where is my cell phone, anyway?" Michael felt his pockets.

"The general may trust his dead zone, but I do not," Marcus replied. "I took it off you while you were unconscious. You won't be in need of it."

Glad Marcus hadn't destroyed it, Michael nodded. He'd have the phone back soon enough.

Marcus removed his jacket and laid it across a table, then moved to a stool. As the man sat, Michael noticed his shirt hitch around his shoulders. It dawned on him that Marcus was not as large as he first appeared, but that he wore a bulletproof vest under his oversized shirt. *What kind of man wears a bulletproof vest all day?* Michael thought of the gun inside his laptop and how to keep it close.

26

On the porch of the Suttons' Craftsman home were a pair of homemade rockers as comfortable as lounge chairs. April knew Van and Claire often spent evenings there watching the day wane, waiting to wave at friends or visit with a passerby. They spoke of how there should be more front porches and front-porch neighbors—that the casual visit was a lost art on the modern backyard society. This evening, April's parents-in-law had waved at several neighbors and members of their ward and also visited with the Wilsons, their backyard neighbors, who had circled the block on an evening stroll. Two extra chairs had been brought out of storage for April and Suzanne, who had joined Claire and Van on the porch after the little girl's bath.

Not liking the long, anxious wait for her husband's return, April had come to stay. The four of them sat watching the last lights of day fade. Claire read a story to her granddaughter, and Van watched bugs dance around the porch lights. April sat quietly, fidgeting with her cell phone. After Claire finished the book, Suzanne moved to her grandfather's lap and began looking at the pictures again.

"The phone will do you no good if you wear a hole in it," Claire said, interrupting April's thoughts.

Looking at her nervous fingerprints covering the phone, April sighed. "I know, but I feel like I'm in limbo. Sometimes I can hardly breathe. I don't know how army wives do it."

"Just like you, dear. One day at a time. Eventually—"

"Don't say I will get used to it. There will never be a next time."

Claire smiled. "I was only going to say it gets easier. The world doesn't stop spinning. You have to be strong for the kids. At least that's how it was when I was young. My mother seldom let us see her upset or doubting Father's safe return. Did Suzanne get to talk to Michael?"

April nodded. "Like I said, he called on our drive over. We pulled over and talked as long as he could." She looked at Suzanne. "We talked to Daddy last night, didn't we?"

Suzanne looked up from the book and grinned. April went back into her thoughts and returned to fidgeting with the phone—never letting it drop below fifty percent on the power meter.

A nondescript gray sedan passed the house slowly, then pulled up to the curb and stopped. Two men got out and adjusted their suit coats. Even in the porch light, April recognized them. She felt the blood leave her face.

"Dad, those are the guys I told you about," she said, trying to keep her voice steady.

Van picked up his granddaughter and set her on his wife's lap. As the men approached the house, he stood and asked, "Can I help you boys?"

"Is this the Sutton residence?" Smith said.

"It is."

Wakefield cleared his throat. "We have a few questions."

Claire stood with Suzanne. "We'll go put this one in bed."

"But Grandma, it's still early!"

Suzanne's protest continued inside the house as the men mounted the steps to the porch.

"Come and sit down," Van said, moving to the far chair. April was seated cross-legged in the chair closest to the steps. The agents politely begged her pardon as they walked in front of her and then sat on the edge of their chairs.

"How can I help you two?" Van asked.

Wakefield began. "We are with Defense Intelligence Agency, sir."

"I know. April told me about your first visit to her home in California."

"So much for a gag order," Smith said with a reserved smile.

Casually, she replied, "Blood is not just thicker than water."

Wakefield turned to her. "We are actually pleased that you're here, Mrs. Sutton, because our questions are about your husband."

April swallowed and prayed for composure. "What about him?"

"We are interested in his whereabouts."

"Business trip . . . overseas," she said flatly.

"We thought as much," Smith replied. "However, we checked his passport and no activity has been reported. It's as though he has dropped off the map, so to speak."

"Has he done anything wrong?" April asked defiantly.

"No . . . not that we are aware of. There was, however, an unexpected passenger aboard a military flight headed for the Middle East—Afghanistan, to be exact. Supposedly, this man was a photographer for the *National Geographic*. We checked and they are unaware of any such assignment."

"Speaking hypothetically," Wakefield chimed in, "if this passenger was a civilian using the army for his own personal agenda, there would be serious consequences."

"Since we are speaking hypothetically, gentlemen . . . " Van pulled his left ankle over his right knee. "Suppose this man had intel that gave him the whereabouts of a certain lost army team and that this man, who hitched a ride aboard one of your planes, was doing what the military refused to do, or was too inept to do."

The agents glanced at each other briefly. "If such intel did exist, we would know about it, sir. We are certain it does not."

Van nodded slightly. "So 'army intelligence' may be an oxymoron after all."

Neither man smiled. "Where did this supposed intel come from, sir?" Smith asked.

"If such intel did exist," Van said, mimicking the agents, "it would come from a reliable source."

Smith and Wakefield stood and straightened their suit coats. Smith stared into the night. "Believe me, it will not be long until you will want to tell us who is feeding you false information."

April lost it. "If the army wasn't so impotently entrenched in politics, Michael would be here now and so would Taylor!"

"April, everything is fine," Van said curtly.

The agents looked from her to her father-in-law. Smith handed a business card to Van. "We'll be seeing you." As they descended the stairs, one of them added, "Don't go too far."

The departure of the two men left a resounding void in the evening. April and her father-in-law sat quietly for several minutes before she finally spoke. "What did they mean, false information?"

Van paused before he said, "I'm going to find out."

27

Under Marcus's vigilant watch, Michael continued working on the general's "small projects." It became apparent that though Marcus was attentive, he had little understanding of what Michael was actually doing. Michael intended to exploit that fact. He knew as soon as he finished the general's projects, his life would be worthless. It gave new meaning to the idea of working against a deadline.

To keep his laptop close, Michael would occasionally type on it and study it so as to maintain the ruse that it was useful. He did that now, then glanced at his captor, who seemed to be dozing. A loud clatter of tools brought the man to full alert, gun in motion. Michael smiled to himself. Silence did him no good; he needed to get into Marcus's head.

"That wasn't ice cream we left those border guards, was it?" he asked.

Marcus shifted his weight.

"Brilliant using green ice cream to hide the C4. What was there, an inch of ice cream and the rest was explosive? And then what a pressure plate, one scoop and—" Michael made an explosion with his hands. "Tell me, why'd you blow it?"

Marcus shrugged. "I was paid to."

"By the general?"

"Does it matter?"

Michael took that as a yes.

"I don't ask questions," Marcus declared. "I just deliver."

"I noticed at the bus stop, you let your accent slip," Michael said.

"I no longer needed it."

"Why did you use one anyway?"

"False presumptions are important in my business. It keeps others off balance."

"Off balance . . . how?" Michael was in. With patience, he'd know how to outthink Marcus.

"When we met, you supposed I was an uneducated, dishonest man. I saw it in your eyes when you looked at my cars. You believed I had acquired my wealth through drugs or some other illegal means."

"And the fact that it was acquired through murder and intrigue is better?"

"It's more honest. I provide a service for those who have ambition and money—like General Rais. I am not biased. My clients have spoken every language, most especially English."

"Hmm. A friend of a friend. You work on referrals," Michael said.

"Of course. I couldn't very well advertise on the Internet."

"Where did you go to school?

"I have a master's degree in business from St. Xavier's in Mumbai," Marcus said proudly.

"Somehow I doubt your current occupation was included on the syllabus."

"Business is business."

"I am surprised you didn't attend a Western college, maybe Oxford or Yale."

"Why?"

"It seems that your English is natural, that's all."

"I can speak many languages and it is best to master the accents as well. The French pay more when I sound French, and so do the British, but not as much as the Italians. Everyone loves to believe they are working with a comrade—or at least a like-minded person." Marcus switched from one accent to another as he said the words "French," "British," and "Italian." "I even tried your Southern drawl," he continued, "but I am certain it lowers the IQ."

Michael smiled. "That's funny. You're probably not a fan of country music then, either."

"No."

Another long silence settled between them. Michael kept on task, wanting to finish early. An hour passed quickly, and then he asked casually, "Do you have children, Marcus?"

"No. I could not bring children into a world of which I am an ugly part."

His honesty surprised Michael. His captor appeared relaxed with no gun in sight, but Michael knew he was a coiled rattlesnake, no different than the ones he had poked with a long stick as a child. Michael returned his attention to a circuit board and said, "What about other family?"

"Only a brother."

"Does he know you kill people for a living?"

Marcus smiled darkly. "I know what you are doing. You may try to become my friend, but when the time comes, I will kill you just the same."

"I have no intention of being your friend. I know why you're here. I'm only interested. You're different than your first impression. Meeting you on the street, I would have never guessed what you do. If we were in America I would say you were an entrepreneur."

Marcus chuckled. "False presumptions, as I said. It also helps that you are supremely naive."

"Perhaps." It was good to let Marcus think he was a brilliant idiot. If he felt Michael was no threat, the sooner the walls would come down.

"The man you were sitting with was not so trusting," Marcus commented.

Michael recalled how McNally's demeanor had changed when Marcus approached. The pilot was no fool. "If I am naive, it is only because of my desire to find my brother," Michael said, then paused before asking, "Where is your brother, Marcus?"

Marcus only laughed. "You just keep digging. All you Americans want to believe people are somehow innately good and peaceful, and that if they are not, there must be something wrong with them. You cannot comprehend that some people are the way they are. Not everyone who takes up the work of death had an abusive childhood or lost their loved ones in some sort of horrible tragedy. God made me just as he made you. I give you Adolf Hitler as an example. He was the son of a middle-class working man. As a child, Adolf was a dreamer but also a leader in embryo—"

Michael interrupted, "I doubt that in those dreams he was butchering thousands of innocent people."

"My point exactly. He was a fairly normal child who had darkness in his heart. Given the right circumstances, the darkness became all-encompassing. If Hitler had been born in America, he never would have grown into the man he was. God put him in Germany."

"Hitler's choices made him who he was."

"I disagree," Marcus said firmly. "Hitler's choices were a product of who he was."

"Regardless, he will pay for his deeds in the hottest corners of hell."

"How can God punish Hitler for what was clearly God's doing? Hitler did not put himself in Germany."

Michael let out a breath. "That rationale may euthanize your conscience, but you have still chosen your own fate."

"Not so. I was still a teenager when in the market I heard of a man who could manipulate the human mind through torture to accomplish any desired result. My heart leaped in my chest and I had to seek this man out. I did not put myself in the market when those men were speaking. I did not bend the universe so that the very next week I met the man who would become my guide in a new world of dark discovery."

"Justify it if you wish, but you still own your choices that brought you here," Michael commented. "When death comes for you, there will be no light at the end of the tunnel, only darkness."

"If that's the way it has to be, I have only fulfilled my God-given potential."

Michael paused and rehearsed the conversation in his mind. Clearly Marcus felt confident in his philosophy, but there was something else. "I noticed you were quick to argue that not all who take up your work of death, as you called it, had an abusive childhood or suffered a tragic loss." Michael paused, watching the man's face. "But you had both, didn't you? What was it? Orphanage? One meal and three beatings a day? No, not an orphanage, but you were beat plenty. And this brother—I'll bet he wasn't just your brother but also a friend. Your only friend. Did you watch him die, Marcus? Or did you kill him, too?"

As Michael spoke he watched Marcus's features twist. With the last question, Marcus exploded from his seat. A gun was suddenly in his hand and pointed at Michael's face.

"Enough!" Marcus barked. "If I was not waiting on half a million, I would kill you now! Get back to work and shut up!"

Michael lowered his eyes and returned his attention to the projects. He had found the man's hot button.

Marcus turned and in anger fired three rounds into a concrete pillar. Once the echoes from the deafening shots faded in the empty hall, he turned calmly and declared, "That will be you soon enough."

Without comment, Michael resumed his task. The EMP was not the long-range weapon the general believed it to be. The disruption would only occur in a very small area. The suitcase nuke, however, was very powerful, with a higher grade of plutonium than expected. It could certainly level a city. Michael would only need a little to pass a validity test. The anthrax was of little consequence if everything went according to plan.

The projects progressed quickly as the night passed. Not long after 3:00 AM, Michael pushed his chair away from the workbench and rubbed his eyes. His hands shook from the caffeine and sugar. "I need some fresh air and to take a leak."

"You know where you can take a leak." Marcus pointed at a bucket at the edge of light. "Fresh air is out of the question."

"I cannot proceed," Michael argued. "I've had too much junk food. I am almost done and I need some fresh air. You can cuff me if you think I'm going to run."

The gun seemed to materialize in Marcus's hand. He pointed it at Michael. "You would not get five meters."

"Fine, then you have nothing to worry about."

Marcus sighed and checked his watch. "Okay. But first . . ." He pulled a pair of cuffs from a pocket.

"I thought you wouldn't need them."

"I am a careful man. You had better use the bucket first."

A couple minutes later, Michael winced as the handcuffs pinched his flesh. They proceeded out of the spotlights and into the shadows. Marcus kept him at arm's length, pistol drawn. It was true that Michael longed for a breather, but more importantly he needed a few minutes in the dark.

Outside, his lungs expanded with cool night air. Above him, countless points of light dotted the sky, and the moon hung low in the east. Out of habit his eyes found the Big Dipper and followed the handle to the North Star, the axis from which the celestial heavens hung. He recalled the maps he had studied before leaving on this little adventure and knew exactly where he was.

"Amazing, isn't it? What a beautiful night," Michael said to cover the soft rattling from his handcuffs.

"If you say so." Marcus did not look up but kept his eyes on Michael.

Michael moved his eyes from the sky to the city lights below. "It wasn't your fault you know—your brother's death." He was fishing but felt confident in the presumption.

"You don't know anything, and it is none of your concern. You need to finish the job." He pushed Michael in the direction of the door, which stood open.

Inside again, Michael rediscovered the stale, tired air he had previously grown accustomed to. Marcus removed the handcuffs and Michael said, "So if wasn't your fault, maybe it was God's."

Marcus landed a solid left hit to Michael's midsection that doubled him over. Kneeling on the floor, he coughed. Marcus squatted beside him, the nose of his pistol on the floor like a third leg of a tripod.

"I said it is none of your concern, but I've been itching to hit you again for hours now. It's funny that you think I would blame God. It was actually a group of insurgents. A southern Afghan tribe. I killed them for it."

Marcus stood and moved away. Michael also stood. He had expected the punch, but the pain was still unpleasant. Taking his time and catching his breath, he made his way back to the workbench. He looked at the clock—nearly 4:00 AM. It would be light soon and he was fast approaching the end of his usefulness. Before long the general would be returning for his three completed weapons.

During the remaining hours while Michael worked steadily, Marcus grew inattentive. He hadn't slept in a long time, and Michael figured his questions had stirred his captor's long-forgotten memories. Michael took advantage of these moments to crack the case of his laptop and slide the pistol into his lap and from there to a leg pocket in his trousers. Then he removed the battery from his laptop to fake a power failure. He carefully moved one of the loaded magazines into his lap. "Can you get me the other laptop, Marcus? I need to see if the batteries are compatible."

Marcus blinked but didn't speak as he moved to the computer.

Moving quickly, Michael loaded the magazine into the pistol. Anticipating the click, he closed his laptop at the same time.

"I'm sorry about my comment earlier." He tried not to sound nervous even though his heart thundered in his chest. "You're right; it's none of my business." He took the computer from Marcus and turned it over. "Ah, the batteries are different—thanks anyway. I will have to get by without it." He returned to wiring detonators.

"You work well," Marcus said. "You are very fast. It is too bad that the sooner you finish, the sooner you die."

"My father always said that a job worth doing is worth doing well." Michael wanted to chuckle at the irony, but the laughter wouldn't come. In truth he was finished, but he stalled, repairing things already repaired and scanning useless components.

It would be day soon, and with the day would come the general.

28

Time moved quickly. The sky outside was no longer black but a dull gray-blue. Michael fought to stay alert. It had been a long twenty-four hours since he'd slept. If he could just hold out a little longer, he would have Marcus summon the general and then he could put his own plans into effect.

Breaking the silence, the outer door slammed shut. Michael heard heavy footfalls and knew the decision of completion time had been taken from him. At the thought of the pistol in his pocket and the weight of his impending death, he felt instantly alert.

The meeting hall grew brighter, and he saw General Rais and his determined walk from a distance. Ten armed soldiers accompanied him. "How are we doing, Michael Sutton?" the general asked once he reached the work area.

Michael nodded. "Almost complete." He looked out at the growing daylight and considered his chances of getting the 10 mm out his pocket and killing both the general and Marcus. The chances were slim, and then there was the general's entourage. Michael would have to stick to his plan.

"Very good, very good." General Rais smiled. "Our enemies will not know what hit them."

After about ten minutes, Michael declared, "I am finished."

"Excellent!" Rais snapped his fingers. A guard pushed forward a small man with round glasses. "Check them!" the general ordered.

The little man moved sheepishly forward with an outdated Geiger counter and some other instruments that should enable him to verify the completion of the bombs without actually arming them. As Michael watched him work, he felt sweat bead on his brow. Lives hung on this inspector's report, and Michael hoped he did not notice some vital components were missing. If this man believed the weapons to be anything but complete and functional, Michael's family would all die.

There was a strained silence as the inspector worked. Lastly, he checked the detonator frequencies. "They are complete, sir," he said after several minutes, then slipped his equipment back into a bag.

"Excellent! You may go."

Instead of scurrying to the door as Michael had anticipated, the inspector lingered awkwardly and after a moment spoke. "You said you would release my family if I did as you asked."

"I will call for their release soon enough. Go before I change my mind!" The general drew a pistol and fired a warning shot that narrowly missed the inspector's head. He retreated without further argument.

After the inspector left, the general turned to Michael. "Do you see what I mean? Everywhere I am surrounded by incompetence. Capable and brilliant men as yourself are not found on this side of the globe." Michael noted that Marcus took the general's comment as a personal affront.

The general said, "Now show me how to arm these weapons. Then our business will be concluded and your family will be safe."

"Release the family of the man who was just here."

The general pulled his pistol and aimed it at Michael. "You are in no position to make demands."

Michael picked up a detonator for the nuclear bomb. "Neither are you. If I push this button the bomb goes now. If you want to know how to set a timer, you better let that man's family live."

The general's vicious glare revealed his desire to pull the trigger. Michael held his breath, hoping his bluff was convincing. Finally, Rais chuckled and growled, "Bleeding hearts." He holstered his pistol, then dialed his cell phone and ordered the release of the inspector's family. As he hung up, Michael put down the detonator.

"Any more games, Michael Sutton, and you will not save your wife and daughter a slow and painful death," the general said, his features slowly returning to their normal color.

"No more games," Michael agreed. He proceeded to instruct the general on the weapons' operation, then packed the items away for safe travel. Through the west-facing windows, Michael saw an approaching helicopter.

"My chariot," the general said, smiling. "Right on time."

Soon, the helicopter landed just outside the door. Looking as pleased as a schoolboy who had just kissed his first girl, the general watched a few of his men carry the weapons to the aircraft. Then, ironically, he offered Michael his hand and said, "It has been a pleasure doing business with you, Michael Sutton. You are everything I expected."

If his priority hadn't been to save the lives of the people he loved, Michael might have spent more energy wondering who had leaked detailed information about him to the general. Clearly, it was someone who personally knew Michael. But it did not matter now. "I wish I could say the same," he said finally, refusing the general's hand.

"Very well. If I had not agreed to let Marcus kill you, I would do it myself, but I am a man of my word. Adieu, Michael Sutton."

The general gave Marcus a nod and turned to leave. One of the general's men came forward and handcuffed Michael before leaving. Marcus's gun again materialized in his hand. Like any tool in the hand of a professional, it seemed almost an extension of him.

"So how are we doing this, Marcus?" Michael asked.

"Turn around—on your knees."

"Really? You're going to shoot me from behind like a coward? Perhaps the general was right and you are as incompetent as the rest."

"Oh, would you shut up!" Marcus shouted. "You've talked till my ears are bleeding. I've killed women who didn't talk so much."

"I can't believe you would take that from him," Michael continued. "If anyone's a coward, he is. But maybe he was right—you're going to shoot an unarmed man in the back. Wow, that takes courage."

Marcus raised his pistol toward Michael's head. "On your knees."

Michael turned around and started to kneel. From under his watch, he retrieved a key he had made while working on the bombs for the general. Earlier, when he had asked to leave for fresh air, he had actually been testing the key on the cuffs while in the dark.

Struggling now at the little lock, he spoke again. "Is this how your brother was killed? Is this how the Afghans did it?"

"Shut up—you know nothing!"

The cuffs fell from Michael's wrists and he tossed them across the floor. He spun and launched himself toward Marcus. His shoulder sank deep into Marcus's abdomen, and Michael pulled the man's legs out from under him. Marcus rolled onto his back and kicked Michael off, but as he did he lost grip of his pistol. Like a cat, Marcus was on his feet and came at Michael.

Less agile, Michael took a kick to the midsection, but he grabbed Marcus's foot and leaned into him, straining the knee. Marcus was still off balance as Michael swung with an uppercut. The punch connected and jarred Marcus's teeth together. Michael followed with several short jabs that hardly fazed his brutal opponent. Marcus countered with a wild left that caught Michael just above the eye, splitting the skin. He followed with a right hook that set Michael on his heels.

Michael swung off balance and Marcus hit him again, sending him to the floor. Marcus inhaled and found his pistol. "That was fun. I haven't had a fistfight for many years." Lying on his side, Michael fumbled in the leg pocket of his trousers.

"But you know," Marcus continued, "you've really made me mad. My brother was all I had in the world. I think I will pay a visit to Lucero Drive. I never work for free, but this will be worth it." He stood over Michael and lifted his pistol. "Goodbye."

In one quick motion, Michael hooked Marcus's left ankle with a foot and kicked at the knee. The knee gave way and Marcus let out a shrill cry of pain as he crumpled to the floor. He fired his pistol but the bullet ricocheted into a window, dissolving it into glass shards.

Michael came to his knees as Marcus attempted to take aim with his pistol. At that moment, Michael aimed his own pistol and fired several times.

Clearly surprised, Marcus searched for the bullet holes in his shirt. His hand came away red.

Michael lowered his gun as he stood over the assassin. "I am sorry, but you left me no choice. To threaten my life is one thing—to threaten my family is something unforgivable. If you had a family, perhaps you would understand." He paused. "Not that it matters now, but it is true that you are a product of both your choices and your environment, just as Adolf Hitler was. May God have mercy on you."

Marcus scowled and tried in vain to lift his gun. A long, gurgling breath slipped past his lips. Turning away, Michael let the pistol drop into his pocket. He didn't revel in his victory, but he was alive and his family was safe . . . almost.

He wiped the blood away from his brow, and with trembling hands found his cell phone in Marcus's jacket pocket. Michael turned it on as he ran for the door.

Outside he searched the sky for the helicopter. After a moment, he saw it like a distant black dragonfly. It appeared to be on the other side of the city and moving northwest. Michael dialed a number into his phone, but paused before he pushed "send." Then, recalling the general's threat to his family and the bombs that threatened the innocent, he pushed the button.

Upon entering the helicopter, General Rais had ordered their destination. Now he sat securely in the cabin with two of his most trusted guards, smiling to himself. He would soon be one of the greatest threats the free world had ever known. He looked out the window to the earth below and saw an army closing in on Mingora, taking over the airfield and crossing the river. Insurgents, terrorists, or whatever the world might call them. To him they were patriots, and Mingora would soon be their capital. He returned his attention to the cases.

Three weapons, three targets.

As directed, the weapons had wireless detonators and would soon be shipped to three strategically chosen cities. He opened the cases and looked at his trophies. It had taken a great deal of time and patience to get them together, but now they were finished. It was a rewarding life.

He reached out and touched the weapons. Suddenly, and in unison, they came to life. His smile disappeared, his glee replaced by a sick feeling of panic. He blinked once in disbelief. Three bombs, three timers: seven seconds on the EMP, eight seconds on the anthrax, and nine seconds on the nuke.

"What did you do?" a guard asked, gaping at the weapons.

"Nothing, you fool. We've been double-crossed!"

"Get rid of the nuke!" the guard demanded.

They fumbled for the door and shouted for the pilot to land—two seconds. The door slid open—too late. The first timer went to zero as the general picked up the case and pitched it out the door. The pulse fried all of the helicopter's circuitry and the craft pitched and rolled. The general was thrown against the opposite door as a powder burst into the compartment—anthrax. General Rais stared in disbelief . . . two seconds on the last bomb. He was thrice dead!

Michael watched as the distant helicopter lost power and then chaotically struggled for life, then exploded in a ball of fire. He stood a moment to catch his breath in the cool morning air.

Finally, he went back inside the building. He had not built a nuclear bomb but only laced the parts with enough plutonium to fool a test. Tucked neatly below the would-be nuke was a good bit of C4. Though he was pleased to have short-circuited the general's plans, taking human lives made it so anticlimactic. But Michael knew he had acted rightly. It was now time to find his brother.

29

Moving through a river of people, Taylor Sutton remembered his forced pleading into a digital recorder. It felt like a dream. The message had brought his brother halfway around the globe. Michael was a brilliant technician, but not famously so. The only person who could have done this was the good colonel, Walter Bracken. Taylor no longer doubted the colonel's hand in these events and could think of nothing the Suttons might have done to deserve such a brutal betrayal.

Tears pooled in Taylor's eyes. For a long time, he had doubted his family's love for him, believing he was only a source of embarrassment and humiliation. But knowing his brother had come so far, with so much at stake . . . Taylor quickened his step. He turned briefly to check his back trail for a shadow. He saw no one that stood out.

On the far side of the city, a black column of smoke ascended into the sky. Somewhere an automatic weapon reported. Was the city under attack? If so, it was all the more reason to get out. But first Taylor had to find Michael.

Climbing the streets that led eastward, the Ranger began to catch glimpses of a sizable building on the descending slope of the eastern mountains. The mountains were nearly barren now with veins cut through the trees for ski runs. The building had to be the abandoned lodge. It was all uphill from where he stood.

As Taylor neared the edge of the city, the modern buildings disappeared and mud huts cropped up. He stopped again to catch his breath, having lost much of his strength in the long weeks of neglected prison life. From this spot, he looked back at the city. Down near the river a battle had begun. He cared little who was fighting whom and doubted either side was American.

In Taylor's peripheral vision, he caught a glimpse of someone ducking out of sight when he had stopped. He had a shadow. He turned to the side, not wanting to give away his destination. After a short distance, the man followed. Hoping to appear lost, Taylor doubled back. If the man had a radio, he would be in contact with others. They would reach Taylor soon. Dressed in guard's clothing, he stood out among the few locals who were left out here. At the outset of the battle, many had disappeared into their homes, and it seemed even more were leaving the city all together.

Taylor slowed, waiting for the man to get anxious. He doubted his own life was worth much, so he had to play it safe. Gathered to watch the battle from the street, a group of men spoke excitedly. Taylor passed them and turned suddenly. Over the shoulders of the gawkers he looked his shadow in the eye. He was a guard from the prison—no doubt about it. Since the guard hadn't yet shot him in the back, Taylor realized the man was hoping to find the rest of the escapees by following him.

The guard had just been speaking into his radio and was caught by surprise when Taylor turned around. Scrambling, the man dropped the radio and lifted a rifle. Pushing through the bystanders, Taylor brought his own rifle to bear and fired first. He shot the man, then retrieved the radio and turned. The bystanders had disappeared. Apparently, the distant battle was suddenly too close for comfort. Taylor scanned the area for others, then pocketed the radio and hurried up the slope.

★

Inside the building, Michael did not look at Marcus's motionless body. He quickly retrieved the sealed canister that contained the plutonium. He was about to leave when he thought about the leftover bomb-making materials still on the table. Sighing, he set down the canister. With just enough material to complete one more remote detonator, he went to work. There was not enough C4 so he had to improvise. Bullets, gasoline—anything and everything went into a nice little pile.

About an hour later, Michael exited the building. From out of nowhere, an armed soldier appeared in the doorway. Both men froze. The soldier stood in full sunlight, and Michael was still in the shadow of the unlit lobby. The soldier panted heavily as though he had just run a marathon. All he had to do was raise his rifle and it was over. Michael's mind raced as he thought about carrying a canister of plutonium while engaged in a gun battle.

Then it struck him that there was something familiar about the bearded soldier. While the crooked nose was wrong, he thought he recognized the eyes peering out from under a hat brim. He took a chance.

"Taylor? Is that you?"

30

On the third floor of the Schwarzkopf building, Vander Sutton paced the floor outside Walter Bracken's office. Some moments in life are far too important for a phone call, and Van needed to speak face to face with his old friend. Michael hadn't called in days, and Van worried he might lose both of his sons. He had to know if there had been any activity in the area or reports regarding Taylor or his team. Van didn't like what the DIA men had said, and in his wildest imaginings he feared some ploy or plot had swallowed both of his sons alive. Walter was the only person Van could turn to.

"You're wearing out the carpet," the secretary said with a grin.

Van stopped to smile back. "I suppose you're right. I'm sorry."

"Michael has your smile," she said.

At the mention of his son's name, the dam almost burst. "You know him?" Van said with a frog in his throat.

"He has stopped by a few times." Probably in her early fifties, the receptionist had shoulder-length dark-brown hair and a desk full of pictures of grandchildren. "He in trouble?"

"It's that obvious?"

"I'm a mother. I know a worried look when I see it."

Just then, the colonel came out of his office. "Van! Good to see you." They shook hands.

"Thanks for seeing me on short notice," Van said.

"You're welcome. Come on in."

"Nice to meet you . . . ?" Van held his hand out over the secretary's desk.

"Wendy. Nice to meet you, Mr. Sutton." She shook his hand, and then he followed the colonel into his office.

"No word from Michael?" Walter said.

"No. Have you heard anything?"

The colonel shook his head. "Nothing. I didn't think you'd drive all this way if all was well."

"Has there been any more intel on Taylor's team?"

"No. Nothing."

"Where did that last information come from that placed the Rangers in Mingora? Were Michael's contacts trusted men?"

"Secure sources, and yes. What's with all the questions?"

"Well, we've had a visit from the Defense Intelligence Agency. They say there never was any intel on the location of Taylor's team. I don't know if I trust them, but it made me doubt everything I thought I knew."

The colonel cleared his throat. "Well, army intelligence is an oxymoron you know."

Van forced a chuckle. "That's what I told the agents. They didn't think it was that funny."

"They also don't have a sense of humor."

"It makes me sound like a crazy old man, Walt, but my gut is telling me something is off. Like maybe somebody lied to you and gave you bad info to get Michael over there."

"It does sound crazy. You've been watching too many movies."

"Probably, but I just have this feeling he was set up."

"Too bad your gut didn't tell you this before you let him go."

"Let him go? What is that supposed to mean? You know he was going, one way or another."

"Then it doesn't matter how you feel. We tried to give him the best chance of returning safely. Soldiers die every day, Van. Men with far more training than Michael."

"What are you saying? I'm not going to just write my boys off for dead, Walt! Are you keeping something from me?"

"No, Van, I'm not. What I'm saying is if Michael doesn't get out of this, there will be nothing you can do. Remember, all this was under the table. Nothing can be tied back to me or the military. If you try to take this up different channels or go public, I will be forced to deny all knowledge of these actions. And no doubt your contracts will be terminated."

Van blinked in surprise. "I don't care about the contracts. I want my boys back . . . alive."

"I know, but I also know that when people get desperate they do things they wouldn't normally consider. Just keep the big picture in mind. I'm telling you this as a friend. This ends here." He pointed back and forth between them. "You cannot involve anyone else. Think of the family you have left. Think of Claire and April. Be strong for them."

Van stood. "I'm giving up on my sons if I do that."

The colonel rose and stepped around his desk. "I'm not telling you to give up. I'm telling you the hard fact is that both your boys might never come home. Just brace yourself for that." After a long pause, he sighed and said, "I tell you what, Van. I have some contacts on that side of the world. Let me make some phone calls. I will let you know what I can dig up."

"Thank you. I'm staying at Michael's place. I'll wait for your call." Van turned and promptly left the office.

The colonel returned to his chair. Vander Sutton was finally getting a taste of reality. It didn't feel as good as Walter hoped it might. Any day now and it would become obvious that both of Van's sons were dead, and of course Walter would need to be outwardly sensitive. He was also prepared to spin this away from himself if Van was so foolish as to go over his head or go public.

The DIA agents worried the colonel. If they found anything that linked him to the failed mission or Michael's disappearance, his hope of being a general would be gone forever.

From his cell phone, Walter dialed a very long distance number, a number he swore he'd never use again. The outgoing call rang into oblivion—General Rais didn't answer. But then he wouldn't. He had what he wanted. Their business was concluded.

Outside the Schwarzkopf building, a fresh breeze stirred. Something was irritating Van about the whole conversation. He did not like that his old friend Walter seemed to write Michael and Taylor off as casualties so easily and acted far more concerned about his public image than their lives. Van had learned years before to pay attention to the whisperings of the soul, as it were. Some people called them gut instincts, others a sixth sense, but Van attributed it to the Spirit of God. The Spirit always revealed truth, and right now Van knew—absolutely knew—that Walter Bracken was keeping something from him. All this "need to know" crap was exhausting. Van needed answers. He got in his car and dialed a number on his cell phone. Seconds later a sharp voice answered.

"This is Wakefield."

31

Tears flowed freely between the brothers as they embraced. Michael had felt so much anger and frustration toward Taylor, but in an instant it vanished. As they stood now on foreign soil, everything that had kept them apart seemed so immaterial. They were brothers, and neither time nor distance could erase that.

Michael stepped back and glanced over his younger brother from head to foot. "You look terrible and smell even worse."

Taylor chuckled. "You've looked better yourself. Is that a cut above your eye?"

"Yeah." He wiped his brow, then pulled Taylor in for one more hug. "I knew you were alive. I knew it."

"We're not out of this yet, Bro."

Michael looked out across the valley toward the Swat River. The fighting had increased. "Who do you think it is? Is it us?"

"I don't think so. It looks more like rebel insurgents. You ready to get out of here?"

"Almost." Michael picked up the canister of plutonium and pointed to the ice cream truck. "I got wheels, if that'll help."

"Yeah, I saw that beauty when I walked up. Made me pretty hungry." Together they walked toward the truck. "What's in the canister?"

"Weapons-grade plutonium."

"Let me guess—General Rais."

Michael nodded. He opened the back of the truck and secured the canister into a cabinet. "That was supposed to go into his nuclear bomb. He had no idea what he had. A bomb like that could wipe out Los Angeles."

"Does the general know he got a fake?"

Michael fought the urge to smile. "He does."

"How'd that go over?"

"With a bang." It sounded like a bad line from an '80s action film, yet Michael couldn't help but say it.

"You're about to laugh," Taylor remarked. "What gives?"

"He was in a helicopter northwest of the city when it blew up."

"You mean you blew it up. I get it—bad joke. Well, I'm glad one of us got to kill him."

Michael's smile disappeared. "He threatened to kill April and Suzanne."

"You did the right thing, Michael. Our first day here, Rais murdered Sergeant Heller in cold blood." Taylor paused as if remembering, then turned his attention to the truck. "How'd you acquire this little sweetheart? I like the cone on top."

"It belonged to an assassin named Marcus. We drove it over from Jalalabad yesterday."

"You and an assassin?"

"Yeah, it's a long story."

"The assassin didn't survive either? You've been busy."

Michael let out a breath. "You hungry?"

"I'm beyond hungry. What do you have?"

"The basics. What flavor of MRE do you want?"

"I dunno. Something chicken, I guess."

Michael handed Taylor a water bottle and a chicken-and-rice MRE. They opened the back doors of the truck and sat on the edge for a few minutes, eating quietly.

"I've been up all night and all they would give me is junk food." Michael shuddered and thought of vomiting. "If I never eat another Twinkie, it will be too soon."

"Yeah, well, I've been eating something like old dog food for the last month." Taylor looked at his MRE. "There's no way I could eat anything with beef."

"We'd better be going," Michael said as they finished the meager meal.

"Before we go, let's scope out our escape route."

"Good idea." Michael handed Taylor a pair of binoculars and kept a pair for himself. They walked closer to the overlook.

"You see how most of the fighting is centered near the capitol building and the river?" Taylor said. Small-arms fire could be heard, punctuated every minute or so with an explosion.

"Yeah." Michael watched a tank obliterate a barricade.

"If we can keep to the south and stay on side streets, we might just avoid it all together. It may not look bad from this distance, but I guarantee you it's ugly down there. Look, here comes some air support."

"For which side?" As Michael spoke, a pair of jets launched several missiles, then banked away to the north. Massive explosions split the air like thunder. There was no sign of the tank.

"Doesn't matter. We want no part of it."

Michael turned his binoculars toward the road. "The only way out of here drops us right into the hornet's nest. Looks like we have some company." There was a man dressed as a guard and three others dressed in traditional Pakistani clothes, one with an arm in a sling, and a woman. Michael noted her boots.

"Well, would you look at that," Taylor exclaimed.

Michael lowered his binoculars and saw his brother staring through his own. "You know them?" Michael asked.

"Yeah. That's what's left of my team, and the woman who helped us escape. They were supposed to be gettin' out of here. Come on, let's go."

Michael was pleased to find the keys in the truck's ignition. He started it and drove to the far end of the parking lot. "I've got something to do before we head out." He stopped the truck.

"Remember that Easter morning when we found a bundle of firecrackers from the previous Fourth of July?"

"Sure. Mom made us pick up every piece of exploded egg."

"Remember wishing we had something bigger to blow up?" Michael dialed his phone. "Watch the building." He pushed "send."

From inside, the building seemed to belch, and in an instant all the windows across the front exploded in a red ball of flame that turned to rolling black clouds.

Taylor whistled. "Why'd you do that?"

"There were a bunch of bomb components left. I didn't want to leave them behind. No telling what kind of nutcase would happen onto them."

Michael depressed the clutch and found first gear. He pointed the truck down the narrow and steeply descending road. "I'm glad this is almost over."

Taylor looked at his brother. "This is far from over."

"What do you mean?"

"The prison warden is after us."

"You guys were being held in prison? The Slohman Gaul?"

"You've heard of it?"

"Read about it. Sounded like an awful place."

"Trust me. It's worse than anything you've read."

"Won't the war will be a distraction for this warden?"

"Not this guy. Our escape will be a personal insult. And it's not just him. We still have Colonel Bracken to deal with."

"What?" Michael nearly ran off the road.

"There they are," Taylor said.

Michael pressed hard on the brakes, but the truck passed the five pedestrians before it ground to a halt.

Taylor jumped out, and when Michael opened his door he heard his brother say, "I figured you guys were long gone."

"You really thought we'd leave you?" one of them replied in a strong accent. "We're in this together, mate. You know the whole 'never leave a man behind' rubbish."

They wasted no time loading up and getting down the mountain. This road would take them into the heart of Mingora. Michael turned his thoughts to finding a path that skirted the fighting. He had studied the road maps of Mingora, but being on the ground was a whole other matter, and of course he had been unconscious on the way in. Taylor and the others rode in the back of the truck, staying out of sight at least until they got outside the city.

As Taylor sat crouched behind the passenger seat, he related to his brother most of what had happened to them since their capture, especially the parts involving Colonel Bracken.

"I don't know if I can believe that, Taylor," Michael said when his brother finished. "Are you certain?"

"Yes, I am. I was sitting with Rais when he called Colonel Bracken on the phone. Think about it. You said he planned your entire itinerary, only to lead you into a trap."

Michael's head spun as he considered the bullet he had just dodged. He forced himself to come back to the moment; he would worry about Colonel Bracken when he could do something about it.

"I only hope we can get out of this alive," Taylor went on, "so I can see his reaction when we all show up on his doorstep." He paused and turned to the others seated in the back of the truck. "I forgot to tell you guys—Michael blew up General Rais."

A barrage of congratulations sounded. Unsure how to reply, Michael remained silent.

After a minute, Taylor said, "I'm curious to know how you whipped that assassin. You got the general with the bomb, but what about the other guy?"

The memory of Marcus taking his last breath made Michael shudder. He swallowed hard, then pulled the gun from his pants pocket. "It was thanks to Dad, actually." He handed the pistol to Taylor. "He concealed that in a laptop. It has rounds designed to pierce body armor."

Taylor chuckled as he inspected the gun and ammo. "Dad always did have a soft spot for James Bond gadgets."

The city of Mingora stretched out like a swatted spider before them. Most of the roads either dead ended or disappeared into the desert. The group trying to flee Pakistan did not have time for a wrong turn. And with the prison warden on the hunt, a mistake could prove fatal.

The trail down the mountain turned into Gumbia Road. Michael got his first real glimpse of Mingora, a filthy little city that looked much better from a distance. Certain areas were still tranquil and green with low-lying earth-tone buildings, some of them probably older than the United States.

Gumbia soon joined a busier highway. Fortunately, there was a sign that read "Peshawar" and pointed left.

"Ha!" Michael cranked the steering wheel.

Just when he had let out the clutch, he had to slam on his brakes as a Jeep and three trucks cut across the highway in front of them. Someone spoke from the back. "Hey, what's going on up there?"

"Idiots acting like they own the road," Michael replied. "Everybody okay?"

Taylor sat forward and stared out the window. "That's the warden sitting shotgun in the first Jeep." He turned to the others. "There goes the search party, guys."

Tension instantly filled the truck.

"Is he coming back?" McGillis asked.

Nasira went pale. "Did he see us?"

Michael watched from the side mirror as the caravan disappeared up the road going the opposite direction. "No. Looks like they're headed up the mountain."

"I had a guard following me earlier," Taylor said. "I'd bet he figured out where I was headed. That reminds me—I have his radio." He pulled it from a leg pocket and turned it on.

32

Aman Shamir cursed under his breath as his new driver took a corner too wide and nearly crashed into the side of an oncoming ice cream truck. Shamir slapped him and swore at him. An accident would cost them valuable time. The driver apologized, and the warden settled back into his seat.

As they continued, Shamir focused on tracking his prisoners. He attempted to contact Mingora's governor to enlist more help for their recapture, but the man was unavailable. The battle had either forced him underground or he was dead, since local leaders always died first in a coup. Either way, Shamir was on his own.

The last and only report was over an hour old: One of the escaped prisoners, dressed as a guard, was seen exiting the city to the east, heading in the direction of the abandoned ski lodge. The report made the warden furious, for he knew Rais had taken the American there to assemble his weapons. Shamir should have realized the prisoners would head there, but at the time he believed only he and Rais were aware of the location. It was obvious now that Nasira also knew of it and had told the others. The eavesdropping little . . .

Contact with the guard who sent the report had ceased. Shamir knew the man must have been discovered and most likely killed. The warden had to anticipate the escapees' next move. He pinched the bridge of his nose and closed his eyes. Something about that ice cream truck at the corner irritated him.

Ten more minutes up the road, smoke from the burning ski lodge came into sight. Shamir wondered if Rais had ordered the building destroyed after the completion of the bombs. It was typical of the self-aggrandizing general to do such things—he reveled in destruction. Shamir, on the other hand, enjoyed the disintegration of the human spirit. It was much more difficult to accomplish and far more rewarding.

The caravan rumbled to a halt before the smoldering building. Shamir quickly ordered an investigation of its interior. Regardless of the smoke and flames, he needed a body count. Six men with scarves across their noses and mouths ran inside. After a few minutes they returned, dragging a single body behind them. Shamir almost smiled, certain it would be the body of some unfortunate American.

Drawing close, he was gravely disappointed. The body, now hairless and partially burnt, was all too familiar. It was an old pupil—a competent and talented killer. Something had gone wrong. "This cannot be! Was there no one else? An American?"

"No one, sir. There was no one else."

Shamir turned in anger. For a moment he considered shooting the messenger but restrained himself. He would need all the men he had to recapture the Americans. He squeezed the bridge of his nose again and closed his eyes. The ice cream truck still hung in his thoughts. Why?

Replaying the moment of near collision, he tried to visualize the driver, whom he had seen only for a split second. Shamir opened his eyes and retrieved a radio. "Look out for an ice cream truck!" he shouted, shaking with anger. "Our prisoners are driving an ice cream truck! Watch the roads out of the city!"

He did not have to order the men back into their transportation. They moved by instinct. Seconds later, the caravan barreled down the mountain at full speed.

With the outbreak of the battle near the Swat River, Mingora seemed to be under a self-imposed curfew, and the caravan moved undeterred through the nearly empty streets. Soon a report came over the radio. The truck had been found—empty.

Aman Shamir slammed the radio down and swore profusely. He had missed them again! He picked up the radio and barked, "All stop!"

The Jeep stopped, then lurched forward. Tired of the jostling, Shamir retrieved his sidearm and shot the driver. Feeling less remorse than if he had shot a stray dog, the warden said into the radio, "Are all exit roads secure?"

He had sent men in pairs to Landaki, Haji Baba, and Bahrain, the three roads that exited the city. He waited for their reports.

Two Slohman Gaul prison guards clambered to the roof of the tallest building on the southwestern edge of Mingora. Landaki Road, the main highway in and out of the city, lay beneath them.

Swinging over the wall, the two men were greeted by abandoned laundry, dry and motionless. They crossed to the far wall, took out binoculars, and began searching for the least likely of targets—an ice cream truck. Landaki Road was no longer a busy highway but a slow-flowing river with schools of people trying to flee the city.

Vazir Bhalli moved his binoculars to the tents and the growing mass of refugees, then worked his way methodically toward the city. The warden's insistence that the escaped Americans were driving an ice cream truck made him think of his children.

Vazir soon spotted a familiar figure with three children. He would know her anywhere, even at a thousand yards and from behind. He had told her to wear her red *dupatta,* and he could see the beautiful scarf with its gold beadwork glistening in the sun. His family was safe.

The guard beside him scanned the streets closer to the city. "An ice cream truck?" he said. "The warden has really lost his mind. I heard he had a young girl locked away in his room. Maybe for years."

Vazir thought of his own daughter and shook his head. "Mind your tongue, Haamid. If the warden gets wind of your contempt, you will be fired, or worse. But yes, I heard the same. The Koran teaches against such practices."

"It is obvious—" Haamid began, but the warden's voice pierced the air and both men jumped. Vazir gave Haamid a speak-of-the-devil look and grabbed the radio from his belt.

"Yes, sir. We are in position. Nothing yet."

"You will call me when you see them!" the warden ordered. "Do not engage until I arrive."

"Yes, sir." Vazir returned the radio to his hip. He peered over the endless tide of evacuees. Almost all of them carried items either on the head or shoulders, items deemed important enough for survival. He knew from experience that most of these "valuables" would be abandoned within two days, creating a trail of the displaced. Part of Vazir hoped he would not see the Americans or the girl. If their only crime was escaping the Slohman Gaul, then Allah bless them.

The sun turned the air into a stifling oven. Haamid offered the older guard a canteen of water. Vazir lowered his binoculars and took a swallow of the warm, metallic liquid. He wiped the sweat from his brow and continued his search. In a sweep of the crowd, he noticed something out of the ordinary. A large truck approached from the west, lumbering and heavy.

"I don't like the look of that truck," he said to Haamid. The men glanced from the truck to the crowd that parted for it to pass through. Vazir searched frantically for the red scarf and could not find it. As the truck drew closer, he and Haamid began to back away from the edge of the building. A kilometer and closing. Five hundred meters—too close!

·At three hundred meters, there was a flash and the truck vaporized. A shock wave rushed across the desert, extinguishing all life in its path and tossing cars like toys and trees like toothpicks.

The concussion of the bomb shook the three-story building where Vazir and Haamid stood. Vazir was knocked off his feet. Several seconds later, he pushed himself to his knees, his ears ringing. His eyes went to billowing cloud above; in an instant the world was a different place. A hot wind blew where before there had been none. He was alone on the rooftop. Haamid had vanished, and even the laundry was gone.

Vazir stood slowly and moved to the side of the building. In the shadows at the foot of the structure lay Haamid, bent and askew. He must have been too close to the edge when the blast erupted. Vazir quickly climbed down only to discover what he already suspected—Haamid was dead.

The warden's voice crackled over the radio. "Does Landaki remain secure?"

Vazir put the radio near his mouth. "Landaki is a crater, sir, and Haamid is dead."

"Who?" the warden said.

"Haamid . . . he was a guard. The blast—"

"I do not care. Watch for those prisoners!"

Vazir put the radio to his mouth, but nothing came out. After a moment he dropped the device. He thought about the woman in the red scarf—his wife—and their children. He had to know if they lived.

Shamir heard the explosion and saw the mushroom cloud ascend into the air. "Keep Landaki secure!" he barked into his radio. "Do you hear me?" No response. He threw his radio to the ground, shattering it. He drew his gun again and fired more rounds into his dead driver. Nothing seemed to make Shamir feel better.

He turned his gun on one of his men. "You! Get to Landaki Road and report at the first sign of the Americans." To the next man, the warden said, "Go with him, but first give me your radio."

It was impossible for the Americans to evade capture forever, and Shamir was not a patient man. As the two guards left, he spoke into the radio. "Where was the ice cream truck found?"

"The cricket stadium at Saidu Road," a voice replied.

The stadium was not far from his current location. Shamir turned to his men. "The prisoners must be on foot or they have stolen another vehicle. We must be quick. There will be a woman with them. Bring her to me and kill the others. You!" He pointed to another guard. "Take some men and go to the cricket field and tell me what you find."

"Yes, sir." After glancing at the dead driver slumped over the Jeep's steering wheel, the guard turned to his men. "Let's go."

Shamir returned to his vehicle and pulled the driver onto the ground. He slid behind the steering wheel, started the Jeep, and sped away. He would find those infidels; they had been elusive so far, but nobody was lucky forever.

Something in his gut told him to head to Landaki Road, regardless of the explosion, and he turned his Jeep there now. With the fighting in the north, and the impassable mountains to the east, Landaki was still the most likely route.

Ten minutes later his radio cracked to life. "Sir?" The voice was meek and nervous.

"Speak."

"We're at the cricket stadium, sir."

"Yes!"

"There is no ice cream truck in sight."

Reflexively, Shamir stomped on the brake and brought the Jeep to a sliding stop. They had fooled him again! He clenched his tobacco-stained teeth. He regretted the earlier shooting of his young driver, for it would be much more satisfying to shoot him now.

He picked up the radio and tried to speak calmly. "You Americans are very clever. The false report on the truck's location bought you time, but you will need more than that to get away from me. I will hunt you until my dying breath! I will find you!"

After a long pause, a voice said in English, "We'll be ready."

Shamir shouted into the radio, "All men report to Landaki Road at the Mingora Bypass!" He threw the radio across the street, where it hit a building and broke into pieces. With the Americans listening, radio communication was pointless.

The warden felt an intense anger he had rarely experienced in his life of cool, calculated malice. Driven by this, he started the Jeep and headed to where the Americans were most likely to be.

33

Parked on the bank of the Swat River, the brightly colored ice cream truck looked at odds with its picturesque surroundings. The low river wound like braided silver strands through the sand bars and marshy soil, surrounded by rich green fields. Above the river to the north, the land rose sharply into rolling bluffs and steep mountains. In a few months, a blanket of heavy white snow would bury the mountains, snow that would melt in the spring and turn the gentle, flowing river into a raging torrent.

The remaining members of the Ghost team had moved away from the truck and sat nearly hidden among the tall grass and reeds. They had emptied the truck of its supplies, the guns, the food and water—all of it. The canister of plutonium leaned against a tree a short distance away. Fulton and Pike were fashioning packs from clothing to carry everything.

Suspecting Landaki Road would be watched, they had driven cross-country until the truck ran out of fuel. When the explosion occurred, they were grateful they had abandoned the road when they did, for now they were at a safe distance.

"Did you have to taunt him?" Fulton said as Taylor tossed the radio away.

"It doesn't matter—he was never going to stop anyway."

"Why throw the radio away?" Nasira asked, marking where it landed.

"The warden wouldn't be so foolish as to use radios again," Taylor said somberly. "Not if he thinks we might be listening."

Nasira had anticipated the warden's anger, but hearing his voice over the radio sent waves of terror through her entire being. It was a voice she had hoped never to hear again. He was too close and too determined. Her hands shook uncontrollably, and when Emilio Gutierrez offered her one of his as if wanting to steady her, she accepted it with a nervous smile.

McGillis said, "We need a plan. Double time."

"We need a route the warden won't expect," Gutierrez added.

"He is smart," Nasira said doubtfully. "There is no route he won't expect."

"I remember a valley that cuts southwest out from the city . . . low ground," Pike declared. "We could stay invisible and make like a possum up a gum tree."

"I have no idea what that means, but I like it," the sergeant replied. "But it could take a week to get out of the country. We need something quicker."

"I know a chopper pilot," Michael said. "I have his number."

Everyone stopped and looked at him.

Taylor exclaimed, "You know a chopper pilot, Bro? You've only been here a day!"

"He gave me a lift." Michael retrieved his cell phone and McNally's card.

The sergeant's brows went up. "You have a phone? You could have mentioned that earlier."

"Stone the crows, you have a signal?" Pike practically shouted.

"I modified my phone . . . it's ringing."

Across the border, in an airbase and just about to sit down to his supper, McNally felt his cell phone vibrate. He didn't recognize the number but answered regardless. "McNally."

"Lieutenant?"

"Yeah."

"It's the muckraker."

"Michael? I didn't think you'd call."

"You said to call if I needed anything. Well, I—we—could use a lift."

"A lift? From where?"

"We're just east of Mingora."

"You're joking. We've heard reports the city is under attack from some terrorists group or rebels."

"The reports are right. A bomb just went off that completely destroyed the only road out of here. We could use some transportation."

McNally had already abandoned his food and was hustling down a wide hallway with countless doors. "Who is we?"

"Myself, the remaining members of a captured team of Army Rangers, and a young woman who helped them escape. Seven in all." Gutierrez motioned to Michael that he needed the phone. "Hold on, the sergeant needs to speak to you."

Gutierrez took the phone. "This is Sergeant Emilio Gutierrez. Who's this?"

"Lieutenant Henry McNally, Air Force chopper pilot."

"It's good to hear a friendly voice, sir. I need you to get a message to JSOC. Tell them LRS team designation Ghost is ready for retrieval. Code word: Tango Charlie X-ray 975—mission complete. Do you have all that?"

McNally had found a room with some area maps and was scribbling down the sergeant's message. He had never heard of a missing team of Rangers, but that did not surprise him. Everything in the military is "need to know." He stood up and read the message back to the sergeant.

"I'll see to it the message gets to JSOC. Other than that, you're going to have to follow the river west. About thirty clicks and you'll intersect Dir Road. Head north on that road and call again when you're in a safe area. It'll help convince brass to send a chopper for you. If not, I'll steal a medical helicopter or something. Just get out of Mingora!" McNally said as he turned and saw a lieutenant colonel named Taney. "And God speed." McNally hung up the phone.

"Planning an unsanctioned flight, Lieutenant?" Taney asked.

"No, sir. I was just speaking with a Sergeant Emilio Gutierrez from an Army Ranger LRS team. He has a coded message for JSOC. Apparently, the team escaped their captors and now needs transportation out of Pakistan."

Taney's eyes widened. "The missing team was classified. What was their call sign?"

"Ghost."

"I'll be . . . How is it that of all the people on this base, this sergeant wound up talking to you?"

McNally wasn't sure how to take that question. "Yesterday I flew to Jalalabad and had a last-minute tag along, a muckraker, so I was told. He said he was with the *National Geographic,* but something didn't feel right so I gave him my number just in case he got in over his head. Apparently, he did. The only way we'll know if this is all on the level is to get this message to Command."

"I agree, but despite the outcome there will be no stealing any helicopters unless you want to spend the rest of your life in a military prison."

McNally smiled. "I gave them my word."

That obviously wasn't the reply the young lieutenant colonel had hoped for. "I'll go with you to see Command. Follow me." Taney spun on his heel.

Sergeant Gutierrez handed the phone back to Michael, who looked at the battery bars—the phone was nearly dead. He stuffed it into his pocket.

Gutierrez spoke with authority. "McNally said we've got a northbound road about thirty clicks due west. Dir Road is what he called it. We get to that road and find a safe place for pick up then call him back."

"Dir Road," Pike repeated. "Didn't it make the list of most dangerous roads in the world?"

Fulton cleared his throat. "We should get going. We have only a couple hours of light left. If we slog all night, we'll be to the road before dawn."

"I agree," Gutierrez said. "Fulton, go left, Pike, right, and make sure we don't have a gunner waiting for us." The men nodded and left. After a several minutes of breathless silence, they returned and reported—all clear.

"Move out," the sergeant ordered. Everybody stood.

"What are we going to do with the canister, Sarge?" Pike asked. All eyes went the canister. It was a danger to carry and even a greater hazard to leave behind, for in the wrong hands its destiny was utter destruction.

"I'll carry it." It was McGillis.

"How are you going to do that with a broken arm, ya dag?" Pike asked him. "It weighs about twenty pounds and will require both hands."

Michael shook his head. "It's my fault we have it. I'll carry it."

"I said I'd carry it!" McGillis barked. "Nobody takes me seriously. Just ignore me. Just ignore the private!"

Everyone watched him move toward the canister. McGillis had cut away most of his long robes, revealing his tattered trousers. He pulled the cut cloth through the canister's two handles and slung it over his shoulders, then called out, "We going to slog out these thirty clicks or just stand around?"

Gutierrez shook his head. "Let's go."

"Whining like a baby," Michael heard Pike mutter to Fulton.

Michael dropped to the back of the group and retrieved his cell phone from his pocket. He desperately needed to make more calls, yet knew the battery wouldn't hold. Calling his father was important, especially in regards to Colonel Bracken, but above all else he knew April would want to hear his voice and know he was alive. Oh, how he missed her.

It took a minute for the connections to be made, but it only rang once and April answered. "Hey, beautiful," Michael said. He heard her breath catch.

"Michael!" She began to cry. "Are you all right?"

"I'm good. So is Taylor. We're almost out. I don't have very much battery so I need you to get a message to my dad."

"All right . . ." Her voice quivered, and Michael could tell she was disappointed.

"Tell him Walter Bracken was behind all this. He sold out Taylor's team and even me."

"Those two guys from the military have been coming around. Do they have something to do with it?"

"They're actually the good guys. Hey, babe?"

"Yeah?"

"I love you. I'm sorry this has to be so short, but if I don't leave some battery for one more call, it'll be a long walk back to Afghanistan."

"I love you too, Michael."

"Kiss Suzanne for me."

"I will."

"Bye," he whispered. "I'll call soon."

"Bye," she replied, crying again. How he wished he could be there to wipe her tears away.

He reached up and wiped his own eyes, then turned the phone off to conserve the battery. He had fallen behind by several yards but now began to pick up his pace. Taylor looked back, and Michael waved that all was well.

Though they needed no encouragement to leave Mingora, their departure was accompanied by an increase of explosions and small-arms fire from the city. The beleaguered band had turned their eyes west, the Swat River on their right. As the battle worsened and the day progressed, the river became a conveyance of debris and the wreckages of war. From time to time, the gentle flow would carry a fallen body away from the place of its demise. Michael watched such a corpse bobbing in the water as the current carried it past. Whatever had been the fighter's purpose in going to war no longer mattered. Silently, Michael prayed his purposes would have a better outcome.

The setting sun found Aman Shamir studying a long procession of refugees as they poured out of the city and wound their way southwest. Peace-loving Pakistanis were vacating Mingora like rats from a sinking ship. Shamir was exhausted. The day had begun badly and was ending worse. He pinched the bridge of his nose. *Where are the Americans?*

From a distance he could see the charred remains of the explosion and hear the survivors' endless wailing. Landaki Road was a crater. No vehicles would leave Mingora for several days, at least.

Amid the chaos, the warden stood alone. The order to reconvene on Landaki Road had not been obeyed. Though it angered him, it did not surprise him. After all, common men were pitiful and weak, which made them so pliable under torture. Shamir imagined the guards running back to their families like frightened children.

"Pathetic," he muttered. He no longer wanted them or needed them. For all he cared, his years as the prison warden were over. The only thing that mattered now was erasing the insult and humiliation left by the Americans—and especially Nasira.

He closed his burning eyes. When he opened them again, he took a fresh view of his surroundings. Fifty meters away stood a three-story building, one of the last tall structures near the blast zone. Carrying a pair of binoculars, he went to the building, climbed the stairs on its face, and went to the edge of the roof. If his breathing was labored by the climb or his face began to sweat, he did not notice. All earthly cares were behind him now.

Holding the binoculars to his eyes, he gazed down upon the refugees and followed their sheep-like wanderings southward. Seeing nothing of interest, he widened his gaze and began to survey the entire area. The sun lingered long on the flat western horizon, and Aman Shamir continued his search for over an hour.

Suddenly, his luck changed. Near the river where the land fell away, he saw it. Like an inverted arrow marking the spot was the ridiculous ice cream cone.

"I have them," he said in a serpent's whisper.

He could not follow the river west to any great distance, but it did not matter. He had the scent of his prey now. They were his! They had always been his—his to desecrate, his to murder and destroy.

34

In a squat, four-story office building in the center of Victorville, California, Vander Sutton sat in a poorly lit lobby on the nearly vacant third floor. This was the address on the card given him by Agent Smith. Van glanced around, surprised by the lackluster appearance of his surroundings. While not a huge fan of TV crime dramas, he had watched enough to make him believe all such offices must be filled with activity and excitement.

Clearly those expectations had been false. In fact, where Van waited wasn't even a lobby but simply three chairs in a hallway. After exiting the elevator he had been greeted, or rather intercepted, by a guy Van guessed was Polynesian. Though Van insisted his business was urgent, the man, whose name tag read "Sammy," had invited him to sit. Van doubted the second invitation would be as pleasant, so he sat—or at least tried to. He found it difficult to be still.

"Did you contact Agent Wakefield or Smith?" he asked. "Did you tell them I was here?"

Sammy said nothing and simply took a bite of a sandwich the size of a dinner plate. While he ate, he studied the security monitors but seemed to always keep one eye on Van.

Van stood again. He craned his neck looking for Agent Wakefield. Low chatter spilled over oddly placed cubicle dividers, the only other sounds the occasional whir and click of a printer.

He had spoken to Wakefield a couple days previous, but the agent was as tight-lipped as ever. If the Defense Intelligence Agency knew anything, they were keeping it to themselves. A few hours ago, Van had received a phone call from April. Michael and Taylor were alive, but that is where the good news ended. To Van's disgust and horror, they claimed Walter Bracken had betrayed them. It took everything in Van not to go straight back to Bracken's office and give him the beating of a lifetime. After Van talked to his wife, a cooler head prevailed. Again he called Agent Wakefield, who agreed to meet.

Several minutes passed before Van saw the agent. Today, Wakefield wore no suit coat or tie, and the sleeves of his white shirt were rolled to the elbows. He merely paused near the entrance to the cubicle jungle and said, "Follow me."

Van glanced at Sammy and then followed the agent. He rubbernecked over the cubicles as he walked, much to the obvious displeasure of some of the occupants. What the office lacked in adornment, it made up for in the latest computer hardware.

Wakefield led Van into a corner office. Once the agent closed the door behind them, Van glanced around. The office was as simple as the rest of the floor—four plain white walls, a simple desk, and one slender window near the ceiling. Van would not have been surprised if the desk folded up for easy storage. The computer, again, was another matter.

"Please sit," Wakefield said. Van did. "Since our first visit, I did some reading up on you. It seems you and Colonel Bracken go way back."

"We do," Van replied, "but the reason I'm here—"

"We'll get to that," the agent interrupted. "We did quite a bit of digging to find this old file." He typed rapidly on his keyboard as he spoke. "We had to have it converted from microfiche, of all things. This file reads like a screenplay from an '80s war movie."

"I'm afraid I missed them," Van said, annoyed.

The agent reached up and with a slight tug removed the monitor from his computer and laid it on the desk. "You didn't miss much. Let's see . . . you and the colonel both volunteered and were going through basic training together. There was a draftee named Stanley Fairweather who completely lost it during the final weeks of training. Stanley began firing his weapon at anything that moved. You saved your friend Walter while catching a bullet in the thigh, subsequently ending your military career before it began. Stanley Fairweather did not survive the incident, and Walter went on to serve three tours in Vietnam, most notably in Cambodia, and has since gone on to become a colonel—a very powerful, well-liked colonel." Wakefield paused.

"And . . . ?"

"You are telling me that a man whose life you saved and who is overdue to be a general sold out his own men as well as set up a plot to get your other son involved? Why? To what end?"

Van felt his face turn red. "I do not know why or to what end, but I am telling you that is exactly what is going on here. Michael has no motive to fabricate this. He is with Taylor's team and they are trying to get out of Pakistan. They have proof that Walter Bracken sold them out. In fact they *are* the proof! I don't care if you believe me. When my sons get home, you'll see!"

Wakefield sat back in his chair. "I like your tenacity. I never said I didn't believe you. I just wanted to be sure of your conviction. My partner says this is a career killer—that whether we are right or wrong, the agent who brings this to light will be shopping mall security before week's end."

Van bristled. "So you're going to sweep this under the rug?"

"I didn't say that."

"So what are you saying?"

The agent leaned forward in his seat again. "That against my partner's objections and maybe my own good judgment, I am going to pursue this."

"Thank you."

"Don't thank me yet. The only reason I'm doing it is because I have high expectations of leadership. Regardless of rank, we should all be held accountable for our actions. I've started digging since we talked. It seems the colonel has covered his tracks well."

Van grunted. "What do you have so far?"

"A lot of nothing. Several encrypted phone calls, text messages, satellites going haywire at precise moments—there's a list but it all goes nowhere. Whoever is behind this has more clout than Colonel Bracken. I think that is what's scaring my partner off."

"I wish I could be more help," Van said. "The most I've seen of Walter has been just recently when he helped us plan this so-called rescue attempt."

Wakefield raised his eyebrows. "Even that took some string pulling. Someone is the puppet master here, and it may not be your old friend."

Van sighed. "I just wish I could help."

Wakefield stood and offered the older man his hand. "You have and you will again, I have no doubt."

Van left the office relieved that Wakefield was an idealist, but also very downhearted that Walter Bracken would do such horrible things. Somewhere in the back of Van's mind, he had almost hoped his sons were wrong, that somehow blame had been wrongly placed on the colonel. Van's family was his life, and to think that somebody—especially a friend—had conspired to take it from him! It was maliciousness beyond anything Van had ever imagined.

Later that night, Colonel Walter Bracken entered his unlit, army-issue apartment at 11:15, his tie hanging from an open collar. Exhausted, all he wanted was a glass of bourbon and a soft bed. The bureaucracy of middle management demanded a great deal; his eyes were set on upper management, where he would be the one handing down all the ignorant commands. In the darkness, he sighed and cursed.

"Time is up," said a voice from across the room.

The colonel froze in place. "What do you mean?" The voice was cold, monotone, and digitally masked, but not unfamiliar.

"You have failed. There has been communication between the surviving members of the Ranger team and a pilot at Bagram. JSOC has been contacted."

"There were unforeseen circumstances. The upheaval at Mingora happened too soon."

"It happened on schedule, I assure you. Your Suttons were a disaster."

"*My* Suttons? It was your General Rais who was a disaster. He was your pawn. I gift wrapped those men for him . . . for you!"

There was a pause. "Regardless, in a matter of hours you will be arrested for treason."

"What? You cannot throw me to the wolves! I'll . . . " The words caught in the colonel's throat. He had no recourse.

"You'll what?"

"Nothing." Leaving the light off, Walter slumped into his recliner.

"You knew the risks. We believed your desire for promotion was enough for you to get this done. But you have failed."

"If I go down for this, so help me, I will find you! There is still some fight left in this old war dog. I won't go to Leavenworth."

There was another pause. "Very well, there is one more chance to at least destroy the evidence against you. Do as I say and you'll never even see the inside of a court room. In fact, you may still have an opportunity to achieve your promotion. If this goes awry, however, you'll have to run."

"Like a coward? I'd rather die."

"Your treason will be worthy of death, if you prefer. But if you change your mind, we have a plan to get you out of the country."

"You'd do that for me?"

"We would. You have been loyal and we reward loyalty. You're a brilliant leader. It is wrong that you have been passed over for promotion for so long."

The subject was a sore spot for the colonel, and he looked away from the voice. "What do I need to do?"

"Because of the turmoil at Mingora, the Rangers will be instructed to head straight across the desert for Jalalabad. Your office will be sent false data that terrorists are heading for that city—"

"I got it." Walter sighed and shook his head—how had it come to this?

"You have reservations?"

"Just regrets."

"Perhaps your commitment is faltering."

"Don't patronize me," the colonel growled. "These are my men. Betrayal does not get easier with repetition."

"It will."

"And if things go badly?"

"If the extermination of the Rangers does not go well, and we will know, there will be a civilian plane sitting on the tarmac waiting for you at midnight. Runway 18. You are on your own, Colonel. We will not speak again."

Walter said nothing. The voice was not a friend or even friendly, and he doubted whether he should trust its owner with his life.

Finally, Walter turned on a lamp. He blinked in the light. The small, lonely house was empty, as he expected. Across the room on the coffee table sat a cell phone. The call timer recorded seven minutes and forty-six seconds, nearly the exact time he had been speaking with the voice. Whoever had delivered the phone had left only seconds before Walter had entered the house. He thought about that as he checked the call history. As always, unknown name, unknown number. Instantly, the phone got warm and went blank. The colonel tried to turn it on, but the phone was dead. *That's new,* he thought.

Across the continent, a man looked out his office window. Red lights flashed at the tip of the great granite obelisk of the Washington Monument. The hour was early, but an orchestrator's job was never done. He crushed out a cigarette as he ended the phone call with the colonel.

Bracken has outlived his usefulness and is in desperate need of retirement, the man thought. *But patience—all such things have a way of working themselves out.*

The man looked about his dark office. Though the colonel had turned out to be impotent, the man could understand ambition. He had ambitions of his own. His current office was square, but one day his office would be oval. He moved to the window in anticipation of the dawn and another glorious day in America.

35

With the sun setting in red splendor, the moon rose as a massive yellow globe and all things changed from brilliant gold to flat gray. Emilio Gutierrez and the others were grateful for the moonlight, for they had only two flashlights and no extra batteries. Also, with the demon at the door, they must remain invisible as long as possible. While they knew it was unlikely, they hoped to escape Pakistan without confronting the warden again.

Sounds of war disappeared into the night as cool air from the river enveloped the small group moving along its bank. Somewhere in the distance, a dog howled and a choir of toads croaked. Faint lights from small villages dotted the slopes along the river, and occasionally a man's voice would rise, cursing or laughing. The toads would pause at the interruption then continue their tireless serenade.

It was three in the morning when the weary travelers finally decided to stop. The river had been their guide since the moon had made it a glittering highway, but now the moon was setting and taking the light with her. During the long walk, Pike and Fulton had kept spirits up with a number of tunes including Joe Walsh's "Life's Been Good" and Bill Withers' "Ain't No Sunshine," but now the singing had stopped. It was time to get some sleep.

Up ahead a wide sandbar opened, as inviting as a king-size mattress. When the group reached it, packs slipped from weary shoulders and dropped inaudibly onto the sand. Seven exhausted bodies scattered themselves like blown leaves across the small white beach.

Before he fell asleep Gutierrez looked at Nasira, curled up and using a pack for a pillow. She appeared so slight in the darkness, yet he marveled at her strength, at all she must have endured over the years. He thought of the silly concerns of other women he'd known and how silly they seemed next to hers. He would do everything in his power to see her restored to her family.

The Sutton brothers lay within speaking distance of each other. "Have you ever seen such a clear sky?" Michael said.

"Only a thousand times from the top of Mt. Timpanogos."

"Sure, but the sky wasn't this clear."

Taylor chuckled. "We can't agree on anything. But they were good times."

"I thought you hated those trips—all you did was complain."

"I didn't hate them as much I said I did. I was just too prideful to admit Dad was right, that I'd have a good time." Taylor paused. "It's a difficult thing, Mike."

"What is?"

"Swallowing pride. It gets stuck somewhere around the diaphragm, making it hard to breathe. And here you come, even after all the things I've said and done, showing up to rescue me like some idiot and almost getting yourself killed."

Michael laughed softly. "You saved my life once. I had to at least try."

Taylor lifted his head and looked at his brother. "Is that what drove you to come? That makes you a bigger idiot yet!"

"Probably, but you're also my brother, and you'd do the same. And it's not like I'm going to make a habit of saving your butt. Next time you're on your own. Besides, April would kill me. Speaking of, we can never tell her about the assassin."

"Is that fear I hear in your voice?" Taylor laughed.

Michael chuckled. "You know it."

After a short pause Taylor said, "I'll only tell her that you made our failed mission a success and that countless lives are indebted to you. How about that?"

"Ugh. Tell her about the assassin instead."

"I should at least say thank you."

"You're right, you should."

"I just did—that was it."

"I guess I missed it."

Both brothers laughed softly, and then there was silence again. Before long, Michael was snoring. Taylor closed his eyes as the night sky, hung from Polaris, rotated above the earth, bringing the inevitable dawn.

Unlike the Swat River, which flows due west, Landaki Road bends south. Once Aman Shamir escaped the ravages near the city and the carnage left by the truck bomb, he followed Landaki until it intersected with Dir Road. He knew the Americans would stay in the lowlands near the river, and that Nasira would be with them. Shamir took Landaki because unlike other crossings, this road had a modern, elevated bridge, giving him an excellent vantage point. This was his land; his ancestors had drenched the soil with their blood for generations. Any moment the land would open up to him and reveal his prey.

Shamir perched hawk-like on the bridge and watched as the sun became a memory and everything turned flat and gray under the moonlight. Making use of night-vision binoculars, he sought with soulless eyes. The escapees would come—that much he knew. He continued his silent searches until the early hours when the moon slipped over the far horizon. Still he waited, brooding and cold, nearly vacant of human emotion.

When the eastern sky began to lighten, it brought only disappointment that he had not exacted his desires during the night. But what did he care, really? Daylight or dark, he would have them.

It was time to act.

Shortly after six when the sun began to bake the sand bar, having given the weary travelers a mere three hours of uninterrupted sleep. The early rays of day found the vertical plutonium canister, and the metallic surface reflected the light into the reeds and brush.

Gutierrez awoke to sore and stiff muscles—the sand had not been as friendly as it first appeared. He reached for Nasira, but she was gone. The sergeant came quickly to his knees. Blinking, he looked around.

"She went into the brush ten minutes ago," McGillis said. He sat cross-legged in the sand and had obviously been awake longer than the others. "Figure she needed to go to the bathroom."

"You didn't go with her? Or wake me?" Gutierrez stood and craned his neck in hopes of spotting her.

McGillis also stood. "She's a big girl, Sergeant. I'm sure she knows what to do."

"You moron! I mean to guard her. We still have the warden out there, remember?"

"I didn't think of that." McGillis lowered his eyes. "Maybe he gave up and went home."

"You wish. People like him don't go home. Ten minutes . . ." Gutierrez grumbled to himself. "She should be back by now."

During the exchange, the others had joined them. Gutierrez turned to face them. "Nasira's missing. Grab a weapon and spread out. Let's hope she's all right."

After thirty minutes of searching, the group rejoined where crop fields and rice paddies spread wide and flat, offering no place for hiding. Their searches had proved fruitless. Nasira had vanished.

"We can't leave without her," Gutierrez said.

"Why? You in love, Sergeant?" McGillis asked sarcastically.

Gutierrez had had enough and laid out Private McGillis with a solid right hook. The force of it appeared to nearly break the smaller man's jaw, and McGillis did not get up for more.

"I believe the rest of us are with you," Ian Pike said. "If it wasn't for the sheila, we would still be in those cells."

"We would be dead," added Fulton. "We owe her our lives."

"How are we going to find her, Sergeant?" Michael asked.

The men had circled to face each other to discuss how they should proceed, when Gutierrez heard sobs from behind them. In unison, the men turned to look where McGillis sat. He was crying.

"I did it again," he whimpered. "I just want to go home. Can't you understand that?"

"We all want to go home, Private," the sergeant said, trying to keep his temper in check. "But if you can't hold your head up when you get home, there is no point in going."

McGillis nodded but continued to sob. "I know . . . I know. But here I am doing it again."

"Doing what again?"

"I'm the reason Cobb is dead." The private held his legs to his chest.

"What'd you say, you stumpy ocker?" Pike took a step forward. Gutierrez put a hand on his chest to hold him back.

"When we were in the torture chambers . . . " McGillis began to rock slightly, cradling his broken arm. "The warden . . . hurt my arm so bad. He promised we'd all go home if I'd just tell him who had killed his guard. So I told him." Tears poured down the private's cheeks. "I just want to go home!"

Pike jumped passed the sergeant's extended arm, clearly ready to avenge his friend. It took Taylor, Michael, and Fulton to hold him back.

"Pike!" Gutierrez growled. "That's enough!" Pike wrenched himself free and walked a short distance away.

"What do you mean, you're doing it again?" asked Gutierrez."

McGillis rocked and tucked his head into his knees. "I just want to go home."

"Tell me what you mean, Private!"

"I thought if we couldn't find her, we'd just go."

"Tell me!"

"I . . . I saw marks in the sand. Footprints, drag marks . . . tire tracks . . . a half a click west. I . . . I'm sorry."

As soon as the sergeant heard the direction, he turned and ran, as did Michael, Taylor, and Fulton. Pike lingered for a moment to say, "This ain't over, ya filthy traitor." McGillis glanced up but continued to rock back and forth.

Just as the private had reported, there were signs of a struggle, with tire tracks heading away. Breathing heavily, Gutierrez looked around in bewilderment. This was a mere twenty or thirty yards from where they had spent the night. "How could this have happened?" he said aloud. "I should have been more careful!"

36

It had been mere happenstance when Aman Shamir stumbled upon the girl in the bushes. From his perch on the bridge he realized a bend in the river was obstructed from his view by a thicket of underbrush. A dirt track used by field laborers ran between the river and the fields. Shamir took this trail, believing it would take him close to the obstructed bend. As he left the road, he had also caught a glint of sunlight from something metallic and this gave him hope.

Not wanting to disturb his quarry, Shamir slowed the Jeep to a crawl. The muffled engine sputtered softly and pushed the tires through the sand. A short distance from the road, he pressed the clutch and let the sand stop his progression. He left the engine running and slid from the Jeep.

Pistol in hand, he had begun to work through the brush when Nasira appeared before him as though she had materialized right out of the earth itself. It was a sign. *She is mine! She will always be!*

Her eyes went wide with horror, and Shamir feared she would scream. She turned to run, but before she could, he was on her as a rabid animal on fresh quarry. He covered her mouth tightly and held the muzzle of the gun to her throat.

"Say a word and you're dead," he whispered. He inhaled deeply. He had almost forgotten how wonderful she smelled.

Nasira squirmed and fought, tears pouring from her eyes. Her first attempt to scream had not even raised a squeak; Shamir smiled as he realized how frightened she was.

Once he got her under control, the warden whipped her around and grabbed a handful of her hair. Looking her in the eye, he pressed the pistol into the soft flesh below her chin.

"If you come with me, I will not kill your friends."

She shook her head.

"No?" he said. "Then you leave me no choice." He let go of her hair and clubbed her in the head, knocking her unconscious, then hoisted her onto his shoulder and moved toward the idling Jeep.

As he trudged through the soft sand, he thought about the Americans. He grimaced under the effort to carry the girl. He could surprise them—kill them. His heart leapt at the thought. He would return and kill them before they knew he was there.

He loaded her into the back of the Jeep, careful not to strike her head against any sharp objects. She was nothing to him dead. Using a rope, he lashed her wrists and ankles together and then to an eyelet in the Jeep. He did not need her running away while he finished off the Americans.

At that moment fate intervened.

As Shamir laid Nasira into the back of the Jeep, a branch that had been pushed up the bank from a previous flood caught between his ankles and the Jeep tire, causing him to pitch forward. The fall was only a minor irritation, but from nowhere a black, oil-skinned serpent appeared and struck him on his wrist.

Fangs tore deep into the flesh before the snake jerked quickly away. On his knees, Shamir watched in horror as the snake slipped out of sight. *Does it not know who I am?*

The warden looked at his wrist, two pinpricks the only evidence of the bite. He needed a hospital right away, but he balked at the thought of leaving. The Americans lay right there, not a hundred yards away. A dozen rounds from his pistol would do the trick. Shamir felt his pulse beat hard in his hand and swore aloud. He hated nothing more than missed opportunities.

After turning the Jeep around, he headed back the way he'd come. He had one, maybe two hours at best. Once he regained the gravel road, he laid into the throttle. Already losing feeling in his hand, he had to focus on grip and movement as he worked through the gears. Landaki Road was not far ahead.

Shamir thought about the snake, a common krait that caused innumerable deaths every year. A man would be better off to have been bitten by almost anything else. He thought about its manner—to strike and destroy so indifferently, then move on without regard. How dare it! If he survived this, he would find that snake and strip its flesh and roast it over a fire while it squirmed for life.

The warden's hand and forearm tingled now as though they were going to sleep. The cool morning air rushed past his face, his sweat making him chill. An approaching sign read "Mingora 50 km." *I can make it,* he thought.

Dir Road merged with Landaki Road and he kept the throttle down. Shamir felt the poison move across his chest and into his other arm. Presently there was a writhing in his stomach that bent him forward against the pain. Cold, emotionless serpents began to slither through his thoughts.

Landaki Road was nearly empty with all the action in the city, leaving the warden free to drive as fast as possible. It took all his strength to keep his hands tightly fastened to the steering wheel.

In the back of the Jeep, Nasira struggled against her own pain. Wind whipped her hair viciously against her cheeks and eyelids. In her aching mind, it felt like stinging bees. She fought against the bees but they kept at her. A hard bounce in the Jeep woke her. The bees were gone, but her hair continued its assault on her pounding head.

Without looking, she knew who was driving and where they were going. She recalled the endless days hidden away in the tiny, dark apartment. Going back there would be worse than dying. She kept her face covered for a long time as she cried. She would not give her captor the benefit of seeing her tears.

The vehicle soon began to slow and then suddenly jerked to a standstill in the middle of the highway. Nasira sat up and looked around. The road was clear. She expected to hear the warden's devilish voice, but there was nothing. She turned her head and saw him slumped over the steering wheel, sweaty and pale.

She pulled at the rope for several minutes but could not break free. It was so unlike Shamir not to have tried to stop her that she looked at him again. He appeared to be very ill.

"Cut me loose," she shouted. "What's wrong? Cut me loose!"

The warden managed to reach back to her with a double-edge knife but lost his grip. The knife toppled to the floor next to her. She quickly retrieved it and with great effort cut the rope.

After extricating herself from the back of the Jeep, she stood. The warden produced a pistol and pointed it at her. "Drive me," he demanded. "Drive me or I'll . . . " His voice trailed off and the pistol fell from his hands to the pavement below.

Nasira looked up and down the highway. It was still empty. "What happened to you?" she asked more out of astonishment than concern.

"Snakebite," he muttered.

She sighed. "You need a hospital." She felt the pity she might have for any wounded animal. "I'll take you."

Shamir stared at her, his face full of perplexity and pain.

"Because I am not like you," she said, knowing his thoughts.

With difficulty she moved his nearly paralyzed body from the driver's seat. She knew that every pump of his heart pushed the poison farther and farther through his system.

"What do I do?" she asked once she sat in the driver's seat.

"Depress that peddle." Shamir pointed at the clutch. "Then twist the key." He groaned.

Nasira started the Jeep.

He pointed at the gearstick. "Start with first gear and then move to second using the clutch."

Nasira fumbled with the clutch and the gearstick, but after several grinding attempts she managed to get the Jeep rolling. She glanced at the warden and marveled how frail and pathetic he looked, curled up against his pain. If he died it would be a fitting end for a man who caused others so much agony. At the thought of his death she waited for feelings of sorrow, but none came.

But I will not have this man's death on my conscience, even if he is a monster, she decided. It would be her last affront to him that, in spite of his cruelty to her, she had remained pure and aloof.

The warden disturbed her thoughts. "You are my angel," he said in a voice that was nearly inaudible above the rushing wind and drone of the tires.

"No, I am not," she replied coldly. "I have been your prisoner and that is all. You are nothing to me, and after you die, I will never think of you again. There is not a soul on this earth who will ever think of you again."

Shamir doubled over in the seat, and though he could not even groan, she knew his soul screamed in pain.

On the outskirts of Mingora at the village of Owdi Gram, Nasira found a large white tent with a red cross on it. Some brave individuals had already set up shop to help those displaced by the fighting. She drove to the tent and stopped just short of colliding with an abandoned car. Shamir jostled incoherently and nearly fell out of the Jeep. Nasira went to the tent and found someone to help her carry him.

"What happened to him?" asked the young man who came to her aid. He and another intern moved Shamir to a gurney.

The warden writhed as if every touch felt like fire. His breaths came quickly and short.

"Bit by a snake," Nasira said. "That is all I know."

"How long ago?" The two men hoisted the warden.

"An hour or so . . . I am not certain."

"We'll do what we can for him." Carrying Shamir, the two men disappeared into the tent.

Nasira turned. She was free to leave. She was free—free forever! The warden was going to die. Wasn't he? She stopped. She had to know for certain.

She went to the tent door and paused. The idea of being surrounded by the wounded and dying made her uncomfortable, but she took a breath and entered.

Inside the hospital tent were dozens of cots and several operating tables, some with curtains drawn. The tent was nearly full to capacity with victims of the war. There was endless groaning and weeping, and Nasira could not help but cry at the sight of so much suffering. She wanted to turn and run from the heart-wrenching scene, yet in her heart she knew she must see the end of Aman Shamir. To know for certain he could never haunt her again. At the far end of the tent she watched as the interns laid him on a table, his body convulsing.

Shamir wanted to scream as the gurney was set down. A needle inserted into his arm without warning felt like a knife. His dying nerves burned, and even the movement of air fanned the flames. Black, consuming serpents now overran his mind, making his whole body writhe. His own silent screams were at once joined by a chorus, a chorus of the tortured . . . and the damned. They felt both foreign and familiar. As the chorus grew, thrashing dragons tightened their embrace on the warden's soul.

Suddenly a visage appeared as if through obsidian glass. The warden knew the face, the angelic face.

A voice said, "It is too late. Was he a friend or family?"

"A stranger," the angel replied. "I did not know him at all."

It was then that the oil-skinned serpents consumed Aman Shamir. He fell away into a scorching blackness to join the choir of the damned.

One of the men who had carried the dying warden reached up and closed the cold, dead eyes. He looked at Nasira and asked, "If you did not know this man, how did you come to be with him?"

"By pure accident," she replied honestly. "Can I exit through the back?" She did not want to look at the suffering and broken bodies behind her.

Outside, Nasira was greeted by a fresh draft of air as though it had just rained. She gasped and then spun around in a circle, her arms extended. She was free—absolutely free! Her heart instantly turned toward home, and she thought for an instant that she caught the fragrance of her mother's perfume carried on the wind. She wondered briefly how to proceed, but then she gathered her wits and remembered the Americans.

Private First Class Todd McGillis sat in the dirt, his face aching and his mouth bleeding. He rubbed his jaw through his thin, blond beard. The sergeant had a strong right hook and McGillis knew he deserved it. He sat there in the silence of early day trying to get his head right.

He had let his desire to go home outweigh anything or anyone. He felt selfish and immature. Ranger training had prepared him for a great many things, but imprisonment and torture in a foreign cesspool had not been aptly covered. That could stand as his excuse, but ultimately the burden of his actions rested with him.

The sun was warm, the sky clear, and sweat trickled into his eyes. He had sat alone for almost a half hour when he noticed the sergeant moving briskly toward him.

As McGillis moved to stand, a drop of blood fell into the dirt near his ankle. He reached for his mouth. No blood, only a fat lip. He pulled his hand away and found another drop on the back of his hand. He felt his nose and found more. *Hmm,* he thought, *the sergeant throws a mean punch.*

He cleaned himself up before Gutierrez reached him. When he was within earshot, McGillis spoke. "I need to apologize for my behavior, sir."

"Save it for later. We gotta go." The sergeant motioned for the private to follow, which he promptly did.

"What's the plan, sir?"

"Not much. The others went to get the supplies. We'll meet up with them in a minute."

"Are we going after the girl?"

"Yes, as fast as we can."

37

Vander Sutton fell exhausted onto Michael's couch. He had gone to Victorville again and visited with Agent Wakefield, but there was nothing new. Granted, it had only been a day, but Van was growing impatient. He was not a young man, and all this activity and stress made him feel older yet. Soon, he rolled off the couch and knelt before his Maker and poured out his heart, pleading that his sons might be speedily delivered home.

Then Van stood and wiped the tears from his eyes. He looked at the clock. He missed his dear Claire, who would be waiting for a report of the day's events. On the coffee table lay his cell phone; he hated how minuscule it was. He went to the kitchen and started the fixings for a sandwich, then dialed home from the landline.

After the second ring, his wife answered with "It's about time."

"I know."

"I bought you a cell phone and you never answer it. You never even turn it on."

"I don't want the battery to run down," Van replied. "Then it would be no good to me if I really needed it."

Claire gave a frustrated sigh but said nothing more about the phone. Van knew it was a sore subject.

He related the outcome of his meeting with Agent Wakefield. Van had always been gifted with brevity, and this took him no longer than two minutes.

"If you could only get Walter to confess," Claire remarked.

"How would I do that?"

"Confront him. It seems to work in the movies. Make him mad. I know you're good at that."

"Thanks for the support," Van said sarcastically. "But you may be right." He looked at the clock. "Ask April if they have a small recorder in the house."

"All right, just a sec," Claire said.

As Van waited, he finished putting together the sandwich that would be his dinner. His wife came back on the line as he took a big bite.

"She said there is a small digital recorder in the spare room upstairs. It'll be in one of the desk drawers."

"Sounds good," Van said, his voice muffled with food.

"Are you talking with your mouth full, dear?"

He and cleared his throat. "No . . . of course not. Actually, I'm eating a sandwich. I'm starved."

"My husband, always thinking of his stomach."

"There's a lot there to think about," he said, laughing. "Hey, I'm going to let you go. I'm going to get that recorder and see if I can get a confession out of ol' Walt."

"Be safe," Claire said.

"I'll let you know how it goes. Love you."

Walter Bracken looked at his watch—12:00 midnight. The problem of running a war on the opposite side of the globe was that eventually one finds himself working too late. He entered the apartment, locked the door, and promptly turned on a lamp.

He waited in the silence for half a minute. Nothing. No soulless voice, just good old-fashioned silence. He let out a beleaguered sigh, pulled his tie from his neck, and went to a shelf filled with old vinyl records. After finding a favorite, he slipped it from its sleeve and set it on an old record player. He set the needle and moved to his bar.

Before Walter had poured a glass of bourbon, Don Williams began to sing "I Believe in You," Walt's favorite drinking song. It reminded him of a time when the world was a simple place.

Between the bourbon and the music, he hoped to forget that under false pretenses, he had convinced the Joint Chiefs to close the Pakistan–Afghan border. The standing order was DSK—or Detain, Stop, or Kill. Nobody was getting across that border, no matter who they said they were.

Walter had just settled into his recliner, where he knew he would eventually pass out, when he heard a knock at the door. He sighed and looked at his watch again. *At this hour?* He set down his glass and retrieved a pistol. "Who is it?" he barked.

"It's Van. Open up!"

Walter stuffed the gun between the seat and arm of his chair, then went to unlock the door and let it swing wide. "Any word from your boys, old friend?" he asked in a friendly tone.

Van promptly punched Walter square in the mouth. As Walt fell back, Van let himself in and shut the door. "Yeah, I heard from them, *old friend.* I just got to know why."

"I have no idea what you mean."

"Stop it, Walt. It's just me and you—two old men getting to the bottom of it."

Walter stood and felt his split lip. "You still have a wicked right, Van. But I can't help you."

"Still listening to Don after all these years?" Van said. "What memory you drowning tonight?"

"I have no idea what you talking about." Walter moved to the record player and shut it off.

"I know you better than you think. The first time you got drunk to that song was when little Mary Rosedale dumped you for Carl Plimpton. We were, what . . . three maybe four weeks into basic? What you washing way tonight?"

"You need to leave, Van."

"Not before I get some answers, Walt. Ever since Stanley Fairweather went off his rocker, you've had a thorn in your side about me. I've felt the animosity to varying degrees over the years but never brought it up. Originally, I thought it was jealousy because of all the attention I received, but it only got worse after you returned from 'Nam. I figured you'd get over it. But here we are, over forty years later, and you still can't get past it. I saved your life that day, Walt. Was that so bad?"

"You have no idea."

"No? So why don't you tell me?"

The colonel went to his recliner and picked up the full glass and bottle. "Look around here, Van. You see any family photos? Any loves lost? No, all I have is the service, and I'm not going to lose her. If I can't make general, I will retire poor and die alone." He set the bottle on his wet bar but kept the glass and took a drink.

"You're blaming me for that? It was your choice to never start a family."

"No, it wasn't. By the time Vietnam was through with me, there was no love left. I killed so many people over there, and not all of them carried weapons. Sure, they promote you for being a good soldier, but that does little to stop the monsters in your head. For ten years after that war, I would wake up in the middle of the night in a cold sweat, screaming. You have no idea how much pain you were spared because you took a bullet for me."

"If it makes you feel better having me to blame, fine," Van said sharply. "But take it out on me and leave my family out of it! My boys did nothing but respect you. When I heard Taylor would be under your command, I was hopeful. I thought you would keep him safe. But you sold them out! For what? So you could become a general? You're a traitor!"

Walter sighed. "You don't get it, Van. If I had taken a bullet that day everything would be different. I would have gone home.

I would have had a normal life and you would be the one in my shoes. You live in a rose-colored world, and it is time you had some cold, hard reality. The best way to do that is by losing the ones you love the most."

"You really don't have a clue about me, Walt. Maybe you never did. Let me tell you something you don't know. I believe my family ties will go beyond the grave. Death cannot take them from me, because of covenants we have made with God in holy places. Unfortunately for you, in the next life you'll still be alone."

Walter Bracken almost choked on his bourbon. "Are you really going to talk to me about religion? You diluted old man. At my word, I can snatch away the life of your boys, and you want to preach to me?" He laughed. "Wow, Van, I have no idea how we were ever friends. Only cowards and women hide behind religion."

Van took a step toward Walter, startling him, and he nearly spilled his drink.

"Yeah, I'm the coward." Van chuckled and moved to the door, but turned to say, "When you go down for this, Colonel, take your medicine like a man."

Walter shattered his glass against the wall, narrowly missing Van's face. Van shook his head and let himself out.

Van stepped out into the night and walked to the parking lot. A firm wind blew from the mountains, moving dirt and dried leaves in waves across the pavement. He got into his car and pulled a small digital recorder from his pocket. He pressed "play."

"Any word from your . . ." said the voice of a man Van had thought he knew but perhaps never did.

He pushed "stop" and started the car.

38

Six men moved in single file down the dirt road at a pace faster than a jog but not a full run. Double time, as they called it. Fulton, who had the longest and steadiest stride, led the others. The crunching of gravel beneath their feet and the lonely buzz of cicada were all that could be heard above the men's steady but accelerated breathing. For almost an hour they had been on the move, since mid-morning. Though the air still felt cool, the temperature was rising and the men were sweating. They carried only weapons and water. Michael was grateful for his habit of taking a morning run, but jogging with a gun in his hand was new.

"So we came . . . halfway 'round the world . . . to chase a sheila," Pike said between breaths. "I could have stayed home . . . and not have to chase them at all."

In the hazy distance, a dark speck appeared on the road. Fulton reported it to the others but never broke stride. The speck grew into an approaching vehicle, and Fulton slowed his pace. Friend or foe, they would know soon enough, Michael thought.

"Should we commandeer the vehicle, sir?" Taylor said.

Gutierrez chuckled. "You not enjoying this run?"

"No, sir."

The words had hardly escaped Taylor's lips before the Jeep, approaching at a reckless speed, was upon them. The men lifted their weapons and signaled the driver to stop. The commandeering was poorly planned and miserably executed, and the Jeep nearly ran over Gutierrez before the driver, obviously out of control, brought the vehicle to a fishtailing halt amid a storm of dust and gravel.

As the dust settled, the driver came bounding out of the jeep, looking as giddy as any girl after her first joyride. "Wow! Did you see me? Driving is fun!"

"Nasira?" said the men almost in unison. She ran to them and wrapped her arms around anyone she could get hold of. Her excitement was contagious and the men began to fire off questions, most beginning with "How" or "What."

Standing in the middle of the road, she explained the events of that morning and especially the demise of her long-time captor. She seemed unable to contain her glee as she reveled in the freedom she had not experienced since she was a child.

Soon the excitement waned and the task of getting home became all the more pressing, for the only thing keeping them from it was a phone call to Lieutenant McNally.

"You should call him, Michael," his brother said. "This must be Dir Road."

"Yeah, and tell him to bring some water. I'm as dry as a drover's dog." Pike was sitting on the bumper of the Jeep with a boot off, dumping out at least a cup of dirt. "Or some stubbies. I could do for a stubby, too."

McNally's phone rang and he pounced on it. "Michael!" he said almost before the line connected. "We expected your call much sooner."

"We had complications," Michael reported. "But we are at Dir Road and have been for some time now. When can we expect a chopper?"

"I'm sorry, Michael. With the outbreak of war in North Pakistan, the powers that be won't allow any air traffic. They're afraid it may be interpreted as hostile."

"What? That's crap and you know it!"

"Yeah . . . yeah I do. I was just sitting in a room full of brass and we all know it's crap. Just more bureaucratic bull, but our hands are tied."

"So what? They expect us to walk back to Afghanistan?"

McNally didn't know how to respond.

"You're kidding me! That's got be a few hundred miles."

The lieutenant heard Michael relay the information to the others. When there was a pause, McNally said, "I'm sorry, Michael, but that's not the worst of it. Put the sergeant on."

A moment later, the voice of Emilio Gutierrez came on the line. "What's going on over there, McNally?"

"I wish I knew. Not only has air traffic been grounded, but DSK has also been ordered for all ground traffic in and out of Pakistan."

"Detain, Stop, or Kill? But not for us, right? They'll let us through if we reach a border check? Lieutenant? What about my message?"

"I don't know. It's a blanket order from the Joint Chiefs. That's the final word. Everything is muddled and confused. All I can do is give you the best route out of Pakistan where we won't be looking."

The sergeant sighed. "Fine. What is it?"

McNally moved to a computer screen where a satellite image was displayed.

"Do you guys have transportation?" McNally asked.

Gutierrez glanced at the small Jeep. "Sort of."

"Good. Since you're on Dir Road, just take it north. Everything to the south is a mess. You'll come to a river and Khazan Bridge. Cross the bridge and take the road west. That is Munda Khar Road. Stay on Munda Khar for about fifty clicks. Another road, Bajaur Road, will take you due west and over the mountains.

Once over the mountains you'll be in Afghanistan and I'll come get you. I wish there was more I could do."

After repeating the instructions, Gutierrez said, "Lieutenant, I need to get another message to JSOC. General Herbert specifically. Tell him we have evidence that Colonel Walter Bracken is a traitor. Also, we need to get in touch with the State Department. Ten years ago, an American girl disappeared in Pakistan while traveling with her parents. Her name is Nasira Habeeb and she is with us."

"I'll do what I can, Sergeant," McNally said. "See you soon."

"God willing," Gutierrez replied.

The line went dead.

"That's it?" Fulton exclaimed. "All they can do is give us directions that will take us back into Afghanistan? We did the escaping. That was the hard part."

"Welcome to the army, mate," Pike said.

They had been so close, or at least they thought so, but now it seemed they were a million miles away.

After a moment of heavy silence, Gutierrez spoke. "It's nearly noon. If we hurry and don't have any problems we might be out of Pakistan by dark. Everyone into the Jeep. We'll drive back, get our supplies, and turn our backs on this dirt trap forever."

The seven of them had a hard time fitting into the Jeep, but with some effort they managed it. In the driver's seat, Gutierrez looked at the gas gauge—the last visible obstacle to a speedy return. There was a half a tank. He doubted it would be enough.

The road back to the sandbar seemed to take an eternity, as is the case when hearts are heavy. Near the river, Sergeant Gutierrez found the side road and took it. Nasira, who sat next to him, was visibly solemn as they halted almost exactly where she had been abducted earlier that day. Gutierrez stopped the Jeep, shut it off, and looked at her.

"Are you all right?" he asked.

"Yes . . . I will be."

"Hey, Sarge, we'll grab the stuff," Fulton said. "Let's go, guys."

Five of them sprang from the back of the Jeep and disappeared into the reeds and underbrush separating them from the river.

"I was just right there." Nasira pointed into the brush. "He was so quick." She shuddered and took a deep breath. "I told him I would never think of him again after he died. But it will be difficult."

Gutierrez looked at her in pity. "Of course it will. He held you captive for a very long time. But one thing I know is that you are strong, and that as you fill up your life with good things, the bad ones will be pushed away."

Nasira smiled.

39

Before they had left in pursuit of Nasira, the Rangers had stashed their supplies at the west end of the sandbar where a heavy branch had landed against the reeds, creating a blind. They doubted anyone would come along but knew better than to take chances.

"Where's the canister?" McGillis asked.

"We buried it in the sand right there." Taylor pointed to a hump in the sand. "Right near that rock."

McGillis went to the hump. As he unburied the canister, he noticed the rock was not a rock but a turtle—a freshly dead turtle.

.At that moment another drop of blood fell onto the side of the metallic canister. "What the . . . " McGillis said as he reached for his nose. The bleeding was an early sign of a painful end.

He turned to the others, who were drinking water and digging for a good flavor of MRE. It was obvious to him now that the canister was leaking. Having made so many poor decisions lately, he hardly trusted himself with this one. If they were traveling in any other way, he would have carried it again, but as it was they would all be poisoned before they reached home. Leaving the canister, he walked to the others.

"What is it, whingey chook?" Pike's tone showed his disgust for the private.

"There's a problem with the canister. I think it's leaking."

McGillis knew he had their attention.

"What makes you think that?" asked Michael, who had been the last steward of the canister.

"I've been getting nosebleeds. At first I thought they were from getting punched by the sergeant, but I just had another one. And there was a turtle crawling near the canister. It's dead."

The men moved with caution to the shallow hole containing the canister. Standing the farthest away, Fulton mumbled, "I'm afraid of only two things in this world. Rats and dying from radiation sickness."

"Only two?" Taylor said. "I've seen the way you jump when it comes to snakes and spiders."

"Okay, four things. But radiation is still on the list. What do we do?"

"We gotta bury it deep," someone suggested.

"Where? It can't be near the water. It'll poison the river if the leak gets worse."

"Out in the desert," McGillis said. "I'll carry it."

Just then Nasira and the sergeant joined them. "What's the hold up?" Gutierrez asked. "We need to be going."

"We have a problem, sir." Fulton still stood the farthest away.

"What now?"

"The canister is leaking, and McGillis has been having nosebleeds."

"There's a dead turtle over here that wasn't there this morning," Taylor added. "I was the one who buried the canister this morning. I remember now that it was warm, too. But maybe that's normal."

Michael shook his head. "It wasn't warm when I loaded it in the truck yesterday. Something must have happened."

"Has anyone else shown signs of poisoning?"

No one spoke up. "All right then," Gutierrez said, "I heard you guys saying something about the desert. I agree we can't bury it here. How we going to get rid of it?"

McGillis walked forward.

"Wait," the sergeant said.

But McGillis plucked the canister out of the hole and carefully slung the strap over his shoulder. He turned, and noticing the other Rangers' disbelieving looks, he said, "Well, let's get going."

"Uh, yes, you're right," the sergeant replied after several seconds. "Everybody stay up wind from the canister. Let's move. The longer McGillis is exposed, the worse he'll have it."

As they approached the Jeep, the sergeant ordered Pike and the others to drive ahead and start digging a hole. Since there were no shovels, they had to use whatever they could find.

"Nasira, please ride with them," Gutierrez said. "I am going to walk with the private." She nodded.

The sergeant looked up at the sun, which was straight up and leaning west. They were wasting time and precious gasoline, but it couldn't be helped. He and McGillis watched as the Jeep drove away.

"Why are you doing this, Private? You're a good soldier—you don't have anything to prove." Gutierrez stayed upwind and ten yards away.

"It's my fault Cobb's dead, sir. It's my fault the girl was taken this morning. Heck, I probably caused this thing to start leaking. I need to prove to myself that I can do something right."

Several minutes passed in silence before Gutierrez said, "My first CO used to tell us something when we let the unit down. He'd say nothing is gained by sacrificing yourself on the altar of self-loathing. You have to shrug off the chains of the past and conquer the moment."

"That's deep," McGillis replied.

"He considered himself a philosopher. Of course he usually followed up by making us run till we threw up. I think that was the 'conquer the moment' part."

McGillis smiled and then asked somberly, "Do you think this canister is going to kill me, sir?"

"I don't know. But I promise you I'll do everything I can to get your ugly butt back to the world. I bet the doctors will fix you right up."

"I hear radiation can give you cancer."

"Try not to think about it."

They walked on, following the Jeep tracks. The tracks left the riverbank, crossed Dir Road, and headed into the desert. McGillis's nose bled again. They had not gone a mile when they saw the Jeep.

"Leave the canister here," Gutierrez said. "Let's go see how the hole is coming."

The hole was going slow, terribly slow. Drenched in sweat, all four men had obviously taken a turn with a rock or stick trying to get through the rocky soil. Pike looked up from digging and said, "Nice of you to join us, sir." He stopped to catch his breath. "I can't imagine anything being better than this. Digging a hole in the middle of the desert on a hot day and there's nothing but rocks. Makes me excited to be alive! And better yet, we're running low on water."

"He's right," Taylor said. "We can't keep going. Even if we had shovels, this would take too long."

"Maybe I could help," Nasira said.

"How could you help?" Pike growled. "You gonna dig?"

She turned and walked to the Jeep.

Pike gave a smug snort and started to dig again. Suddenly a grenade landed in the shallow hole. Pike fell back and scrambled away.

Nasira chuckled. "I didn't pull the pin!"

Everyone laughed, and Pike sank to the ground in obvious relief. "I'm going to kill her," he mumbled. Then he shouted, "Why didn't you tell us there were grenades in the Jeep?"

"I tried, but you would not listen."

A few minutes and a live grenade later, there was a hole sufficient for the canister. Gutierrez and the other Rangers marked the coordinates with a pile of rocks in hopes that one day the plutonium could be recovered.

Having wasted valuable time and energy, they climbed into the Jeep and continued on. A mere twenty miles later, the sergeant realized the half tank of fuel was not going to get them across the border. Loaded, the vehicle was rapidly sucking the gas tank dry. Gutierrez pulled to the side of the road and shut the engine off. He leaned forward on the steering wheel.

"What's going on?" Michael asked.

The sergeant sighed. "We're nearly out of gas. There is no way we will make it across the border in this thing."

"Not to mention the seating arrangement sucks," Taylor said. Everyone had spontaneously unloaded when the Jeep stopped.

"Even if we could top it off, it is just rotten on mileage with all of us in it." The sergeant glanced at the sky and then back to the earth. A small car approached on the road, but the driver must've seen the men with guns getting out of the Jeep, because the vehicle sped up until it was well past them. "We probably won't get much help from the locals." Gutierrez motioned to the car. "Not to mention we are running out of supplies."

"There is the hospital where I took the warden," Nasira said. "They may have fuel. Or better transportation."

The sergeant nodded. "What do you think, McGillis?"

Everyone turned to the private, who seemed surprised anybody would ask his opinion.

"I'm with Nasira. The hospital sounds good to me. I don't feel well." At that moment he turned away and threw up.

"Blimey, the wee chook's not lookin' good," Pike said.

Everyone climbed back into the Jeep, and with Gutierrez at the wheel, they turned once again toward Mingora. Forever afterward, the men would look at that city as the earthly equivalent to a black hole.

40

It was near dusk when the Jeep stacked with Americans reached Owdi Gram and sputtered to a stop in front of a hospital tent. The gas gauge leaned heavily toward empty. Unlike before, no one came out to offer help. Nasira pointed out that there were now three tents where there had only been one. It appeared every available hand was busy.

Fulton and Pike helped Private McGillis from the Jeep and into the nearest tent. Gutierrez was about to follow when Michael stopped him. "Sergeant, I have an idea."

"All right."

"I was thinking Taylor and I should go get the ice cream truck. It will fit us all, and McGillis could even lie down if needed."

"I thought it was out of gas."

"It is, but I'm certain we can get enough fuel along the way to fill the tank. We just need a gas can and a rubber hose. Taylor used to specialize in such activities and was almost arrested once."

"Hey, I was barely involved in that," Taylor protested.

The sergeant smiled tiredly. "I don't see you being barely involved in anything, Corporal." He turned back to Michael. "It's a good idea—as long as you are armed. Anarchy may well be the current ruling power inside the city. Keep your heads down."

The two brothers retrieved some weapons from the Jeep and disappeared into the failing light. Gutierrez turned to Nasira, who had been clinging to his arm. He reached up and clasped his hand around hers. She was trembling.

"Are you cold?" he asked.

"No."

"What is it then?"

"I cannot go in the tent." She paused. "I just cannot go in there again."

"That's okay," Gutierrez said tenderly. "Wait here. I will be right back. I just need to check on the private. Perhaps you could find us a place to rest before the sun goes down."

She nodded and he kissed her on the forehead. He wondered if he should have done that.

In the tent, the sergeant was accosted with the horrid images and stench of war. He was glad Nasira had waited outside.

As the Sutton brothers walked away from the hospital, Michael laughed. "Barely involved? You are so full of it! You were a hair's breadth from going to juvenile hall."

"That's my story—barely involved—and I'm sticking to it. So where are we going to find this gas can and rubber hose?"

"Give me a minute." Michael went to a nearby car and lifted the hood. "You have a knife?"

A folding knife appeared in Taylor's hand and was instantly open. "Found it in the truck."

Michael took it and cut a small radiator hose from the car. Water began to pour onto the ground.

"I hope that car is abandoned," Taylor said.

Michael smiled. "We'll return the hose later."

"And now for a gas can, Copperfield."

"Copperfield?"

"You're a magician, like the one when we were kids. Remember he supposedly walked through the Great Wall of China."

"Yeah, I remember. That was so fake, even for then."

They found an old man emptying a large plastic jug into the massive generator that powered the lights and equipment in the hospital tents. He had his back to them, and when they walked up, he turned and gave a start.

"Hey, we're sorry. We didn't mean to scare you," Taylor said.

"Scare me?" replied the man in a British accent. "I thought you were spirits. Ya nearly killed me!"

"Sorry. We're just in need of your can there. We'll return it."

"Sure. My name's Pete." He stuck out a friendly hand and the brothers shook it. "My friends call me Petrol Pete."

"Well, Pete, my name's Taylor and this is Michael. We have a truck—"

"Jus' call me Petrol. You sure neither of you's spirits?"

"Pretty sure."

"Ah, too bad. You're welcome to the can. I seen some, you know."

Taylor couldn't resist. "Seen what?"

"Spirits!"

"You don't say. Where?"

"Well, it wasn't me personally, but my da', he seen 'em—"

"Sir, we'll return this in the morning," Michael interrupted. He turned Taylor around and they began to walk away.

Pete said, "All right, in the morn'."

Once the two brothers were out of earshot, Taylor said with an English accent, "He's a nutta, that one."

Michael chuckled. "Too many gas fumes. Nice of him to lend us the can, though. How far do you think we are from the truck?"

"Maybe two clicks. I can't believe we've been trying for two days to leave this city and the farthest we can get away is what, fifty miles maybe?"

"Well, you know what Dad always says—there's a reason for everything."

Taylor chuckled. "Oh yes, Dad and his view of the world."

"It's a pretty good view. God is not just the God of one moment."

"Wow, now you're quoting Mom. It's no wonder you and I never saw eye to eye."

Michael laughed briefly, but as they drew nearer the city, a sense of unease brought him to listen more and talk less. The noises of unrest and war wafted across the distance, seeming louder as sounds tend to do in the evening hours.

Taylor pointed out a truck with saddle-mounted tanks. "You bring a flashlight?" he whispered.

"No, but the moon should be up shortly."

Taylor spun the cap off a tank, releasing the pungent smell of gasoline. "We're in luck." He inserted the hose into the tank, started the siphon, and let gravity work its magic. While they waited, he said suddenly, "I haven't asked how April and little Suze are. Everyone well?"

"Yeah, they're good," Michael replied. "Suzanne is getting big—you'll hardly recognize her. April still hates you."

Taylor nodded. "I can understand that."

Nothing was said for a minute as they listened to the trickling of the fuel into the container.

"How about you? You have a girlfriend?" asked Michael.

"Nah. Four or five, maybe. Too much man for just one."

The brothers chuckled softly and then Michael said, "You're still full of yourself and full of crap."

A few minutes later, the can was full.

Taylor tested the weight of the full can. "You know, we should have gotten a little closer to the truck before we filled this up."

"There are two handles. I'll take one. We only have a mile . . . maybe."

The moon, a bright-orange ball, had just risen above the mountains in the east. With the full can between them, Michael and Taylor walked awkwardly toward the river where they had abandoned the ice cream truck. Hoping to avoid any fighting, they skirted the city. But violence loves the dark. The quick report of machine gun fire stopped the brothers short and they took cover behind a mud hut. Michael recognized the sound of the AK-47 or one of a dozen copycats. There seemed to be a small band of insurgents fighting an even smaller band of defenders. The gun fighting came in waves as the AK-47 and all its cousins fired 600 rounds a minute but were limited by 50- to 100-round clips. The occasional stray bullet clipped the edge of their shelter, bringing showers of dirt.

"How long do you think this will last?" Michael asked Taylor.

"At the rate these guys are spending rounds, I doubt it will last long. One side or the other is going to run out of ammo. You smell gas?"

"Yeah, actually, I do." Michael checked the can in the dim light and saw a dark and growing puddle beneath the container. "Great. There's a hole."

"Is it near the bottom?"

"Yeah."

"Let's turn it over."

"That's a good idea. Just pray the lid holds."

The brothers kept their firearms ready and eyes alert. The powerful 10 mm Colts would be worthless in dead men's hands.

"Come on, you guys," Taylor said, "you've got to be nearly out of ammo." Soon the torrent of gunfire became a mere trickle then disappeared altogether. Michael watched him work his way to the edge of the shelter and glance around the corner.

"All's quiet—let's move," Taylor said.

The upside-down gas can was even more awkward, but they managed to get it between their shoulders and used the handles to hold it upright. As they moved, Michael's eyes darted from side to side, and he knew Taylor was on the lookout at well.

After several minutes, there came from the shadows a childlike whimper followed by a sob. Michael motioned that they should check it out.

Taylor shook his head. "No way," he whispered. "It could be a wounded soldier ready to shoot the first man he sees."

"That was no soldier. It sounded like a kid."

"Kids will shoot you too."

"Come with me or I'll go alone."

Taylor grumbled. "All right, but let's not be stupid and get ourselves killed."

They set the can down with the hole at the top and went quietly toward where the whimper had originated—a shadow was created by a low rock wall that lined the street where the fighting had just occurred. When they got near, Taylor tossed a rock over the wall. A whip-crack of a small pistol replied.

"I told you," Taylor whispered.

The whimper came again.

"Ha! I told you too. Somebody's wounded."

"Probably just a militant. Come on, let's get out of here before we join him." Taylor moved to leave.

Michael grabbed his arm. "You saw the hospital tents full of wounded. More innocent people are getting killed than militants."

"That's what you don't get. Anyone could be a militant."

"If there is a chance we could help someone, we need to try. Tell them to throw out the weapon and we'll help them. What do we have to lose?"

Taylor shook his head. "Only our lives." Then in his best Pakistani he said, "We are Americans. We are here to help you. Throw out your gun."

Seconds later, a pistol flew from behind the wall. Michael slugged his brother in the arm to say "I told you so."

Taylor called out, "Here we come." He tossed another rock—nothing. They moved closer to the wall and glanced quickly over.

There was no soldier, only a woman. She sat against the wall with a child on her lap. The child was bleeding and moaning. The brothers leaped over the wall and squatted near the woman. Taylor spoke to her and she replied. After a minute Taylor spoke again.

"What is it?" Michael asked.

"She's hard to understand, but it seems her child was wounded earlier today, and when she heard there was a hospital outside the city she began to carry him there. Then the gunfire started, so she ducked in here but twisted her ankle and cannot get up. She was ready to die here with her son when we came by."

"Tell her we can get her to the hospital."

"I did. She doesn't trust us."

"Tell her we are Americans again. Perhaps she thinks you're one of them with your beard and all."

"She knows we're Americans. It's more obvious than you think."

Michael moved in to take the boy from the woman's lap, but suddenly she pointed a gun at his forehead. Michael raised his hands and made as if to back away, but then snatched the weapon from her trembling fingers. The gun clicked but did not go off.

"I'm not going to let her child die because of her mistrust of us. Hold your gun on her, Taylor. I'm taking him."

"You're insane."

Regardless of the gun, the woman began to fight Michael off. "Point the gun at the kid."

"This isn't going to help her trust us," Taylor argued, but he did as his brother asked and the woman quit fighting.

Michael pulled the boy to him. "Help her up."

"This is only going to slow us up."

"I know. You're carrying the gas can."

Taylor helped the woman to her feet. Without the load of carrying the boy, she could manage a hobble. Michael swung his long legs over the wall, but Taylor had the task of helping the wounded woman.

"I'll bet her ankle is broken," Taylor said. He hefted the gas can onto one of his shoulders.

"You're probably right."

In the dim moonlight, it was difficult to tell how badly the woman and child were hurt. In spite of the language barrier, Michael spoke to the child, reassuring him. The boy only moaned, but at least he was alive. The Swat River was still a half mile away and Michael was stretching his stride. Taylor informed the woman of their destination and she followed, trembling.

The moon was shining when the truck came into view. To Michael, it was a glorious sight. He stepped quickly to the vehicle, and though Taylor protested, Michael promptly opened the back doors. He gently laid the boy on the floor of the truck and turned to go back for the woman.

"You're a fool," Taylor said.

"What?"

"Someone could have laid claim to this truck while we were gone and been ready to defend it to the death. When people are kicked out of their homes, they will live in just about anything."

"I didn't know."

"I tried to warn you, but you never listen," Taylor growled.

"Are you done? I need to go help the boy's mother."

"Fine. I'll put the gas in the truck, but I'm not going to explain to your wife what happened when you get yourself killed. Like grabbing the gun from the woman—that was stupid."

Frustrated, Michael turned and walked away. He knew he had been foolish and lucky. In fact, his insides still quivered, but he was running on adrenaline and didn't want to stop and think about it.

Almost a quarter mile back, he found the mother of the child crawling. She was weeping and wailing, and Michael knew the thought of losing her boy was more than she could bear. He came to her side and helped her stand. Trembling, she grasped him and kissed him, her tear-soaked face touching his. He imagined that her husband had been killed and her home destroyed, and that her son was all she had left in the world.

Prying himself from the woman's clutching arms, Michael began to help her walk. She leaned on him heavily and the going was slow. Soon headlights bore down on them and the old ice cream truck pulled up beside them.

"You look like you need a lift, Brother," Taylor said.

"You have no idea."

A few more steps and Michael opened the back doors of the truck. The woman crawled in next to her child, and the boy muttered what must've been akin to "Mama." They embraced.

After Michael shut the doors, he joined Taylor at the front of the truck and collapsed in the front passenger seat. "I'm glad you're driving."

"So much for not making rescues a habit, huh, Mike?"

Michael smiled. "Just shut up and drive."

41

Gutierrez came out of the white hospital tent and found Nasira waiting for him. He had been an hour inside with the private, and it was late. Seeming relieved to see him, she asked, "How is McGillis?"

"Sleeping. They have some medication for him. It's not the best stuff but it will help him."

She nodded. "He is a hero."

"He was brave to do what he did," Gutierrez said, not wanting to disclose that guilt had been the private's motivation. There was no harm in letting Nasira believe the best in others, since she had certainly seen the worst for the majority of her life.

"The other two have a tarp laid out so at least we can rest," she said. "It's about fifty yards from here, so it is not so noisy."

"Sounds great. It's been a long day."

As Gutierrez and Nasira worked their way through the darkness, Pike hailed them. "Over here." He shined a flashlight in their direction.

"Easy with the light, Corporal," Gutierrez replied. "You just blinded me."

"It's not the Ritz, but at least we won't get dirt down our drawers tonight," Fulton said.

The sergeant chuckled. "We're all getting used to sleeping on the ground, but what I wouldn't give for a king-sized bed."

"King size? You plan on having company, sir? Perhaps a young refugee?"

"Shut up, Pike."

Pike flashed the light in his face. "I'm just joshin' you, mate."

It was nearly eleven when an ice cream truck stopped in front of the three hospital tents. As it happened, the truck's headlights came to rest on a young man in a lab coat, holding a flashlight. Taylor spoke to the man and asked him to help with a wounded boy and his mother.

The intern moved to the back of the truck and quickly examined the boy. "He's lost a lot of blood," he said. "Let's get him inside."

The boy's mother tried to follow and nearly collapsed. Michael braced her up as she shouted after her boy. A female hospital worker came to her aid.

"She's broken her ankle," Michael explained.

The hospital worker shined her own flashlight at the woman's foot. "I'd say it's broken—nearly broken off."

The woman's foot dangled and Michael had to look away. He wondered how she had walked at all. She was carefully helped into the hospital tent.

Michael shook his head. "You know, in a better light I may have thrown up right then."

"I know what you mean," replied Taylor. "What now?"

"We should find the guy who lent us the gas can and explain that he won't be getting it back, and try to borrow another one."

"Ol' Petrol Pete! Mr. I-see-dead-people."

Michael chuckled. "No. Mr. My-dad-saw-dead-people."

"Oh, that's right."

Taylor borrowed a flashlight from a table near the door of the tent. Around the back of the tent, they found Pete leaning back in a chair snoring like a hibernating bear, a gas can in his arms.

"That's a little odd," Taylor said.

"I told you. Gas fumes."

They shook the old man. He awoke with a snort and said something about a woman named Bernice. The gas can in his arms fell to the ground. He looked up and said, "Spirits?"

"No. We need to borrow another can. The last one got shot," Michael said.

"Which one of you's a spirit?"

"Neither of us." Michael looked at Taylor, then shook the old man again. "Wake up, buddy. Did you hear us? The last can we borrowed got shot."

"Oh, that's too bad. I liked that one. Whatcha doin' with it anyway?" Petrol Pete sounded intoxicated.

The brothers looked at each incredulously. "We needed to get some gas for our truck," Taylor said. "What else would we be doing with a gas can?"

The man shrugged. "That's your business."

"We need another can for more gas," Taylor said impatiently.

"Oh, well, why didn't you say so? Come on. Bring your torch." Petrol Pete stood and walked a short way to a dark tent behind the others. He pulled back the tarp to reveal a tanker truck.

"Got to keep her under wraps. Don't need no crazies trying to blow her up. She's got about four hundred sweet gallons in her," slurred the old man. "Take what you need."

Taylor gasped. "Are you kidding me?"

"I never kid about petrol, laddie."

"We thought you only had a little and that's why you were using cans."

"No. I jus' like cans."

The brothers looked at each other and Taylor discreetly traced circles around his ear with one finger.

"Thank you very much, sir," Michael said.

"I'm glad you lads woke me up. I need to add some petrol to the generators anyway." Pete picked up a can and filled it from a valve on the back of the truck. Then, humming a tune, he turned and walked away.

"I bet by morning, Petrol Pete will have no memory of giving us the gasoline," Taylor said with a chuckle.

"I agree. We'd better fill up the truck now and not wait for dawn. I can't believe we went siphoning when we had a tanker within spitting distance."

"I'll get the truck," Taylor said.

"While you're doing that, I'm going to check on the kid and his mother." Michael entered at the back of the tent where he'd seen them taken earlier. Inside, he quickly understood why both ends of the tent were open—ventilation. Not every bed was full, but there were several people with severe burns, one to a large portion of his body. He writhed in agony as doctors wrapped him in treated bandages.

Michael's eyes searched the beds for the boy and his mother. To his horror, he found them huddled together on a chair, their faces a ghostly pale. She held a bloody cloth against her child's wound. Her ankle was now purple and swollen. Michael looked from them to the empty beds.

"Who's in charge here?" he bellowed. No one really looked up until he asked the question another two times and with increasing fervor. Finally, a middle-aged man with wire glasses walked up. His pepper-gray hair rolled back from a high forehead like the ocean waves.

"My name is Dr. Kingsley. What can I do for you, sir?" His voice was calm and dignified and his pronunciation perfect.

"I would like to know why this woman and her child sit here unattended. The boy is bleeding to death."

"We only have so many beds, sir."

Michael looked around. "There are three empty."

"Sir, I am sure that in your profession you do not let strangers tell you how to do your work. I have a very complicated situation here and a very stringent employer. Please let us do our jobs."

"You have an employer? Does he realize you are neglecting the wounded? You are a doctor, or at least you look the part. Is that boy going to die in your care?"

"I am acting on orders from my employer," the doctor said as he adjusted his glasses. His voice remained calm even though his pasty complexion was growing red. Some of the other doctors and nurses seemed uncomfortable as Michael pressed the issue.

"I would like to speak to your employer before the boy dies of blood loss and his mother from gangrene."

"You cannot, sir," Doctor Kingsley said. He invited Michael to go outside.

"I will not." Michael remained planted like an oak. "I want to know why you are not helping this boy and his mother."

Another doctor walked up beside Kingsley. For a second Michael thought he was about to be outnumbered, but surprisingly she turned on the senior doctor.

"Why don't you tell him, Kingsley? Tell the man why you won't allow us to help them."

"Stay out of this, Doctor Sheridan. Get back to work."

Doctor Sheridan turned to Michael. "We cannot help them because they are Sunni."

"What?" Michael could not believe his ears.

"Doctor Sheridan, get back to work!" Kingsley had lost his composure.

"We did not carry this boy and his mother out of the city so they could die in your tent because they are from the wrong branch of the family tree!" Michael barked.

Sheridan pulled on fresh gloves and went to the wounded boy and his mother. "Doctor Sheridan!" protested Kingsley. "We have our instructions! They are to wait!"

"I did not sign up for discriminatory doctoring. You said we would help the refugees. That is what I'm doing."

Doctor Kingsley went to physically remove Sheridan and was cut short by a pistol in his face.

"You need some help, Bro?" Taylor asked. He had entered quietly and stopped the doctor short of his objective. Kingsley's eyes went from the pistol to the man holding it steady.

"I think we're fine here, Tay. The good doctor was just about to give some first-rate medical attention to his new favorite patients. Isn't that right, Dr. Kingsley?"

The entire medical tent fell silent in anticipation of the doctor's reply.

Dr. Kingsley cleared his throat. "Go ahead, Dr. Sheridan," he said meekly, then adjusted his eyeglasses and left the tent.

After a moment, the hospital workers resumed their tasks. With the help of a young intern, Dr. Sheridan moved the boy and his mother to adjacent beds. The brothers lingered for a moment, and then Michael spoke.

"Are you going to be all right, Dr. Sheridan?"

She glanced at him. "I shall be fine. Dr. Kingsley will not return tonight. He is a prideful man and you embarrassed him."

"We wouldn't have hurt him," Taylor said.

Michael nodded. "But no one should be allowed to die in a hospital just because they are Sunni."

"No, they should not, but regardless, I disapprove of violence even to accomplish worthwhile tasks. You two had better go fight your war, wherever it is." Dr. Sheridan inserted a syringe and tube into the woman's ankle, and a bloody fluid began to drain.

Michael looked away.

"I am sorry to be rude," the doctor continued. "And I am thankful that with your help we can now save their lives. But you cannot stay here. Don't worry about me. Kingsley knows my worth."

The boy was now hooked up to an IV and an intern began cutting away his crimson clothing. Given a shot for her pain, the woman deliriously mumbled to the brothers what Michael knew were words of gratitude. He came to her side and took her hand.

"Goodbye," he said, then thanked Dr. Sheridan.

Outside, Taylor turned to his brother. "Just making friends wherever you go, aren't you?"

"It's a gift. You fill up the truck?"

"What do you think I was doing while you were starting a fight with the doctor? I also borrowed another can from Petrol Pete. I don't think he'll miss it since there are about fifty of them in that tent."

"He said he likes cans." Michael yawned. "Should we go find the others and get out of here?"

"You know, I almost forgot McGillis is in that other tent. I should go and check on him."

"He's probably asleep."

"True. Wish I was."

"Me too." Michael yawned again. "Asleep in my own bed."

On the far side of a bluff, Pike, Fulton, Nasira, and Gutierrez lay silent but not sleeping. Nasira spoke after a long time. "I wonder if my parents still remember me."

"I am certain they do," Gutierrez replied.

"It has been so long."

"What is the first thing you want to do when you get home?"

Nasira did not have to think. "Kiss my father and mother. I have worried for many nights that the last morning before I went out to play I had not kissed them and told them I loved them. What are you going to do?"

"I don't know," Gutierrez replied.

Pike piped up. "You cheeky liar. You said you were going to kiss the first girl you laid eyes on."

"Thanks for that, Pike."

"No worries, cobber."

Fulton suddenly sat up. "Somebody's comin'." Everyone looked toward the oncoming headlights.

"Fair dinkum . . . the Suttons made it back," Pike said.

The lights stopped just before the crest of the bluff and a car door slammed shut. A figure appeared with the headlights behind it. "Anybody know where we could find a bunch of ragged army dogs in desperate need of a bath?" It was Taylor Sutton's voice.

"Sutton, you don't smell so good yourself," Fulton replied. "Tell your brother to shut off those lights."

Taylor motioned to his brother, who turned off the lights and the engine. The Suttons joined the others on the tarp. Darkness and a cool western breeze enveloped them as the moon and night's speckled blanket draped across the sky.

"What's the plan, Sarge?" Taylor asked.

"Did you look in on McGillis when you got back?"

"No, we figured he'd be asleep. Could they help him?"

"They put him on a potassium-iodine drip," Gutierrez explained. "They said it would counteract the radiation faster than pills."

"How long till he's well enough to travel?" Michael asked.

"As bad as that kid wants to go home, he'll travel long before he's well enough."

"So we kidnap him and the drip, cross the border, and Bob's yer uncle, we're at the airbase in time for supper," Pike said. "You know he'll get better care there, mate."

"I agree," Michael said. "We may not be too welcome here tomorrow since Taylor pulled a gun on the head doctor."

"What?" everyone said in unison.

"Hey, wait a minute. Michael picked the fight." Eyes shifted from one brother to another.

"You two are the Fighting Suttons, aren't you? If it's not with each other, it's with everyone else."

Michael laughed. "It was for a good cause."

The sergeant shook his head. "Sounds like our minds are made up then. Let's go round up some supplies, kidnap McGillis, and head out."

42

Lieutenant McNally found it impossible to relax. The thought of good men stranded because of bureaucracy made his blood boil. It reminded him of the men who actually went through the horror portrayed in the movie *Black Hawk Down*.

He lay on a cot in his barracks and stared at the ceiling. It was 4:00 AM. There had been no word from Michael or the Rangers, and they should have been across the border by now. McNally hardly knew Michael but knew his type. The type that sacrificed everything for what was right, and never with guile or with expectation of praise.

The lieutenant sat up and rubbed his bristled chin. If there was one thing he hated, it was letting someone down. He thought about the pandering administration he had witnessed the day before—high-ranking military officials tied down by foreign policy. Obviously, those in command did not share his convictions. Armchair generals, he called them. Handing down orders from air-conditioned office buildings about matters they had long since lost touch with.

Lieutenant McNally sighed. What he had the itch to do would surely be the last thing he ever did as a pilot in the military, yet what did he really have to lose? He never saw any action, he kept to himself, and he had no real friends left in the service. Most of all, he'd simply been in the military too long.

It was time to end it—to throw in the towel, and in a way that mattered.

In an Air Force Tactical Operations room on the far side of the base, a young man at a computer monitor spoke up. "Sir, we have a vehicle headed for the border in sector twelve."

"Put it on the main screen, Corporal," said the operations major. When a large screen came to life, he grunted. "Just a small vehicle. Are there any signs of weapons?"

The screen zoomed in. "Nothing on the exterior, sir, but there is a cone-shaped object on the roof." The corporal punched a few buttons on his keyboard and the screen became a rainbow. "There appear to be slight traces of radiation—possibly bomb residue."

The major shook his head. "The cone may be a guidance apparatus or perhaps even a missile. Thanks goodness for modern technology. We have our orders. Let's send up a UAV." He picked up a phone and said, "I need clearance to fire on some possible hostiles looking to cross the border at sector twelve." The major paused, then replied to the person on the phone, "Yes, sir." He turned to the corporal. "We have weapons hot clearance. Launch is a go."

A mile from the tactical operations room, an MQ-9 Reaper came to life, fully armed and fueled. The drone taxied toward a short runway. The small prop at its tail roared to life and the radio-controlled sentinel was airborne and headed east.

Unmanned aerial vehicles were the Air Force's new kid on the block, and a launch or mission never went unnoticed by Bagram's younger residents. Older pilots like McNally didn't approve of turning war into an emotionally detached video game.

Shortly after 5:30 in the morning, McNally stood in the grub line at the mess hall waiting to get a breakfast he doubted he'd eat. He had been for a run in the cool morning air—three miles in an amount of time when he used to do five. He didn't know if it was age or if his heart just wasn't in it. In the mess hall he heard chatter about another UAV launch and tried to pay no attention.

From behind the lieutenant, a voice spoke up. "You hear? A Reaper was sent on another seek and destroy this morning. The target was neutralized, of course. Feels like time's running out for you old guys, don't it?" McNally turned to find a pudgy-faced UAV operator named Willis smiling widely.

McNally glared at him. "Why you smilin'? Find a cupcake in your pocket?" Someone behind the staff sergeant snickered.

Willis's grin fell. "I heard they're comin' out with helicopter drones next. One day all you old-timers will be a thing of the past."

Ignoring the younger man, McNally shifted so they no longer faced each other.

"Anyway," continued Willis, who talked too much and too often, "terrorists won't be trying the roads through sector twelve anytime soon."

McNally turned to him again. "What sector did you say?"

"Twelve."

Without another word, McNally ran out of the mess hall.

The pre-dawn sky had faded to a dull blue, the eastern horizon ablaze with the coming day. Michael Sutton and Emilio Gutierrez sat in the front of the ice cream truck with Michael driving, his knuckles clenched white on the wheel. Bajaur Road's tight switchbacks and hairpin turns had made their overnight descent of the mountain especially rough. Motion sickness had taken on new meaning during the night, as everyone got sick at least once.

With the truck's dim headlights, the group only knew they were on the right road because it continued to head west.

Sergeant Gutierrez tapped Michael on the shoulder. "Hey, man. I gotta take a break. Let's find a place to stop."

At the next level spot in the road Michael stopped the truck and shut off the engine. Not needing an invitation, someone opened the rear doors. Pike and Fulton seemed to willingly fall out the back.

Taylor crawled forward. "What's up? Why we stopped?"

"Time to take a breather," the sergeant said.

"It'll be good to switch drivers," added Michael. "I've had it."

Everyone had gotten out and scattered for the sake of privacy when from out of nowhere a rocket thundered into the front of the truck. The vehicle exploded in an engulfing cloud of flame and smoke. The seven lucky passengers immediately dropped to their bellies and peered into the lightening sky as a nearly silent Reaper banked north and disappeared over a cliff.

"No way that just happened," said Fulton in total disbelief and amazement.

"What's goin' on, Sergeant?" McGillis asked. "Why are they shooting at us?"

"I don't know. Maybe they think we're someone else."

"It's Colonel Bracken. He can't let us come home." All eyes turned to Taylor, who stood a few steps away.

"How's one corrupt colonel able to do all this?" Fulton said skeptically. "To circumvent JSOC and get the Air Force involved? It's impossible!"

"It only means he has help," Michael said in defense of his brother. "You keep communications jumbled, wires crossed, and anything is possible."

"What're we going to do now?" McGillis asked pathetically.

The question hung in the air as all eyes returned to the truck, and the long black finger of smoke rising into the atmosphere. The exit had been so immediate that there had been no chance to save anything. All their supplies, their food and water, were instantly gone.

Someone turned a rock with his foot, and Nasira kicked at a weed. Grim realization struck the sergeant. They were a hundred miles from anywhere with nothing more than the clothes on their backs. Had they come so far and done so much to die in the desert, killed by their own?

Their destination lay in the west, and without speaking they all turned and began to walk.

43

McNally made a beeline for the Air Force's Operations Room. Covering the distance, nearly a mile, in half the time he had during his morning run, he missed a dozen opportunities to salute his superiors along the way. He burst through the doors of the Hoover building and after glancing at a sign that said "Ops," turned to the right. An MP blocked his destination but saluted as the winded McNally approached.

"I need to see the operations major," the pilot managed.

"I am under orders, Lieutenant. No one is admitted."

"Tell the major they are shooting at Americans. There are Americans trying to cross at sector twelve . . . Army Rangers to be exact."

The MP shifted his weight. "All right, I'll call him." He pulled a radio from his belt and spoke with a female corporal inside the room. After a few minutes, during which McNally worried if he'd even be able to get through, the MP handed his radio to him.

"Major, this is Lieutenant McNally," he said quickly.

"How can I help you?"

"Sir, somehow you have bad orders. A team of Army Rangers and two civilians are trying to make their way out of Pakistan. They were told to use the road through sector twelve just last evening."

"Lieutenant, I have orders as of 0400 that instruct me to stop any activity attempting to cross the border. The Rangers must be in the clear."

"Major, I am telling you they are not. I have not heard from them. No one has."

"Last I checked, Lieutenant, Rangers do not report to you. Have a good morning, sir."

"Major," McNally said. No response. "Major!" Nothing.

At that moment, another corporal in the operations room spoke up. "Major Perkins, the occupants of the previously destroyed truck have survived and are proceeding to the border. What would you like to do, sir?"

The major moved to see the corporal's screen. "Determined, aren't they? Let's take a closer look at them if we can." He needed to know if McNally was right.

The corporal moved a mouse and the satellite zoomed in on seven people walking through the Pakistani desert. "Do any of them look American?" asked the major.

"This view is primarily downward, sir. One or two could be American, but the others appear to be locals or paramilitary."

The major sighed. He had been trained to obey orders and he reviewed them in his head. The men the lieutenant had been concerned about must be in the clear—they had to be. The major felt the corporal watching him, waiting for direction.

"Send the UAV back and get a better look at them. Perhaps a few more rockets will turn them around."

The corporal spoke into a headset. The previous reaper had already returned, and another one, fresh and ready, moved onto the tarmac.

Outside, McNally handed the radio back to the MP, then measured him up. There was no getting around the younger, stronger man, though twenty years ago McNally probably would have tried. He decided to find a more direct solution to the problem.

Those men in the desert needed him. Then and there, the lieutenant decided today would be his last in the military. It might also be his last day as a free man, yet it seemed right. His feeling of listlessness was gone, replaced with drive and purpose.

He left the Hoover building and inhaled deeply. He had to get to the airfield but was tired of running around like an overzealous private. Soon, he found a car with the keys in it. As McNally drove, he considered his options. He must be prepared for anything. He might need to return fire and would have to carry survivors. After his mind scrolled through a list of possible candidates, he finally settled on a Black Hawk. Not any Black Hawk, but a sweetheart used by Special Ops. The HH 60G Pave Hawk—a veritable flying tank. And he knew exactly where to get one.

McNally chuckled to himself. "I guess if I'm going to steal something, it might as well be something worth the effort." He pulled onto the airfield and soon stopped near a hangar. Dozens of mechanics worked busily on countless planes and helicopters. McNally's eyes scanned for a particular guy and soon found him pushing a helicopter into a massive hangar. The lieutenant crossed the warming concrete and began to help push.

Noticing him at once, the mechanic said, "How are you, Henry?"

"Could be better. How about yourself? Where's the truck?" McNally asked as he leaned into the helicopter. "Pushing stuff around is for the birds."

"Broke down. Parts won't be here until tomorrow."

McNally grunted his sympathy. "How's the wife?"

"Good. Just had baby number two."

"That's great, Malcolm. You name him after me?"

Malcolm laughed.

They soon had the helicopter parked in the corner of the hangar, after which half a dozen mechanics tore into it like ants into a dead dragonfly. Malcolm and McNally turned back toward the entrance and stopped where sunshine met shadow.

"You're not here to talk, are you?" the mechanic said.

"Nope."

"Figured. You want to fly my girl again, don't you?"

"Yep. You owe me."

"I know. You seem wound up. I don't want to know what you're doing, do I?"

"Not unless you're looking for trouble."

Malcolm sighed and wiped the sweat that glistened against his black skin. "Fine, but when you're arrested, I'm going to tell them you were only supposed to test the gyros. Got that?"

"Gyros . . . got it."

"She's sitting a hundred yards over." Malcolm motioned to his right. "But you better bring her back in one piece!"

"I see her. She armed?" McNally asked as he began to walk away.

Malcolm shook his head. "Of course . . . but not that you're going to need it, right?"

McNally kept walking and merely waved over his shoulder. He walked steadily toward the Black Hawk's evil twin. Even sitting on her landing gear, she looked squatty, mean, and heavy. The HH 60G was twenty thousand pounds of angry she-bear. He had flown her once a few years back and fallen in love with the big, clunky beast. She was a nightmare to handle but came fully loaded. A particularly useful item was terrain-following radar, which allowed the Pave Hawk to fly very close to the ground. The aircraft also had a signal jammer. McNally intended to use both today.

Not "trained" to fly her, it had taken some planning for McNally to get into her cockpit, but he had learned long ago that a man in need of a favor will do almost anything. Less than a year ago Malcolm had needed some extra leave time. The young couple was gunning for a second baby, so McNally had given his leave time to Malcolm. Apparently, the mission had been a success.

As he climbed into the cockpit, McNally's heart pounded. He strapped in and fixed his headgear, looking over the endless gauges and switches. A few flips of carefully chosen switches and the she-bear awoke from hibernation with a growl.

"I missed you too," McNally said.

44

The road descending the Pakistani mountains followed a wide, fast-flowing river with settlements surrounding the river and the road. After centuries of cultivation and careful irrigation, these villages were green and lush, a stark contrast to the desert around them. When the grade became too steep, the road would depart both river and settlement and the tightly wrapped switchbacks would return.

Though no one got sick, traveling by foot was arduous. Shale rock, as slippery as soap, could send a person over a cliff in a flash. For seven souls bent on home, walking was painfully slow. Above them the sun followed their westward progression, bright and unblinking upon their heads.

Michael calculated they were somewhere between seventy and a hundred miles from Jalalabad, as the crow flies. After the loss of their truck, they had not gone far before falling upon the mercy of the mountain villagers, who were very gracious. They seemed little concerned with the affairs and wars of the people on the desert floor. By virtue of this charity, the Americans now had a leather canteen full of water, and chunks of a flatbread cooked on hot rock. It wasn't much, but they were grateful for it.

Currently, the hot desert floor drew closer with every step. Away from the river, the ground was parched and rocky. Little dust devils sprung up and promptly died, and unseen desert life clicked and buzzed, but the monotonous sound of shuffling feet dominated Michael's senses.

Away from the river and man's cultivation, the land was void and nearly empty of life. Clearly when clouds did gather and burst, the ground was wholly unprepared for the much-needed moisture. The parched earth had nothing by which to harvest the water to promote growth. Little trickles gathered into deep cracks, all of which found their way to natural canals cut in the earth by previous downpours.

The seven weary travelers stopped where some of these canals had converged and washed out a large section of road. It dropped at least ten feet down, and the gap was twenty feet across. At first Michael and the others merely stared at the cavity through sun-washed eyes.

"Did we get off course?" Pike asked.

Gutierrez turned to look back. "I don't think so, We're still heading west."

"Looks like last year's rains washed out the road," Fulton commented.

"There must have been a lot of water," Nasira said.

Michael nodded. "That's the problem with deserts. What water it does get just erodes the land and washes away any topsoils."

At that moment, Gutierrez pointed out a small gray object in the western sky and said, "We need to hide."

"This is getting ridiculous," Taylor said.

"Take cover in the wash!" The words had scarcely left the sergeant's mouth before a missile dropped from the UAV and raced toward them with a screeching whistle. The rocket slammed into the ground where they had been standing, but they were ten feet below as a cascade of dirt and rock showered down. The UAV buzzed overhead and banked as if coming back for another run.

McNally had just arrived upon the scene when the first rocket became a ball of flame on the earth. It was a Hellfire missile, rightly named. He was flying low, very low thanks to the terrain-following radar. He could see the drone swing around for another pass. He was in range and flipped on his signal jammer. Too late—the Reaper launched again. McNally launched a counter measure. The second Hellfire exploded midair.

He targeted the UAV. "This is how you spend eight million dollars in five seconds." A little trigger brought to life a massive machine gun, and seconds later the drone popped like a bug on an electric zapper. "I hope that smart-mouth Willis was piloting."

McNally set the heavy Pave Hawk down next to the cavity, sending up a duststorm. He idled down the rotor. After exiting the helicopter, he came to the edge and peered over. With eyes shielded from the sun, seven dirty faces looked up at him. He had been right. "You all need a lift somewhere?" he said in jest.

"McNally!" Michael said, choking on the dirt. "You're a sight for sore eyes." Instant relief was coupled with exuberant laughter.

"How did you know?" Gutierrez asked.

McNally squatted on his heels. "Well, after we talked, the Air Force zipped up the border like a parka in the Arctic. I tried to tell them we had men out here, but they wouldn't vary from their orders. So I came out." He turned back to the helicopter, where he hooked a long ladder to an eyelet and kicked it over the bank.

Nasira came up the ladder first. McNally took her hand. "Ma'am," he said with a nod. "Go ahead and get in."

"I'll wait here," she replied, and for a moment McNally thought she was going to hug him.

McGillis went next, and soon everyone stood around McNally, shaking his hand and slapping his back. There was a barrage of thank yous and tear-filled eyes. McNally smiled. Except for the day he became a father, it was the best moment of his life.

★

Michael watched the dirt-covered faces in the back of the helicopter as it carried them home. Tears flowed, heads hung in relief and prayer, and there were wide smiles.

Nasira, who had been away from home the longest, clung to the sergeant's arm as might a child. The intrepid young woman who had dressed in her captor's clothes and later watched him die seemed shrunken in this moment. Her strength and nobility were gone, and for the first time Michael saw her as a lost nineteen-year-old girl in desperate need of love. He thought of the five Army Rangers who owed their lives to her. No doubt, they would love her until the day they died.

Michael noticed Taylor looking back at him with a smile on his face and asked, "What?"

"Studying faces again, aren't you? Trying to figure out what everyone is thinking. You haven't changed a bit."

"Once you find a niche that works for you, you just go with it."

McNally spoke over a speaker. "Just to let you all know. I radioed in to let the base know I was bringing in a bunch of strays, but when we land at Bagram there might be some excitement. You see, I just shot down an eight-million-dollar drone with a helicopter I was only supposed to take on a test flight. Just a heads up."

Everyone looked at their pilot and then each other.

Michael laughed. "I knew there was something I liked about you, McNally!"

It was as the lieutenant had predicted. Every member of the military police on the base awaited their arrival on the tarmac. Touching down, he cut the engines, and as the rotors slowed to a stop, armed guards closed in.

Over his speaker, McNally announced, "Thank you for flying Con Air. It has been a pleasure being your pilot." He laughed then said, "Seriously, I'm grateful to know you. See you all in court." With that he opened his hatch and was immediately accosted by the MP's.

As the MPs led McNally away in handcuffs, the side door of the HH 60G slid open and the seven weary and filthy passengers were invited to step out. Surrounded by military police, Gutierrez spoke up. "We are what's left of an Army Rangers LRS team designation Ghost, with the exception of Nasira Habeeb and Michael Sutton."

"We know," an MP replied. "We have orders to take you inside for debriefing."

Nasira turned to Gutierrez. "Has there been any word about my parents?"

The MP answered before the sergeant could. "I wouldn't know, ma'am. Please come with us."

The sergeant made one more request. "While we are in debriefing, Private McGillis needs medical attention. He has had a lethal dosage of radiation."

"I can relay the message. That is all I can do," the MP said.

The seven individuals being loaded onto a personnel truck were quite a sight. Three of them wore paramilitary fatigues that didn't fit; three others, including the woman, wore filthy and tattered traditional Pakistani clothing. The last of them, an obvious civilian, was dressed in common jeans and a polo shirt.

45

Sergeant Gutierrez was the first to be debriefed. The others—except McGillis, who went to the hospital under guard—sat in a small white room that resembled a doctor's waiting room. There were two doors: one led out into a hallway, the other into the debriefing room. A small TV tuned to BBC played low in one corner, and a table with magazines sat in the middle of a dozen armless and uncomfortable chairs. Thankfully, the room was air conditioned.

Fulton and Pike had already fallen asleep on the floor, and Nasira was curled up across a row of the chairs. Michael and Taylor sat slouched in their chairs, staring at the TV but not really watching.

"What a long week," Michael said with a sigh.

"It's been a longer three months for me," Taylor replied. Pike was snoring loudly now.

"Guess I have nothing to complain about." Michael paused then said, "What is a debriefing like?"

"Just a lot of questions. They'll probably be nicer to you since you're not military."

"Huh. You mean other than the fact that I used military transport to get all the way from California to Pakistan?"

"Yeah, they may not like that, but that was also Bracken's doing. I know you're not the kind to boast about accomplishments, but the military is just as big on meting out honors for bravery as they are punishments for cowardice, so don't skim over the encounter with General Rais or how you helped us get out of there alive. If it wasn't for you, there would be devastating weapons in the hands of a madman."

Michael shrugged. "I did what anyone would do. I just hope they let us call home soon. April has got to be going crazy."

Suddenly, the door that led to the hallway opened about three inches. Young eyes scanned the room and then rested on Michael. The door opened just far enough for a head and arm to slip inside. Michael recognized the head as belonging to Corporal Scott.

The young man spoke quickly. "I heard you were back. I took care of your stuff like you asked . . . no charge, just happy to help CIA. Remember me if you ever see an application with the name Everett Scott." Then the door closed and Corporal Scott left before Michael could set the record straight.

"CIA?" Taylor said.

"Yeah, that's my second job." Michael laughed as he opened the bag. "Uh, well, it just seemed easier to let people think what they wanted as long as I got to you before it was too late. Looks like I'll have a change of clothes at least."

Right then a news report came on the TV that caught their attention. A reporter stood next to a burned-out building. "Hey, isn't that . . ." began Taylor.

"Yeah," Michael replied.

The reporter said, "I am standing above Mingora, a city in Northern Pakistan, where only days ago insurgents overran the city and took control. The city's government has fled, as have most of the half million occupants. As you can hear by the gunfire, some pockets of resistance still fight in the city below. Behind me is a burned-out structure that was once a popular ski lodge. Why this building was destroyed is unknown." The camera panned from the city back to the blackened remains of the ski lodge. A yellow tarp could be seen rustling in the wind and the reporter went on. "A single body was found here. It is believed he was an innocent casualty in this bloody, bloody battle—"

Michael raised an eyebrow. "Innocent casualty? If she only knew. I've seen enough. How about you?"

"More than enough." Taylor got up to turn off the TV. Instead of sitting back down, he lay on the floor and appeared to quickly doze off.

Michael leaned his head back against the wall and stretched out his long legs. Soon he too was asleep.

Aside from snoring, silence prevailed in the windowless room. Five people looked dead except for the heaving of their chests as they slept. The cool air and silence were glorious.

Nasira jolted awake with a sudden feeling she was back in the prison—that the warden was still alive and the escape all had been a dream. To her relief she was safe, and four good men slept soundly near her. If it was safe enough for these men of action and ability to sleep, it was safe enough for her.

She closed her eyes, but the terror from the dream had filled her body with a familiar anxiety. She had grown so accustomed to the presence of the anxiety that she had not noticed it until it had returned again. As she sat up, the snoring stopped. She glanced at Pike and found him looking back at her. He stared for a brief moment and she held his gaze.

"I was dreaming," he said as he sat up.

"So was I," Nasira replied.

"I was dreaming I was back in that prison, but gratefully I'm here and free. There were so many times I dreamed I was free and then woke up a prisoner. I never appreciated air conditionin' like I do now, sheila."

Nasira smiled. Just then someone could be heard at the door leading to the hallway. It opened and a young female private entered. Though she seemed to try to hide it, it appeared her senses had been affronted by an unpleasant odor.

The door opening and the presence of the private startled Michael and Fulton. Red eyed, they sat up. Taylor continued to sleep.

The private moved to Nasira. "I am Private Hannah Webster."

Nasira smiled pleasantly. "Hello."

"Would you like to come with me and get away from these smelly men?"

"No," Nasira replied quickly.

"We can get you cleaned up and take your fingerprints," Private Webster explained. "If they are in the system, we can search for your family."

"I will go if they can go with me." Nasira motioned to the others.

"They cannot leave yet."

"I will wait then."

Private Webster took a seat next to Nasira as if determined to return with her. After a minute, Nasira moved to a chair closer to Pike.

Minutes later, a door opened and Sergeant Gutierrez entered, his long debriefing finished. He was followed by an austere, middle-aged officer whose features were weathered like overripe fruit, crow's feet extending from dark piercing eyes as though he were looking into the sun. Or your soul.

Fulton kicked Taylor. "What?" Taylor snapped.

"General Gibbons."

Taylor quickly stood. Everybody but Michael and Nasira came to attention and saluted.

The general returned the salute. "At ease."

Nasira came and stood next to the sergeant as a child might a parent. She was glad he didn't seem to mind.

"So which one of us is next?" Pike asked.

"You," Fulton said. "I'm going to finish my nap."

"Actually, I have asked General Gibbons to let the rest of you simply write out your statements so that we can all get cleaned up and rested," Gutierrez said. "I think it was my smell that convinced him."

"It was," General Gibbons replied dryly.

"Does that mean we can hit the showers?" Pike asked.

"It does." Everybody turned to leave and Gutierrez spoke again. "All except the Sutton brothers."

Michael and Taylor hung their heads and the rest began to file past.

"Sucks to be you, mate," Pike said.

"Sorry, but you two are the only witnesses to Colonel Bracken's role in these events, and General Gibbons is very interested in what you know," Gutierrez explained.

"I am going to need a chainsaw for this beard," Fulton declared as he started down the hallway.

"There may not be enough water in Bagram for the shower I'm about to take," Pike said.

Outside the small waiting room, Private Webster came to the sergeant. "I need to speak with you, sir. Alone."

He turned to Nasira. "Wait here a minute." He and the private took a couple steps away.

"Nasira needs to come with me," the private said.

"She is free to do what she wants."

"She will not come with me unless you or one of the others is with her. I am assigned to get her cleaned up and fingerprinted so that we may find out if indeed she is a citizen and, if so, help her find her parents."

Emilio Gutierrez looked at Nasira, who glared at the private. "She has been through a great deal for the last ten years and doesn't trust you," Gutierrez said finally. "Though she should hate men for what she has been through, she seems to trust us. It may be a form of Stockholm Syndrome, but I'm no doctor. Tell you what, the other guys and I will take turns getting cleaned up and sitting with her. After I am done, we will go with you. Sound good?" He knew Private Webster had little choice in the matter.

"I will dig up some clothes that fit her and be back in an hour," she said, then saluted.

Gutierrez returned the salute, and the private turned to leave. "One more thing," the sergeant said. "Regardless of what happens with the fingerprinting, she is coming home with us."

Private Webster nodded.

46

News of the rescued Army Rangers flooded the military communication channels. Initial details were sketchy, but five members of the LRS Ghost team were alive and well. Colonel Walter Bracken received the news while in a meeting with other military commanders. Publicly, he smiled and applauded their safe return, but in the recesses of his guilt-riddled mind he contemplated a prompt departure. He recalled words in the dark: *Runway 18 . . . a civilian plane . . . midnight.*

In the midst of the jovial banter regarding the missing team's good fortune, Walter Bracken checked his watch. It was 8:00. Four hours was a very long time, and yet the thought of running—running for the rest of his life—made his heart sick. Was he that kind of man? Had he become everything he'd once hated about the military? Was he not truly and genuinely happy that all the nefarious plans had failed and good had triumphed?

As to not draw attention to himself, he waited half an hour, barely listening to the items of discussion, then excused himself. A matter of urgency had come to his attention. He drove to his office and collected a few items, including a matched set of Civil War era black-powder pistols with ivory handles. From there he drove home and began packing his things.

An hour later, the colonel came to himself, sitting alone on the edge of his bed holding one of his ivory-handled pistols. It was a large and clumsy instrument, but beautiful too, a relic from the troubled rebirth of a glorious nation. He felt unworthy to even hold it.

He knew what he should do. He went to his closet and withdrew his formal attire. The buttons and medals gleamed even in the dull light. He began to undress.

After two days of trying, Van Sutton finally reached Agent Wakefield. The two men met on the third floor of the Victorville office. It was getting late, nearly 11:00. Van crossed the distance between the elevators and Wakefield's office like a speed walker. He found the agent getting ready to leave for the night.

"What's so urgent it couldn't wait until morning, Mr. Sutton?" Wakefield glanced at his watch.

"I've been trying to get a hold of you for two days," Van replied, mildly irritated at the agent's indifference.

"I've been busy. Bracken isn't the only case on my desk."

"I realize that, but I had to let you know I made a recording of a conversation with Bracken. He confesses, more or less." Van set the small digital recorder on the desk.

Wakefield just stared at the device. "I told you to stay away while I built this case. Unless he flatly admits to his crimes that recording may not be admitted into a military court. There are rules as to how recordings are to be acquired."

"So this may be worthless?" Van asked in frustration.

"Play it for me." Wakefield sat down and rocked back on the hind legs of his chair.

After the recording finished, Wakefield smiled. "It's good but not great. It'll help prove motive. Nothing will beat your son's—"

Just then the phone rang.

"You expecting a call?" Van asked.

"No," replied the agent. The phone rang again and he picked it up. "This is Agent Wakefield."

Van heard one side of a very quick phone call. Wakefield listened briefly and replied, "We are. He's what? Where? I'm on the way." He hung up the phone and began to put on his suit coat.

"Who was that?" Van asked as they went to the elevators.

"My boss. Someone informed him that Colonel Bracken is trying to skip the country. He's at Edwards and about to catch a plane with an unlisted flight plan."

"I'm coming with you."

"You'll have to stay in the car, Mr. Sutton. No grandstanding." Wakefield pushed the call button on the first elevator.

"You don't know me very well."

The elevator dinged and doors slid open. The elevator was not empty. Dressed in full regalia with his hat tucked under one arm and his white hair perfectly combed, stood Colonel Walter Bracken. As the colonel stepped from the elevator, Wakefield drew his firearm.

"There will be no need for that, Agent." The colonel spoke with perfect calmness. "I have come here to report my crimes."

"Are you carrying a sidearm, sir?" Wakefield had yet to lower his gun.

"No, young man, I am not. You may check if you like." He held out his arms, and Wakefield put away his gun and checked the colonel for a weapon.

"How did you know where to find me—find us?" Van asked.

"Since our last meeting, I've kept tabs on you."

"We just received a call that you were trying to skip the country," Wakefield said. "We were on our way to prevent that."

The colonel lowered his eyes and muttered something about a double cross.

"What was that?" Wakefield asked.

"Nothing you won't hear in my statement."

"Are you ready to make one now, sir?"

"I am," the colonel replied.

47

After what felt like days, Michael and Taylor left the debriefing room. It was unclear whether Michael would face charges for unsanctioned use of military property as well as falsifying of legal documents. At the moment, the brothers were just happy to be given the opportunity to shower, shave, and eat.

Unlike his previous visit, Michael and his brother were shown to in-house barracks where they had access to a bathroom, and Taylor had a clean pair of fatigues waiting for him. Since Corporal Scott had been so diligent in returning his property, Michael now had his phone charger, and he quickly found an electrical outlet. He let Taylor use the bathroom first as he sat on the bottom bunk near the outlet and dialed his wife.

When the call was picked up, Michael said, "Hey, beautiful, I'm so sorry I haven't been able to call sooner. We've had a time getting back to this military base. Hello? April, are you there?" He heard sobbing, but finally an inaudible response came.

"I'm here," she whispered.

"I wish I was there with you right now," he continued softly. "I really do." He knew he would never understand what she had been through, not knowing whether he was alive or dead.

To his surprise, the line went dead. "April? April? Hello?"

Michael hung his head. Either she was too torn up to speak or she was seriously mad at him. The thought alone of losing her was enough to make him physically ill. As he was rubbing his forehead, a clean-shaven Taylor walked in. Where his beard had been, the skin was three shades lighter than the rest of his face.

"Everything all right, Mike?"

"Yeah, I guess. I hope. April hung up or the line went dead. I'll give her a couple minutes and call back."

"Wish I could help." Taylor collapsed onto his bunk. "But female matters are beyond my scope of ability. I can barely keep a girlfriend."

"Maybe it's because you were always chasing the wrong kind of woman. What about that Private Webster? She was eyeing you, even with your scruff on."

"Hmm . . . maybe. She was good-looking."

"Did you notice the ring on her finger?"

"No. You trying to hook me up with a married woman?"

Michael chuckled. "No! On the other hand was a CTR ring. She's probably Mormon."

"Well, in the military that stands for 'Corrupt the Righteous.'"

Michael shook his head. "Why don't you get out of here while I try to call my wife again? I'm going to have to do some serious kissing up and don't need you around making fun."

"Fine, I got it. You fly halfway around the globe and still wind up taking over the room. Some things never change."

Michael grinned. "Would you just get out of here?"

"All right, I'm going, I'm going," Taylor said, obviously in a good mood.

Michael dialed the phone again and prayed April would pick up. To his surprise, she did on the first ring. "I was wondering when you were going to call back," she said with a smile in her voice.

"You hung up on me."

"Sometimes a girl has to have a good cry."

Michael slowly let out a breath. "I thought you were mad. I was ready for some serious kissing up."

"No, but you can kiss up if you'd like."

Michael laughed. "Wow! I miss you!"

"Ditto. So, tell me all about it. There's no way you're getting off this phone until you tell me everything."

So Michael started from the morning he had called her, when the whole adventure was ahead of him and he honestly feared the outcome. He told her about McNally and Marcus, glazing over the latter's violent end, and the arrogant General Rais, and on and on. Before Michael knew it, they had talked away his day and her night. Taylor had returned and fallen asleep, and little Suzanne had woken up. Michael talked to his daughter and of course said he would bring her a gift.

"You have to promise me one thing, Michael," April said as the conversation wound down.

"Anything."

"That you will never, ever leave me like this again."

"I promise," he said.

"Good. Now get some sleep and get your butt home!"

"I love you too."

In a vacant cafeteria, Nasira sat at a round table, slumped to one side and staring at a soda can. She had not seen a soda for ten years and hesitated to open it. As she watched, condensation began to collect around the outside. She ran her finger around the cool surface. Soon a drip formed and ran down the side. She knew how the soda can felt, for she too wanted to cry.

She looked from the can to her blackened fingertips. She had scrubbed unsuccessfully at the fingerprint ink. She wondered if she would ever find her parents. She wondered at her memories. Were they real? Or had the warden's mind games been triumphant? Was she certain her father's name was Aamir and her mother's Mysha? Nasira thought of the photos that had been taken of her. When her parents saw them, would they recognize her?

"You haven't touched your food, Nasira," Emilio Gutierrez said. "You look worried." He took another bite of his dinner.

She didn't say anything, afraid she would join the soda can in crying.

He spoke again. "The woman who took your prints and photos said she was going to work on this all night if need be. You've come this far and waited this long. Just a little longer." He reached out and touched Nasira's trembling hand. "Regardless of the outcome tonight, you are not staying here. You are going to America."

"With you?" she said.

He hesitated before replying, "Yes, of course."

"Do you love me?"

Emilio choked on his food and spit it into a napkin. Nasira stared at him, completely sober and expecting a reply.

"I'm not going anywhere, if that's what you're worried about. I care a great deal for you, but let's just take this one step at a time. The first one is finding your parents. Remember how it felt to drive that Jeep? The wind in your hair? The freedom?"

"Yes." Nasira smiled again. "Sorry I almost ran over you."

He chuckled. "My point is that everything from here on out is going to be like that Jeep ride. It's all brand new for you. Everything is going to be an adventure. Including finding your parents."

Just then Private Webster rushed into the room, out of breath. "Nasira! We have found them!"

"You have found them? You have found my family?" Nasira quickly stood.

"We have . . . they're on the phone!"

Suddenly forgetting her doubts, Nasira rushed toward the private. "Take me."

In an office filled with high-tech digital devices of every variety sat a simple telephone. Through a web of incomprehensible connections that seemed almost magic, two ends of the earth were miraculously linked. Nasira picked up the phone and listened to her mother speak tender words as she might to a child, and Nasira realized that in her mother's mind, she was still ten years old. Nasira replied briefly and softly as tears ran silently down her cheeks. Suddenly she was alone in the room, and her mother said she was handing the phone to Nasira's father.

"Papa? Papa, are you there?" she said after several seconds of silence. Finally a voice came over the line and she exclaimed, "Papa! I'm coming home! I have missed you!"

"I have always been with you," her father said. But his voice, calm and measured, was not how she remembered it.

"What do you mean?" Nasira asked. She looked around the room again but saw no one.

"You know what I mean."

"Who is this?" Her voice quivered with panic.

"You know who this is. I'm right here with you."

Nasira looked up and saw the warden holding a phone to his ear. He was standing in his apartment, and she was there, too. A cold shudder coursed her body when he put the phone down and stepped toward her. She screamed as his hand grabbed her, and suddenly she was awake. A man stood beside her and she fought him back.

"Nasira . . . Nasira . . . Easy . . . It's Emilio. You were crying in your sleep . . . easy. You're all right. You're okay. I'm here. You're safe."

Nasira curled into a ball as he held her tight. He sat with her for the remaining hours of the night, during most of which she cried. There had been no quick reply to her search for her parents, and she had gone to bed feeling desperate and alone.

48

Time, it is said, marches on, but in reality it seems to go at a dead sprint, racing toward a distant unknown future. And so it was that before the Sutton family knew it, more than a year had passed. The tragedies and triumphs of that fateful summer and fall were behind them and filed away into the annals of the past.

It was Thanksgiving, and the great oak in the backyard had shed many of its red and golden leaves, which now decorated the roof and yard. The air felt crisp with the coming winter, but the sun shone warm and bright.

Claire floated around the kitchen as she prepared dinner, humming to herself. To her, every opportunity to get the family under one roof was a festive occasion, regardless of the time of year. Little Suzanne sat next to Michael on a barstool, and Van had been sent to the store for more rolls.

"Mom, didn't you say you cooked two turkeys this year?" Taylor asked as he walked into the room. He had been outside on the phone.

"Yes. Somehow both your father and I took a turkey out to thaw. We're getting senile or something. Why do you ask?"

"What's senile?" Suzanne asked.

"It's when your start forgetting things, sweetie," Michael said with a chuckle.

His little daughter nodded. "Oh. Mommy's senile, too."

April slugged Michael. "What?" he protested. "I didn't say it."

His wife laughed. "Yeah, but you're the reason she said it."

Taylor sat down next to Hannah Webster, put his hand in hers, and winked. She wore her blond hair in a pixie cut and a perpetual smile in her hazel eyes. Michael smiled to himself, proud of his matchmaking abilities.

"I sort of invited some friends," Taylor said in response to his mother's question.

"Oh, how many?"

"Four."

"Oh . . . oh!" Claire turned from washing vegetables in the sink. "This isn't like the time you invited . . . "

"No!" interrupted Taylor, his face suddenly red. "It's nothing like that. It's my old Ranger team. They are all on their way home but had a flight delay and wanted to stop in. I told them you'd never let them leave without eating so they had better bring their appetites."

Hannah looked from Taylor to Michael. "Why did Taylor blush?" she asked. "What happened the last time he invited someone to dinner?"

"I don't have any idea," Michael lied.

"I'll tell you," April said with a grin.

Turning even redder, Taylor looked at his brother. "You told April?"

"It just slipped out." After a quick pause, Michael said to Hannah, "Don't worry, we'll fill you in on all the good dirt. Speaking of dirt, Mom, you haven't brought out the baby book yet."

"I had three older brothers," Hannah reported. "Why do you think I joined the military? If I could survive them, I could survive anything. Even Taylor." She kissed him on the cheek. "So where's the baby book?"

"I thought I'd save it for after dinner," Claire said.

"Ah, no, Mom," Taylor groaned. "All the guys will be here then. I'm going to have to disappear."

"You're not going anywhere," Hannah said playfully.

A rumble could be heard from the direction of the garage. Michael's father had taken the 'Vette to the store. He came in with dinner rolls, Canada Dry ginger ale, ice cream, and two more pies.

Claire frowned. "All I said was rolls."

"Yeah, but I invited some company," Van replied.

Her mouth fell open.

"We already have guests coming," Taylor said. "My old team."

"You talked to them?" Van asked.

"Yeah, not ten minutes ago."

"Good, I was afraid I was buying all this food and tricking your mother into cooking two turkeys for nothing."

Claire gasped. "You tricked me into baking two turkeys?"

"Well, sure. Otherwise we'd have argued all day about how many people one turkey could feed."

She grabbed the first thing she could get her hands on, which just happened to be a spoonful of potato salad. It shot across the kitchen with deadly accuracy and hit her husband in the face, then plopped onto his shirt.

At first, Van just stood there as if awestruck, but the potato salad kept coming. He grabbed a saucepan lid and used it to shield the onslaught. Michael and Taylor moved their loved ones back to a safe distance.

"Hey! You're wasting food," Van said from behind the lid. "Didn't I say I was sorry?" He moved in and grabbed her waist, wrapped her up in his arms, and planted a kiss on her. The food fight was in a ceasefire until he rubbed his mayonnaise-covered face across hers. After that, he retreated.

Michael and April laughed until they nearly cried. Suzanne giggled and said, "Silly Grandma!"

Chuckling, Michael's mother moved to the sink and wiped the salad from her cheek. She seemed to have regained her composure by the time she picked up the bowl and said, "Salad, anyone?"

"Only if you're going to put it on a plate," Hannah replied.

Shortly, Van returned with a different shirt on and a smile from ear to ear. April and Hannah had moved in to help clean up the war zone.

"So, I'm confused," Taylor said. "*You* invited the guys over for Thanksgiving?"

"That's right," Van replied.

"I thought I invited them. I just—"

"I invited them weeks ago. I wanted to surprise you."

"And apparently your mother, too," Claire interjected.

"I thought this was a good idea. You haven't seen each other since Bagram, and I thought it would be sort of like a reunion. It's not likely you'll ever serve together again. I also invited Henry McNally, but he's having Thanksgiving with his son. He said to wish you well." Van moved to where Taylor and Hannah sat. "Think of it as a welcome-home party from the old man."

Taylor reached over and hugged his father. "Thanks, Pop."

"It is good to have you home, Son. Even better that you brought Hannah with you. I think I'd trade her for you any day." Van winked at her, then asked, "How long are you two staying?"

Hannah glanced at Taylor. "We thought we'd stay through Sunday and maybe go to church with you before we head back."

"Of course you can stay," Claire said, looking as if she might cry. She rounded the counter quickly and enveloped Taylor and Hannah in a tight hug.

Taylor pulled away. "It's just church, Mom."

"It's an answer to my prayers, Son." She kissed Taylor and Hannah on their cheeks and squeezed tighter.

Van reached over and pulled his wife into an embrace. Michael knew the idea that Taylor was back in their lives and also returning to the Church they loved was nearly overwhelming to both of their parents. Michael could still hardly believe it himself.

After giving his parents a minute, he changed the subject. "It's too bad they forced McNally out of the military. He was the only one willing to buck the system to save our bacon."

"It could have been worse," Taylor said, clearly happy to take the attention from himself. "The fact that they gave him an honorable discharge in exchange for his silence tells you how embarrassed the military was."

Van cleared his throat. "Nobody has it worse than Walter. He won't live long enough to finish his sentence."

"Brought it on himself," Taylor replied coldly.

The room fell silent until Claire said brightly, "On to happier thoughts!"

Just then the doorbell rang. "That's them," Van declared.

"I'll get it!" Suzanne bolted to the door and pulled it open wide. Four men stood on the porch.

"Come on in," she invited. "Be careful—my grandma's been throwing salad."

Walking out of the kitchen, Claire said, "Only when people deserve it, honey."

Van stood next to his wife and extended his hand. "Come in, come in." Ian Pike entered first, followed by Delray Fulton. Todd McGillis entered third, and finally Emilio Gutierrez.

Everyone congregated at the entryway and greeted each other with warm handshakes and hugs. Michael hardly recognized the guys without their beards and grime from weeks in the Pakistani prison. Fulton, Pike, and Gutierrez had gained back the weight they had lost in captivity, but McGillis still seemed a little frail. He had lost all his hair, but bald suited him.

Once Claire brought out the extra bowl of potato salad, everyone gathered at the table for a two-turkey Thanksgiving feast. They all bowed their heads as Van offered a prayer recounting the matchless blessings of the past year and the miracles of love and forgiveness that brought them together as friends and family.

"So this is the plan," Claire said after the blessing. "As we pass around the food, everyone has to tell us one thing they are grateful for or something new that has recently happened. I know some of us have been itching to spill the beans." She turned to Hannah, who sat at her left. "You first, dear."

"Oh," Hannah said a little nervously. "Well . . . Taylor has asked me marry him." A round of congratulations followed, along with "Good on ya, mate" from the Australian.

"Thank you, thank you," Hannah replied, smiling. "I just haven't decided yet."

"Oooh," said the men in the room. Hannah laughed.

"She said yes, she said yes," Taylor informed them. Hannah leaned over and gave him a kiss.

"Okay, your turn, Taylor," Van said.

"Let's see, you already know the good stuff. But I also took a position as a Special Ops trainer so I can stay home."

"That's great, Son," Van remarked. Claire reached over and patted Taylor's hand.

Delray took a roll and some potatoes, then said, "I'm leaving the service altogether. I'm going to open a shooting range next to my dad's church. I'm going to call it Hellfire and Damnation."

Everybody laughed. The plates grew increasingly full as the platters progressed around the table.

McGillis cleared his throat. "Right now, I'm just thankful to be alive, but I've also taken a position as a recruiter." He smiled a little uncomfortably.

"Good for you," the other Rangers said in turn.

"I'm stayin' in the squad," Ian Pike declared as he took a double serving of sweet potatoes. "Thankful to be a Ranger."

Next at the end of the table, Van said, "I'll be last."

All eyes went to Suzanne, who had insisted on sitting next to her grandpa. April leaned over and whispered in the little girl's ear, and Suzanne burst out, "I'm going be a big sister!" Everyone laughed again.

"When are you due?" Hannah asked the beaming April.

"Next June."

"How about you, Michael?" Claire said.

He smiled and kissed April. "It's hard to top that. Just grateful for family. Your turn, Emilio."

"First, Nasira was reunited with her family not long after we left Bagram. She's with them now. She's been visiting a counselor and is doing very well." Emilio glanced at Taylor and Hannah. "We're also engaged to be married. Just haven't set a date yet. And lastly, I'm also leaving active duty to take a post as drill sergeant."

After another round of congratulations, Van stood. "Thank you all for coming. It is wonderful to share this meal with you. I would like to tell Taylor and Hannah how proud I am of them. Claire and I will be expecting grandbabies soon.

"And I also will take this moment to tell Michael and April that I am selling VAS Engineering to them."

Michael gasped and looked at his wife.

"As long as you always leave a spot open for your brother if he wants it," Van continued, "and you agree to send your mother and me on vacation at least once a year."

"Done," Michael said with a chuckle.

Van picked up his glass. "Also, although nothing here is alcoholic, I'd like to raise a toast."

Everybody stood with glass in hand—even Suzanne, who had a glass of milk.

"I'd like to raise a toast to family and friends. May we forgive every trespass and look for the best in others. May those we've lost live forever in our hearts, and may we live true to their memory."

All present raised their glasses.

"All right," Taylor said. "Enough gushy stuff—let's eat!"

As everyone moved to sit down, Michael smiled. "I couldn't agree more."

48

Colonel Skip Martin awoke to the sound of a thunderclap. His wife moved closer to him, but he pulled away and stood to retrieve a handgun from under the mattress. His wife stirred. "Is everything all right, Skip?"

"Thunder . . . or something. I'll be right back." Since the days of active duty, he had grown to dislike thunder. It reminded him of diversion tactics or a sound made to cover something else. His friends called it paranoia; he called it survival. After twenty-five years, his wife usually slept through it.

Skip moved carefully in the dark. Something seemed amiss in the house, a foreign presence perhaps, or perhaps nothing at all, but his instincts were on fire. He checked the spare room, opening the door only as far as he knew he could before it groaned. Nothing.

With all the lights still off, he moved to the kitchen and front room. Lightning flashed and thunder rolled. His night vision was ruined by the flash, and the house seemed instantly darker. As he reached for the light switch, he heard a voice.

"Colonel Martin . . ."

Afraid someone might have a bead on his back, the colonel spun and squatted on his heels. "Who's there?"

"A friend."

"I don't have any friends who would invite themselves in, even on a stormy night. Give me a reason not to kill you."

"I know you have been overlooked for the posting as general for the last three years. I have the connections you need to be recognized by the Joint Chiefs. The Armed Forces Oversight Committee meets in six months. There is time to get your name on the list of candidates."

"So this is how it is done . . . conversations in the dark?" In the blackness, Skip's eyes searched for the source of the voice. He saw no one. "Keep your connections. I'll take my chances."

"I had been led to believe that we were kindred spirits—ambitious, patriotic, and willing to do what needs to be done."

"I am all of those things."

"Then we can help one another."

"You have not told me who you are. I don't deal with faceless politicians."

"You're certain I am a politician?"

"If you are not, you are just as bad." The colonel had not turned on the light but had nevertheless found the source of the voice. "Whatever you have read or heard about me, you have mistaken ambitious service for ruthless aspiration. At my wife's request I have sought the posting for general. She believes I could do well there. I would not betray her for you, whoever you are.

"If I have learned anything in my twenty-five years in the service, it's that men who seek favors in the dark are a Trojan horse. Your glossy smiles and waxed features only hide your cancerous, gangrenous souls."

There was no reply, and a figure appeared in the darkness. "Who are you talking to?" asked his wife from the hallway.

"Wrong number." Skip took the cell phone and dropped it into a drawer, sickened that someone had been in his house to leave the device. Whoever it was knew him well enough to realize he would be up in a thunderstorm checking the house. Skip would make it his life's mission to find out who this man was.

In a dark, rectangular office overlooking the Washington Mall, the man blew a lung full of cigarette smoke into the air. He had terminated the call when he lost control of the conversation.

Idealists, he thought. *Oh, how I loathe idealists. They have little understanding of how the world really works. But for every idealist there are a dozen men willing to do what is necessary. I will have the Oval Office yet, and then there will be no turning back.*

ABOUT THE AUTHOR

Kristoffer Neff first took an interest in writing as a sophomore in high school, but he didn't see himself as an author until he won a short-story contest while living in Utah. He writes whenever he can find a spare moment, which sometimes amounts to a only a few hours a week since he operates his own business. His first novel was *No Place to Hide* (2010, Granite Publishing).

The idea for *Home of the Brave,* which is based on the parable of the prodigal son, came to Kristoffer one afternoon while he played with his young sons. He and his beautiful wife, Melanie, live in Arizona and have four children. For more information about Kristoffer and his books, please visit kneffbooks.com.